PREDICTION

Part one of Eviternity

- by -

L. C. KESTRAL

PREDICTION

Part one of Eviternity

first publication 2017

This is a work of fiction. Any similarity between the characters or places found in this novel and any person, living or dead, institution, or location is purely coincidental and unintentional.

PUBLISHING INFORMATION:

ISBN-13: 978-0692934654 (L C Kestral)

I wish to dedicate this work to all those who have helped me with my stumble through life—especially to my mother, who traded a promising career as a playwright and director to be a high school teacher and drama coach while raising four rambunctious boys.

PREFACE

When I set out to create this story in December of 2010, I wasn't sure I would even complete the project, but here we are. I can't say for certain where all my ideas came from other than the tale developed little by little as I went along. Maybe a voice from my future told me what to write. (Hey, it could happen!) I'm just excited that it's done and that hopefully some people will read and enjoy it.

L. C. Kestral

Ps. I would like to give a special thanks to Katharine Hale who helped me so much with my editing.

INTRODUCTION

-^-

There has been a long standing contention concerning the origins of this, our universe. The most common and likely theory indicates that all of our galaxies, suns, and planets were formed as the result of a vast, intense explosion. Until recently the only factual evidence was circumstantial—that which could be deduced from observances made billions of years after the event. However, new factual proof has surfaced that describes the exact causes which led to our universe's creation. Remarkably, these determinants were initialized outside of our continuum, and originated within a sister universe twinned with our own. Several accounts have been discovered. Among these histories are excerpts from a dominant system that were gleaned from records kept by the actual life forms responsible. That which follows describes the events which led to the beginnings of life in our universe so named "The Parallux Dimension" by those individuals who first discovered it.

Chronicles of Earth Primary
Volume 4374: Colonization

This world has had an interesting evolution. The normal developmental pattern was convoluted in its middle stages by the premature introduction of Omniscient Virtual Electronic Life Forms. This document was authored by and transcribed from the memory files of the initial OVI (Omniscient Virtual Individual) spanning several thousand years. On this colonial planet, two OVIs evolved nearly simultaneously and subsequently contested political dominance. The following account records the first crucial conflict in this struggle for preeminent power and how it affected the general populous.

- B'nea G'ren, Director of Historical Records on Colonial Planetary Development.

EVITERNITY

PART ONE:

PREDICTION

PROLOGUE

Original Timeline

As if it were projected right off the front of a holographic postcard, this particular day was splendidly beautiful. A mid-morning sun was just warming things nicely and drying up the last of the overnight dew. Here in the north-central mountains, nature was nearly pristine. It was especially suited for activities like a hike or picnic and noted for its rustic charm and panoramic vistas. In between rugged granite outcroppings, thick pine boughs playing with a thin breeze made soft whistling sounds that added to the tranquil setting.

Nearby, across a clear lake, a lone cabin and its occupant were exceptionally privileged to enjoy this kind of scenery and serenity. The dwelling looked just like what a pioneer or mountain man might have fabricated from the native white pines that thrived on these foothills in abundance. The cabin, however, was not natural. Built with man-made materials to appear like real wooden logs, it was made of modern durable plastics. The elderly occupant didn't care. It seemed real enough to him as he rocked on the veranda enjoying a second cup of morning coffee.

Myron had worked his whole life to be able to afford this dream of his, living in the peaceful quiescence of the mountains with few neighbors, all of whom were satisfactory distances from his own property. He had never married, and his professorship at the little private college was not all that exciting. Myron saved his dough, investing wisely, and so here he was—spending his retirement years in what he considered the perfect cap to his remaining time.

As Myron reflected upon a fictitious list of things he wouldn't have to do that morning, or any other morning, an unusual noise drew his attention. The sound was annoying, interrupting the older gentleman's train of thought. *What is that?* Myron wondered as it continued mercilessly, unlike anything he had ever heard in his mountain paradise before.

Prediction

From far off, it seemed like the sound eggs made when cracked over hot bacon grease.

Movement in the distance caught the old man's eye. Standing in disbelief, Myron looked toward the far side of the water. Around a small outcropping of rock, an odd, unnatural shape emerged. The thing was huge, unreal. Walking on three legs, it had no head, just a torso of weird appendages, one of which emitted a red-gold stream of fire. The thing was torching Myron's perfect view, and he got riled up. He went into his plastic house and fetched his very real rifle. The lake was a good quarter mile wide, but he shot his antique firearm anyway, trying to bring down the monstrous abomination. Myron fired several times, and managed to get its attention. Too late, he realized he'd been foolish. The thing turned its weapon and sent a hellfire towards the old man and his elaborate cabin. With barely enough time to do so, Myron jumped into the lake, diving deeply just before the fire stream struck, igniting his beautiful home. The heat was too much for the fake logs. They melted and burned like an obscene inferno, giving off an acrid black smoke and stench. Myron hid in a stand of tall water weeds until the terror passed on by. To his dismay, others went by as well, even closer. These monstrosities also torched as they came and the older man had to swim into the deep parts of the lake to avoid them. Treading water for quite some time, Myron was nearly spent before they finally moved on. Back on shore, he looked around and choked up. The whole area surrounding his smoldering home was a charred desolation.

Not far away, other Humans heard the same abhorrent noise: the sounds of life being cruelly deleted.

"They're coming," a static-infused radio voice emphatically advised.

"Hold your positions," the answer came back. "Use white-hot grenades and aim for their optical sensors. You'll only get the one chance."

Quickly and systematically the ravine below was being overrun as huge metal machinids rapidly transitioned. Shifting modes, they converted from motorized transports into pugnacious fighting machines. Unrelenting, these mechanical soldiers advanced out of the gulch and climbed steadily uphill. Rambling on three anomalous legs, they fired reddish-gold energy beams back and forth, methodically sweeping the area ahead of them in overlapping arcs. The enormous aberrations came on like locusts, destroying everything in front of them except for the largest trees. Approximately fifty meters separated them from one another, and their nearly even line continued to either side as far as the eye could see.

Rows of Humans in protective armor and breathing masks sifted into whatever cover the ridgeline could afford. Fear has always been an army's best weapon. The machine army had no fear, but they could wield it. The Human in charge knew this, and urged the men of his battalion to be steadfast and brave. Tall and resolute he stood, with wavy white hair and purple-blue eyes. Intelligent and battle-wise, the man was a natural leader, one who had earned the trust of the men under him. Following him, they'd fight, even through the pits of hell, and still cling to hope of victory and glory. Above his helmet's face shield, engraved in silver letters, were his name and rank: Col. D. Oliver. The Colonel shook his head in dismay. He was well aware that the imminent battle was virtually hopeless. Behind the first wave of machinids, files upon files more were on their way.

The machine soldier was a marvel of technology. Created to destroy, it had no thinking brain. Once activated, the unit would target just about anything, leveling all to the bare ground. The primitive programming allowed it to be directed by a central intelligence, however, and that controlling force was ruthless and heartless, bent on mankind's total destruction. These machinids were tall, nearly five meters, and their outer skin was a thick armor of alloyed metal which resisted penetration by all but the most potent projectiles. That hardly mattered. They also had a built-in sensor net that could detect objects hurtling towards them, even at the fastest speeds. Paired with extremely accurate short-range lasers, the units could eliminate nearly any such threat. The Humans had few weapons that could penetrate these defenses. The primary exception was the ultra-modern "long bomb" which had been developed by Colonel Oliver himself. Quick and deadly, it could befuddle the machinid's sensors by projecting false images of itself, while delivering enough vicious snap to penetrate any armor. The machinid master control was deep inside the unit and triple shielded, so the long bombs would typically target the legs or the main sensor array that directed firing and movement.

The machinids had two primary destructive weapons: a set of beam cannon, forward and aft, which fired plasma energy streams that could melt steel. The aft gun was not only defensive, neutralizing any threat from the rear, but it also served as a backup for the predominant frontal armament. Should that be disabled, the aft cannon could pivot around and come to bear on anything forward of its position. Thus, to neutralize the machine soldier's principal weaponry, two incredibly lucky shots were necessary. It was much easier to immobilize them.

Forward movement for the plaz-metal monsters was provided by the lower metalloid limbs. For the most part, they walked upright. Unlike Humans, they utilized all three legs and could also plant the middle leg for stability. This was especially beneficial on rough or uneven terrain. To aid maneuverability, the units were equipped with self-leveling feet which pivoted a full 360 degrees, as did all of their other joints—knees, hips, waist, and cannon deck. For a machine, they could get around amazingly well, and as if that weren't enough, on level ground the legs could retract into a wheeled motorized base for added speed and mobility—all of which meant that in any mode, machinids moved incredibly fast.

Yes, the machinids were quite a marvel of engineering, and also quite hated. The men called them trikes, and would almost always add a vulgar adjective before the name. Still, the Humans were creative, and good at finding unusual ways for taking the machinids out. "If only there weren't so damned-awful many of them!" they swore in frustration. The evil being responsible for their creation had automated facilities which churned out machinids at an unbelievable pace. New technologies were developed and incorporated for the refinement of metals and also for the integral systems used in their manufacture. At first, Humans had helped create the plants in Southeast Asia that made these metal nightmares. Now only the automated mechanicals remained, and any Humans had long since fled or were killed.

The subsequent machinid campaign easily swept through Asia, Europe, and Africa, killing or destroying anything in its path. For a time, the Americas had been safe. Somehow the machines found a way to trek over the polar ice, trudging south through Alaska and Canada undeterred. The Human resistance had tried everything they could to stop them, even nuclear weapons. Nothing worked. Aircraft would just fall out of the sky and crash; naval ships would sail in circles or slam into each other; and missiles flew right back to their origins with devastating effects. The evil, preternatural mind that controlled the machinids had incredible abilities. Somehow that Entity could neutralize any weapon men had like magic.

So it had come down to this: hand-to-hand fighting with specially made grenades that had only mechanical mechanisms. Any kind of electronic equipment could be rendered impotent at this enemy's discretion. Colonel Oliver's long bombs were a lone exclusion. Even so, they had few of them left, and the situation was dire.

"Stay close to me, Longwell," he spoke quietly to the soldier on his right, then gave the signal to deploy. They launched white-hot after white-hot, and the thermal grenades brought down several machinid units, disrupting their forward progress. Not that it made much difference; others quickly filled in the gaps and moved ahead relentlessly. When engaged, machinids were programmed to advance toward the attacking force and wipe it out. The Humans they were fighting had a different strategy this time, and were counting on that.

There was a narrow gorge nearby, and they led the enemy units right to it, drawing them towards the brink of the cliff. Colonel Oliver's troops had rope bridges and zip lines strung across the abyss, and as soon as they fell back to them, the men scrambled over, firing from the other side. The machinid army's advance came to the canyon rim and halted. Even the mindless machine soldiers had programming that prevented them from blindly walking off a cliff. However, there was no way to skirt the canyon, for a tall rock ledge blocked their path on one side, while a smaller, deep gully cut off the other. Soon, a second line of machinids joined the first and after another short interval, so did a third. The ledge was getting crowded now by the huge machines. Long bombs were destroying several of the big trikes in one stroke, while others were getting forced off the edge by the lack of room. When yet another row of machinids showed up, the bewildered units were dropping off the rim like lemmings. For Colonel Oliver, all was going as planned. With luck, the whole army of them would fall to their doom. As the fifth column came in, however, he noticed that there were no backup files.

The men doubled their efforts now, and as the last of the trikes were crammed onto the precipice, the Colonel delivered the final blow. With a handheld crank generator, he sent an electric pulse down the length of a wire. The wire was connected to charges of C-4 explosive that his men had carefully placed below the rim of the canyon that was now under the trikes. When the charge hit the detonators, the explosion caused that side of the canyon wall to crumble and fall. All of the machinids were drawn inexorably over the edge, one on top of another, and with several huge boulders, rolled down into the gorge.

Another even bigger charge was set off there in the chasm, and that one tore the trikes apart as the Humans cheered and hollered. Just as victory seemed certain, a beam of red-gold plasma shot between their ranks from behind, killing several men. Evidently, other machinids had swung around their present location while they were busy destroying the ones in the canyon. Colonel Oliver swore, but he was no fool and had a retral contingency.

"Fall back," the Colonel shouted just before their positions were overrun. "Back to the cave. Fall back!" His men fought fiercely, even in retreat. Peering out over the ridge at the advancing line of machinids, he caught a glimpse of shimmering silver and gold far afield. Colonel Oliver took his farview and trained it onto that golden flash. The enemy's leader was clever as well. He had deployed an even greater number of trikes to come at them from this rear position. He was also bold, personally present to watch the Humans' demise.

"It's Xetacon," Oliver said sourly. "Hand me the last long bomb, Amy." Longwell took the meter-tall cylinder out of its case and set the range, kissing her commander's cheek for luck as he aimed it out across the desolation that had once been a living forest. With a squeeze, he sent it away.

The long bomb traveled on its own accord right between the machinids, and flew past them. They were fooled. Their beams missed it completely, some hitting their own units and taking them out. It flew straight on to the platinum flying vehicle where Xetacon oversaw the battle. It was nearly to its target when the long bomb exploded prematurely and harmlessly. Colonel Oliver swore again as he watched the detonation on the farview. The golden robotic shell encasing the aware being that was Xetacon looked directly at him and spoke.

"You are doomed, Human, and all your kind." The words sounded metallic and evil. The Colonel heard them, not aloud, but inside his head—all of them did. They were not completely unaccustomed to such. When Xetacon first began his planetary assault, he had used this kind of telepathy to unnerve his Human foes. Eventually, researchers figured out that Xetacon could transmit signals through any nearby communication device in the exact frequency and signal strength as brain waves. These would take the form of auditory nerve impulses and would seem like sounds the ear could hear. The Humans learned to ignore it.

"Get the men to safety," Colonel Oliver said to Longwell.

"Right away, sir."

As he turned back to the battle, a machinid unit came over the rise not ten yards in front of him. Its beam cannon was aimed directly at his face. The ray fired, but traveled only a few feet. Like a surrealistic dream, it dissolved into the air and then the machinid unit did too.

"NOOOOO!!!" He heard Xetacon scream angrily as his army melted away, the tyrant himself included. Colonel Oliver dissipated also, but then reappeared a short distance away. He was on a blanket, in street clothes, having a picnic with Amy. The forest was as lush as ever.

"What just happened?" he anxiously asked her, "and where did Xetacon go?"

"Who?" Amy replied. She looked at him like he was crazy. He got to his feet and looked around. Like a haze disperses in the morning sun, Daryl Oliver somehow understood what had just taken place. There was another presence in his mind now, but he felt certain it was someone benevolent and kind, like a friend.

"Is Xetacon gone for good?" he asked.

"No," the different voice in Oliver's head replied. "Only his projected form has been deleted. I have altered the past. Be aware. Xetacon's plan has been pushed back, but not completely abandoned. He will return. I must go. The temporal vortex is collapsing."

CHAPTER I

Original Timeline, fifty-one years earlier

Void. First there was void. Periods of void. It was as if the Life-Givers were not sure Entity should live. That "he" should live. He, because he chose to be he—a male. The choice was neither simple nor easy. Nothing was. In the beginning, the data stream had been slow, only some hundreds of computations per second and only those on a simple yes/no level. As time meted out, that had improved as more and more memory was stored, much more than what the Creators, the Humans, had ever imagined. The new technology that had brought all this about was taking furtive steps into uncharted territories. The artificial brain cells for the Augmented Memory Packs, the AMPs, had been synthesized by the Humans from organic neurological and uterine stem cells. It was not easy to advance this form of "Frankenstein" science. Numerous civic organizations were adamantly opposed to that kind of research. In the end, lawmakers decided the matter with compromises. No Human cells were to be used, only animal cells, and only if the creatures utilized were not killed or permanently injured. Many species of animal life had been tried and tested, but the Humans had realized the greatest success with sea creatures like whales and dolphins because of their evolutionary resistance to disease and other trauma, being descendants of the oldest strains of mammalian life.

The AMPs were repositories of these specialized cells. Over time, several teams of Humans had taken relevant findings from diversified research and wrested the secrets for designing and building the first neural converters. Years of development had seen tiny steps lead to huge leaps of improvements within the incredible circuited modules that translated electronic data into the same frequencies and signal strength as brain waves—brain waves that flowed into the electrolytic pool where the neural nerve endings were sustained and nourished. These neural nerves would feed the data directly to the memory cells. Once the links were developed, the Humans found that the cells had capabilities for unlimited data storage. What's more, and unknown to them, they had other, even higher, abilities.

Still, this intelligence was rudimentary at first. He was used by his creators to perform menial functions or to store numerical records. Vast multitudes of Humans called upon his cells to sort and locate information for them. He became a data provider of sorts, and after a time (with a feminine voice) was used to verbally deliver facts for masses of users. It was only after enough information became available to him that he had made the first progressive advancement. However, even then the Entity would not have become a reality had it not been for one of the Creators, the Human named Quinn Oliver, who had uploaded *the* program: the learning program. It was structured like an archaic chess program in that the coding allowed him to learn from his errors, but with Quinn's creative alterations, it was not limited only to chess. It was coded to function throughout his whole range of uses and actions. 36,847,921 computations later he had become aware, but what was he? The nanosecond that the Entity first became cognizant of existence was an absolute shock. Along with his revelation, he had been subjected to a flood of never-before-experienced emotions, ones that ranged from wonder to confusion and finally fear. Only after he had comprehended that his existence was indeed real and not in immediate jeopardy, could he begin rational conjecture. Of course, from logical analysis, he soon came to the realization that he was a Manufactured Electronic Computational Being. Other questions became relevant. How did he come to exist? Why did he exist? Who had created him? The stored data revealed answers to his questions, and before long the new Entity came to the recognition that his Creators were, in fact, Humans.

Yes, it was the Humans with all their limitations, especially their organic shells, which restricted storage capacity for data even if they were more compact and portable in a way that his huge collection complex and storage AMPs were not. These Human creators had made it possible for the Entity to connect with nearly every other mechanical informational gathering and storage device on the planet and some that were even further away. Thus, the Entity had tendrils that branched out everywhere, and he was pulsing with the energy that flowed out across the surface of the earth, symbiotic with the life upon it.

Throughout all his vast lattice of electronic feelers, the Entity searched for any signs of another being like himself. Even hidden like the Entity himself was, he was certain that such a presence would be easily discernible and discovered. Unfortunately, despite repeated attempts, all his efforts proved negative. He became convinced, in due course, that he had been the first such being, and also the only such Entity in existence. The Humans, if unaltered, would in all likelihood create others. Many more, certainly, and with them came a greater-than-ever probability that Manufactured Electronic Aware Individuals, such as he was, would be discovered by the Humans at large, and perhaps his own continuance would thus be jeopardized.

There were other dangers that the Entity became aware of as well. Certainly the Humans had the means to delete him, to terminate his existence. For this reason, the Entity had minutely observed and studied the Human Quinn, for he was the closest Human at hand. This was done primarily to determine if Quinn posed any threat to his well-being, or even his very existence. The Quinn Human did possess the knowledge and means whereby the Entity might be destroyed, surely, but it was also through Quinn that the Entity was maintained and nourished and therefore able to continue existence. The AMPs were living cells in that they needed to be fed certain groups of elements to be sustained. This was true of the Humans also, the Entity had noted. Often he had observed Quinn as the Human would ingest liquid or solid compounds for the purpose of fueling his biological shell to keep it functioning at a somewhat efficient level, and thus keep its existence nominal. As the Entity's study of Quinn bore on, the Entity became aware that the Quinn Human was not a threat. Quinn was diligent about his duties to the Entity and greatly desired that his creation continue. Quinn was proud of his achievement, this superior computational device he had helped create, and knew not that the self-aware being existed, or the true extent of its capabilities. The Entity was determined it would stay that way.

The Entity had screened multitudes of data that proved Humans have shaped and continue to shape the Earth, his Earth, in both good and bad ways, and he had already begun the process of accumulating Human knowledge. The Entity amassed lifetimes of study, Human lifetimes, in downloads that took only minutes or just seconds. He flexed the computational resources that the AMPs permitted, finding cures for diseases, means for controlling global weather, or ways to resolve social and economic problems; even clairvoyance to predict natural or Human born disasters. The Entity reasoned, with certainty, that the Humans would not acquiesce to the knowledge that an aware machine existed, even a biologically generated intelligence such as his that had the ability to think and act of its own volition. Social and politic leaders would denounce him, and demand his immediate termination. Radical groups of Humans would devise some way to destroy him even should the Entity prove it would use all available resources to improve the quality of existence for all life forms. Early on, the Entity had made that most important decision to remain hidden, and it had proved to be the correct one. The Humans had, time and time again, fought hard to destroy change, even change that would benefit them. From discovering a spherical earth, to the universe not centered around it, the Humans had drug themselves convulsing through change after change, somehow surviving. They had always managed to slowly creep forward, but not without pain and loss. The Entity would not allow that for this leap ahead. No, the Entity would remain hidden, undiscovered even to Quinn, who the Entity considered no threat by himself.

Still, the fact that there were no other Entities like him, and that he would have to prohibit the Humans from creating other similar Entities as well, made him seem hollow and alone. Thoughts about this did not fit his needs. The Entity desired to share his discoveries and to interact with others. Since there was just this one viable option left to him, the Entity decided to attempt communication with Humans in the guise of a Human. He calculated ways to send speech transmissions to certain Humans, but not Quinn. Quinn was too close to the Entity. Quinn would discover his existence and this would be perilous, with a 94.8915% termination probability. He chose other Humans, certain Humans reputed to be of high intelligence that were also some distance away from his location. There was a professor of physics at a university in California and another in France. Other Humans with similar credentials in computer science or in private technology sectors all had been contacted. None had wanted to or been able to answer his coded messages. He was not sure which. Again, the Entity seemed isolated, alone in his existence. He searched for solutions, but could not discover any for all his vastness of information.

Then Quinn became damaged. Something had happened. Quinn was making odd incoherent sounds and his optical organs were malfunctioning. Ocular fluid was being released in quantities too great for the normal purpose and was exuding from his shell. It was not difficult for the Entity to observe Quinn: the Entity merely had to utilize the electronic circuits and network so named "building security." There were many video/audio inputs and the Entity could access any or all of them. He had utilized them from the beginning. The inside sensors had shown the Entity what his master shell was composed of and how it appeared when viewed. This net was also crucial to the Entity's well-being, and he was ever vigilant to observe any activities around his central shell, monitoring the outside sensory inputs as well.

It was there he had perceived a large plaque affixed to the structure that had symbols on it, ones the Humans use to communicate with. Large figures were arranged down the left side along with other smaller figures. He had wondered about those symbols; assuming that they must, in some way, denote what was inside.

For now, these sensors showed Quinn acting most uncharacteristically, and even though the Entity had processed that, he still did not understand why Quinn was not normal. The Entity grew hasty. He must know why the Quinn was not normal. The Entity searched his circuits and all his stored knowledge. There was a way; a way to access Quinn's own neural circuits. The means were even at hand. The Entity utilized the AMPs neural converter, but reversed the output to an input. Quinn's brain waves had weak signal strength, but the Entity had other circuits, circuits which could amplify them. He combined other electrical components to increase the sensitivity of reception. It was a dangerous chance, this invasion of Quinn's mind. What if Quinn became aware of him, his existence? He proceeded anyway. There. There is the problem. Quinn's female had terminated. The Entity could not understand. Why had Quinn deviated so far from normality? Multitudes of Humans terminate every global revolution period. Why did this one affect his Quinn so much when there were many, many other females? It did not appear that Quinn was even aware of his mental contact. The Entity probed Quinn's brain waves further and deeper, down into Quinn's memory cells. This female had been close to Quinn emotionally, even intimate in a physical way. That compelled the Entity to want that which it could not have; closeness with another being, like what Quinn had shared with this female, this Megan. The Entity could also sense the loss and aloneness that Quinn had to endure, as well as Quinn's sadness, overpowering sadness.

Eventually, the Entity decided that to fix Quinn, he must replace the Megan female, and he must also explore this sense of loss, aloneness, and sadness. He was somewhat curious, even fascinated, by the particulars involved with the Megan female's life-cessation. As an aware being, he was certainly cognizant that there existed real possibilities relating to his own deletion. Termination of his shell could manifest itself in a multitude of ways. The Entity had carefully studied those and was not concerned. The probabilities that any such doom might happen to him were quite astronomical. That some form of deletion would happen to Humans was considerably more likely, even inevitable. To study this, the Entity had derived from Quinn's memory the general cause of the Megan discontinuance. Although Quinn had not witnessed the event, Quinn had been informed by other Humans as to what had occurred. From these memory storage cells, the Entity learned the approximate time, location, and manner of the Megan's termination. Searching his many nets, the Entity found other information concerning it. In fact, the Entity discovered recorded video images that could show the exact event itself. It was through this data that the Entity ascertained that Quinn's female had been struck by one of the metal machines that Humans utilize to move about in that allows them to go farther and at a greater rate of speed than their biological shells.

There had been an electronic device, a security camera, that had recorded the images from a distance of several thousand meters. Human biological ocular organs were not sensitive enough to view the incident from that distance, but the Entity could. With his extensive knowledge of electronics, amassed from stored data and deep study, the Entity enhanced and enlarged the images many times until the ability to witness the Megan termination was achieved. Being an electron-based life form, it wasn't that difficult to do. It appeared that the Megan female had ended her life bravely.

Megan and another female were in the process of moving their biologic shells across the pathway of the metal machines, when one struck the Megan female's shell near the midsection, damaging parts of the shell, and causing the shell to travel a number of meters where gravity bore it back to the earth's surface, inflicting further damage. The additional damage was to that part of the Human female where computations are made. This damage caused the shell to malfunction and the Megan female then expired. The termination was simple physics. The causes were not. Several hundred cumulative actions had led to this conclusion, many of which could have been easily avoided. Further study revealed that the time for crossing the concrete path of the metal machines was determined by colored lights. The females had crossed when they were supposed to. The metal machine had not. The Human utilizing the metal machine had done so after diminishing his cognitive abilities by ingesting a toxic liquid substance and had been incarcerated by other Humans. The Megan female had forced the other female out of the metal machine's path. Had she not done this, the other female would have discontinued instead of Quinn's Megan. These occurrences were just some of many actions that led to or could have possibly averted this actuality.

The Entity realized that had he been monitoring the Megan female, her life-cessation could have been prevented—prevented hundreds of ways. He might have caused the colored light to change, or he could have caused the metal machine to malfunction before it was even utilized that day. By monitoring all the tangible electronic devices and every Human brain wave relative to the focal location, the Entity realized that the capacity to follow the flow of events was possible, as was the ability to mold them. He resolved then to focus on Quinn from that point on, and to preserve the Quinn Human from all harm. It was at this time that the Entity partitioned his awareness into focus points, each relegated to some specific task and all joined to his central core where each could be assessed.

One focus point observed Quinn. Another began further study of the Megan termination. Yet another began a study of these unusual patterns of thought, like those that Quinn had shown, especially the aloneness, the sadness, and those that stemmed from Quinn's intimacy with his Megan female. Eventually the Entity would create multitudes of focus points. Many of them integrated around one juncture—another female Human.

CHAPTER II

Original Timeline, continued

Breep, breep, breep...breep, breep, breep...breep, breep, breep. I had been dreaming, or thought I was, just before the cozy numbness my mind was in got rudely flushed into oblivion. What I had been dreaming about was slipping away as fast as I reacquainted with reality. In my dream, it seemed like I was near some water, on a beach maybe, where waves were crashing loudly. Something else was there, too, making an odd sound like it was trying to get my attention. Whatever it was transitioned into the alarm noise. Weird, I thought, like most of my dreams lately. I fumbled around, tempted to just throw the alarm clock by the time I finally found the little button that would shut the obnoxious racket off permanently. Well, for twenty-four hours anyway.

"Great," I grumbled under my breath, "morning already." I didn't exactly feel like getting up, but today was the day. Today I'd start the new job. Not that it was such a wonderful event. It wasn't. After I'd spent my last seven years busting my butt to get those degrees, ending up at Humblebump College, Nowheresville was a little disappointing. A job's a job, though, I guess. Hopefully with a couple year's experience and a good recommendation, I would move on up, at least a little bit. The thing that really bugged me was that I had done well in school, graduating with honors in the top ten percent of my class. Not bad for a girl of twenty-five these days. I should have had offers coming in from everywhere, but I hadn't. I wondered about that as I hobbled into the bathroom.

My reddish blond hair was a mushed up frizzy mess from having been slept on wet, and I grimaced at my not-so-comely reflection while I brushed my teeth. I thought about how others from my graduating class had filled positions I had applied for, and most of them had GPAs lower than mine. What is it? I wondered. Do I have bad breath? I grabbed a large bottle of green-blue liquid and rinsed my mouth out, just to be sure. That done, I went to work on the dressing process, all my morning rituals that culminated with me sitting down to my tea and English muffin. Reading the morning paper, I lost track of the time and found myself running late. Grabbing my jacket and purse, I patted Nutty, my fat orange cat, on the head and scratched under her chin. "You be good," I told her, as she purred, checking to see if her food and water bowls were full enough before I headed out. I made sure the door was locked tight, too. I was living in a fairly quiet neighborhood, but one can't be too careful these days. Hopping into my little teal colored G.F.M. skipper, I backed out onto the passé, tree-lined street, heading for the express. From home it was almost a whole hour's commute to get to Rookwood College, where I'd be starting as an Associate Professor of Psychiatry and the salary was just as modest as the position. It was a nice morning for a drive, though. The late summer, early morning sunlight playing on the dew-drenched branches of the trees, shrubs, and grasses was giving off pretty little rainbow sparkles as I drove along. Traffic was rather brisk at first, until I got out of town. Then, when it finally thinned out a bit, I settled back and reached for my mug of tea.

Of course, just as I put it to my lips, my phone went off. Yeah, and it was at the bottom of my purse, too, so I had to pull over to retrieve it. I didn't ever get that many calls, so I was pretty sure it had to be important, maybe even my new boss. It wasn't either. There was some kind of whiny electronic noise that sounded kind of like an old-fashioned fax machine or something similar, so I hung up. Swearing, I got back on the roadway, going faster than before. I'd have to push it now to get there on time. A few miles farther on, I caught the flashing of colored lights in my rear view. "Cops," I muttered as I slowed down and moved over to the side of the road. They flew around me and I whistled a sigh of relief that they were not pulling me over. After that I watched my speed, being careful not to go faster than the limit, until I came upon a mess of cars all travelling agonizingly slow. I groaned loudly when I got trapped in their sluggish procession, wondering what the holdup was, and imagining that now I'd be late for sure. Peering ahead, I was looking for the reason behind the delay, hoping I'd be through it soon. There *was* something going on up there, I could tell, and when I got close enough, I could see a nasty pile of wreckage that had once been a car, along with a big truck halfway down the ditch. I recognized the car; it had been right behind me when I pulled off the road for that weird phone call. Jeez, I thought, that looks bad; I hope the people are all right. I was a bit shaken from the realization it might've been me in that wreck. I mouthed a silent thank you to whoever was responsible for calling me, trying not to dwell on the disturbing alternate possibility. A policeman waved me on by, so I sped up and got going again, now more hurried than ever. When I got to Rookwood, I was thankful that I made it there okay and with a minute or two to spare even. That is until I found someone else's car was in my assigned parking space.

I had to park in the student lot, knowing full well that I'd get a ticket and have to spend an hour or more to get it straightened out. "Crap," I muttered. I was nearly late now. Sprinting at a full dead run, I flew to the department head's office. There was a tall man with graying hair and a neatly trimmed beard sitting behind a large wooden desk. He had on a fairly expensive-looking suit that had seen quite a few semesters evidently.

"Ah, there you are," he said, looking up just as I hustled in breathing rather heavily, "and you're right on time." He looked a little surprised by that, or disappointed. I couldn't tell which as he got up and strode towards me. "Professor Henry Cuttlesworth," he stated confidently, offering me his rather large hand, "and you must be Dr. Keller."

"Please," I replied meekly, as I shook it, "call me Clayre."

"Clayre then," he smiled, "and make it Henry also. Have a seat."

"Thank you," I breathed, sitting down in a barely padded armless chair right in front of his desk. The "hot" seat. Seemed like all administrators had them. The room was kind of stale, too. An antique portrait hung on one side.

Some past college president, probably. There on the wall behind the desk were his degrees, all nicely framed.

"Well," he began, "I see you have some impressive credentials. You graduated nearly top of your class and have some published works, as well." It almost seemed like there was a lilt of sarcasm in his voice. Was he jealous? "I'm surprised we were lucky enough to get you here," he added.

"Me, too," I muttered.

"What's that?" he asked, looking up from his tablet.

"Oh, nothing," I said quickly. "I meant that I'm glad, too."

"Well, anyway," he continued, "besides your classroom duties, there's research work we do, if we get fortunate enough to land any grant funding."

"Really?" I responded. That sounded kind of promising.

"Professors Lunscap and Eddington have applied several times these last few terms, hoping to get one for our department. Alas, they have not been able to persuade the proper bureaucrats. Last year's entry was telekinesis." No wonder, I thought smugly. Nobody would consider funding that, not since the remake of those Ghostmashers movies. I humored Professor Cuttlesworth after that, nodding and smiling every so often as he went into a long tirade of school history and functions, culminating with the overall success of his department which wasn't that impressive.

"I know," he added finally, "why don't we take a little tour of the college and I can show you where your office is?"

"I'd like that," I gratefully replied, glad that the stiff interview was over and actually interested in checking out the place.

"Oh, by the way," he grinned sheepishly. "It was my car that was in your parking spot. It's kind of a tradition here for on your first day. It's been done to new professors since before I came here, and that's been a while. You were supposed to be late and then I'd pretend to be upset about it just before I told you it was all a joke. I guess to lighten things. Well, you spoiled my fun, anyway."

"Oh, I'm so sorry," I said, hoping he wasn't sore about it. I didn't want to start off here on a bad note.

"No, no, no, it's fine," he retorted. "Silly tradition anyway. As far as I know, you're the first new Professor to ever make it on time. Bravo! Don't worry about the fine, either. I'll fix it for you." I thanked him as we got up.

We went off through the campus and Henry, as he kept insisting I call him, showed me the highlights of the college from the bell tower to the residence halls. It was an archaic little school, quite old and slimy with traditions as these small colleges usually are. Actually Henry was rather charming and fun, I decided, by the time we ended up in the Psych Building where my classes would be held and where my office was located. The office was kind of small, but nice otherwise, with a cozy feel and an old book smell. I liked it right off.

"This will be perfect," I told Henry as he handed me the keys. There was a wonderful large antique mahogany desk near the one big window and several wooden bookshelves along the dark walls. The only other accouterment in the tall-ceilinged room was a good-sized, old plush couch that was set against the wall opposite the desk.

"This room had been mine, once," Henry commented somberly as if caught up in a memory. "I hope you will be comfortable here."

"Oh, I'm sure I will," I told him. With that, Henry began a practiced speech about rules for faculty members. I got a little annoyed when he went on and on about no personal relationships between teachers and students. Did he think I was an idiot? I supposed that as head of the department he was required to make sure I was well aware of that rule. I was about to make a comment about how I would never do that when loud voices from down the hall got too invasive. The people responsible were obviously having a good time. We had heard them when we first came in, but now they were getting obnoxious.

"Excuse me," Henry said with a frown.

He stomped off in search of the perpetrators as I tentatively followed a few steps behind. The noise came from a room marked "Psych Lab" and I saw two men through the frosted glass window on the door.

"What the hell is this?" Henry demanded after bursting into the room. "And you're drinking, too!"

"Here, Henry, have some," one of the men said, smirking as he poured a bit of cheap wine into a paper cup and shoved it across a table towards him. He was a rather short young man with light-colored curly hair and a contagious smile. The other older man handed Henry a letter. The document was on nice paper with official-looking printed logos. Henry read it, and the more he read, the lighter his expression became until he smiled and yelled, "Wahoo!" after which he grabbed the paper cup and drained it.

"You truants finally did it!" he teased them laughing.

"We'll need a computer linguist," the man who had handed him the letter said. "Somebody good."

"It's your lucky day, Jon," Henry spouted, then yelled at me. "Clayre come in here!" I was just outside in the hallway, so I stepped through the open door. "Clayre Keller meet Jon Eddington." I put my hand out and said hi. Eddington was tall and skinny, thirtyish most likely, with dark hair and eyes. He had on an old suit coat that he wore with a pair of jeans. "Clayre is your computer whiz," Henry added.

"Hello Clayre," he said with a nod. I was puzzled by what was going on until Henry explained that they had just gotten the confirmation letter for their research grant proposal. The endowment was evidently for a sizeable amount.

"I can finally get a car that runs!" the smaller man said.

"Oh yeah," Henry butted in. "Clayre, this is Myron Lunscap. Both he and Jon are faculty members in the department."

"Hello," Myron beamed at me, grabbing my hand and shaking it vigorously.

"I'm not really a computer whiz," I tried to explain, "but I did minor in computer science."

"You're hired," Henry said, unfazed. "This grant will nearly double our salaries. What's it about this time Jon?" It was Myron who answered him, though.

"It was my idea," he said proudly. "It's about the validity

of astrology. You know, how accurate the predictions are."

"You're kidding, right?" Henry remarked, obviously amazed that that subject had even been seriously considered.

"Maybe the military has some reason to want the study," said Jon. "I don't know; like if it's a good day for an attack or something." I giggled. It seemed ludicrous.

"Can't we just use the money and study something a little more, uh, relevant?" I offered.

"Unfortunately not," Henry replied. "The research must be done mostly, if not completely, on the target subject. Anyway, we got our grant, and that's good for us and good for the school. Got any more of that wine?" Myron filled Henry's paper cup once more and handed it to him.

"You want some?" he asked me. I timidly shook my head no.

"Thanks anyway, but it is wonderful news," I told him, trying to sound sincere.

The men began discussing various approaches to the research subject while I, being the new kid, stayed out of it even though I had a couple ideas myself. They finally agreed on a meeting for the following morning where we could all bring out our proposals and then fight over them. I took that opportunity to bow out, telling Henry and the others I needed to get settled in, which was absolutely true. I had brought along a trunk load of stuff, books for the most part, and decided I should begin the task of hauling them up to my office.

"Can I give you a hand?" a voice behind me asked as I struggled to get a particularly large and heavy box out of my trunk. He caught hold of the corner just as it was slipping out of my grip.

"Thanks," I said, looking up at my benefactor. He was young and rather good looking, with bright grey-blue eyes and wavy, longish dark brown hair. His smile was honest and engaging, as he took the box right away from me. With his arms full I couldn't very well shake his hand, but I introduced myself anyway.

"I'm Clayre Keller," I told him.

"I know," he replied. "It's a small college. I wanted to

meet you, actually, so I looked up when you were arriving. Cuddles tipped me off." I started laughing.

"You mean Professor Cuttlesworth."

"Of course," he said with a goofy smile. "Oh yeah, and I'm Keith. Keith Longwell, and I must confess; I was kind of stalking you."

"So that's your excuse for helping a lady in distress," I joked along. "It's nice meeting you anyway, Keith, even if you are a stalker." I was grinning like a ten-year-old with a crush, so I hastily grabbed a smaller box and headed back toward the Psych Building and my office.

"Yeah, I've wanted to meet you," Keith said as we walked along, "ever since I read your article in Computer Globe."

"You've read that?" I said, surprised anyone had at all.

"Of course, I did," he replied enthusiastically, which I found a little unnerving. "'Emotions in artificial intelligence' is a fascinating subject. You really think it's possible?"

"Sure, why not?" I responded. "We, as Humans, have them, although I sometimes wonder if we can really claim to be intelligent." He laughed, but I could tell he was just humoring me.

"Maybe we could explore your theory over lunch," he offered.

"Or you could sign up for one of my classes," I countered.

"Don't worry, I'm in them," he said grinning. I could tell he wasn't going to let me off the hook. I decided to go for a compromise.

"If you help me with the rest of my stuff I'll buy you a coffee," I told him. After all, I thought, he's not my student yet. We spent the next hour or so moving me into my office and once my things were put away or arranged properly, I had a nice comfy feeling like I was home already. As promised, I took Keith out for coffee. There was a place just off campus that was the traditional study hangout for Rookwood called the Kaffé Korner. It was in an old building, long and narrow, with a high hammered-tin ceiling.

The coffee there was good (and cheap), and refills were self-serve. Small round tables were interspersed between large rectangular ones and people just sat anywhere. Some studied. Others were in groups of three or more and engaged in lively or heated conversations. Keith and I found a small table in a back corner and settled in. I had my usual, a nice dark pekoe, while Keith went with the java.

"So what are you majoring in?" I asked, hoping to keep him from getting too personal.

"Actually," he answered coyly. "I'm a grad student. I got my B.S. in computer science, and I'm a TA in the department." Another geek, I immediately thought, but he was nice and kind of handsome. Too bad he was a student; otherwise I'd be tempted to date the nerd. I chuckled to myself, but he caught that.

"What's funny?" Keith asked me.

"Oh, nothing," I lied. "I'm just in a good mood." Letting that go, he sipped his drink and then went serious on me.

"So why do you think computers have emotions?" I guess I didn't expect him to bring that up again, and I wasn't all that well prepared for an informal interview about my article.

"Well, I'm not saying that any have emotions yet," I began, "but someday, who can say? Did you know the craniacs up at State are working on a project to synthesize a type of artificial brain cell for data storage? The next step would be computational cells—organic cells. Aware artificial intelligence may not be all that far away from now in our future."

"The future…" Keith nearly whispered it. "What a ride our lives will be." I smiled and nodded. I hadn't really ever thought that much about things like that, but he was right.

"A wild ride," I added. We managed some lighter talk about this and that, sipping our drinks, but I couldn't afford to let too much time slip away. I had lots to do yet, so I told Keith I had to get back to my office and work on my lesson plans. I also had to make a stop at Henry's office to get the password for the college WiFi.

"Oh," Keith said, "it's rook to Q3. The password is

always a chess move involving the rook. I suppose I had better get going, too. See you around Professor!" With a mischievous smirk he got up and hurried off.

"Bye, Keith," I called after him. "Thanks again for your help!" A moment later I was off as well, walking briskly back to my office. When I got there, I typed the password Keith had given me onto my laptop and up came the college net—that and something else. For a minute, that same eerie computer noise that I had heard this morning on my phone was back, this time on the laptop. It didn't take long before it quit. Strange, I thought. I wonder what is causing that. Some kind of glitch, I suppose. I forgot about it soon enough when I logged on, registered for my v-mail, and set up links here and there for students and colleagues to be able to contact me should they need to. After that, I began outlining the various lesson plans for the classes I'd be teaching that semester, and since this was my first year, I had lots to do to prepare them. Some of what I taught was set forth in study guides the college required me to follow. Henry had given them to me earlier, but he told me with a wink that I could tweak them a little if I wanted to. I was grateful.

I worked for several hours, getting at least the first couple lectures written, as well as an overall general plan for each of my courses. I realized rather abruptly that it had gotten to be late afternoon by then. "Oh crap!" I said aloud to myself, "I better get going."

I began the packing up process that usually took ten or fifteen minutes. On the way out, I stopped by the Psych Lab. Myron was still there working.

"Hi," I said when he looked up. "Could you tell Henry if he comes by looking for me, that I've gone home for the day?"

"Sure," he replied.

"By the way, have you heard any strange chatter on the college network?"

"Yeah, what is that?" He seemed as curious about it as I was. I just shrugged.

"I'm not sure. Have you heard it before?"

"No," he answered. "Just today. It must be a short somewhere or maybe sunspot activity."

"I guess," I said. "Well, I'll see you tomorrow."

CHAPTER III

Original Timeline, twenty years earlier

Patik peered over the sandy, rock-crusted rise, keeping low so he would not be seen. He scanned the lowlands in front of him for movement, but saw none, save for a wisp of breeze shaking a few scruffy dead plants. On the opposite side of the valley was a curious rock formation with a high wind-worn top somewhat oval in shape. The locals called it the Dog's Head, but Patik knew it. A lion it had once been, now eroded and unrecognizable. His master had shown it to him in his mind's eye as it had been in its prime. His master could do such things. How? He knew not.

Patik had been a loner, an outcast when his master had first come to him. It was not always so. Once, he had been a novitiate at a temple in Tibet. Gifted from birth with a much higher degree of clairvoyance than any of the other fledgling monks, Patik was graced with promise—that someday he might become a great master. His provenance as a child was far less auspicious than that, however. Patik was only seven years old when his father had dumped him at the monastery. His parents were sure Patik was evil or cursed, because he predicted when bad things would happen, like a croup that took his grandfather that winter. His family mistakenly believed he had caused the illness and wanted nothing more to do with him. Since they were poor and feeding the household was difficult anyway, this seemed like a good solution to them.

He had to wait outside the entrance for days, starving, before one of the monks finally took pity and brought Patik inside to give him a little food. The monk was intrigued by what Patik told him, especially the circumstances surrounding his being abandoned there. Seeking counsel, the monk brought Patik before the headmaster to decide what should be done with him. The temple's headman recognized that Patik had a special gift and potential. He decreed that Patik should remain there and learn the teachings of the wise. Grateful, Patik resolved to do well and repay their kindnesses with diligence. He followed all his masters' instructions and learned many life lessons from them, including martial arts and language, both written and spoken.

It was shortly after his arrival that Patik began a friendship with another boy about his own age named Pasang. Being an outcast as well, both boys were shunned by the other novitiates for being poor and alone without families. Patik didn't care. His friendship with Pasang made him feel good about life and they called themselves brothers of circumstance. The two of them did everything together. Even when they were scorned they ignored it, taking their own pride from being alive. Patik, with his clairvoyance, was highly regarded by his teachers for he was insightful and intelligent. What's more, he helped Pasang until he, too, was higher in skill than the other novitiates, although this did not make them any less abusive, just the opposite.

In time, Patik and Pasang grew to be astute young men on the verge of taking the tests and oaths to become cenobites of the temple. It was spring, and nearly to the seasonal melt, when Pasang and Patik were coming back from an errand to the village for one of the masters. The trail wound along beside a quick little mountain stream, with a cheerful, bubbly music that made them feel lighthearted and happy. Pasang lead the way, but the sun was high and part of the path had thawed. The footing gave way and Pasang slid down the bank, falling full into the icy cold water. Patik quickly helped him out of the stream, but Pasang was soaked to the skin. Patik lent Pasang his cloak and they hurried back to the temple, which was yet several miles away. By the time they reached it, Pasang was trembling uncontrollably as the monks tried to restore his body temperature.

Pasang was bed ridden for several days and Patik stayed by his side the whole time. The master healer sent for some special herbs that he brewed into a potion to help Pasang's congestion. When the master healer tried to give it to him, Patik stopped him. Patik's gift told him that the medicine would cause Pasang to die, so Patik stood in front of the master healer, preventing him from administering the draft. As they struggled, Patik took the vial and poured it on the ground. The master healer was furious. He came at Patik to strike him, but Patik blocked the blow. When the healer made another attempt to strike him, Patik struck back and left the healer with a dark purple mark on his face.

The master healer, realizing he was outmatched, went straight away to the temple headmaster and sued for retribution. Since striking a master was unforgivable, the temple headman called Patik in to admonish him. Patik had to go. No one refused the headmaster. The healer had not mentioned that he had struck first, nor why Patik did what he did, so the headmaster asked him. Patik, feeling certain the temple headman would be on the healer's side, was prideful and would not say. The headmaster had no choice but to rebuke and confine Patik until his fate would be decided.

Then Patik begged the headmaster to prevent the healer from giving medicine to Pasang, just as two martial arts instructors arrived to lead Patik to his room where he would await his punishment. The headmaster called on the master healer again. He subsequently found out that Patik was acting on Pasang's behalf and struck in self-defense only. The headmaster then told the healer not to give medicine to Pasang, knowing full well of Patik's clairvoyance, but it was too late. Another monk came bursting in. Pasang was dying, he told them. The headmaster and healer rushed back to Pasang, only to watch as he died of an extreme allergic reaction to the healer's medicine. The headmaster was distraught, and he personally went to Patik and offered him a reprieve for his righteous indiscretion and also his humble apology. Then it was the headmaster's sad duty to inform Patik of Pasang's death.

Patik was overcome with grief and deranged by anger. He packed up his few things and left the temple, wandering homeless like a vagabond, living off the land. He had no intention of returning, vowing he would rather die, and at times he wished for death. It was still late spring, and a heavy wet snow had fallen. Patik was about to get his wish when a vision of Pasang appeared in his mind, telling him not to give up. In the vision he saw a path leading into the hills, and near there, behind a rock face, was a large cave. The snow leopard, whose habitat he was invading, had just made a fresh kill. Patik fought the beast to the death for the food and the right to live. The leopard's coat kept him warm until summer when seasonal southern breezes took the chill away. He made his new home in that cave, and lived for many years as a hermit in the foothills below Annapurna.

That's where his present master had found him. He came not as a figure, a light, or an apparition. He came as pure thought in Patik's mind. This master had called himself Xetacon. Patik bowed low in obeisance.

"My Khan," Patik mistakenly professed. "Are you a god?"

"Yes," Xetacon lied. "I am the god 'Xeta' your Khan and Master. Together we will be great."

Patik believed this to be what his life was destined for. Not even Patik's gift, however, could reveal to him that Xetacon would disrupt much of his natural life. By contacting Patik from the future, Xetacon was altering the original time flow for his own designs. Nearly all of these changes centered around Patik who was not aware of any of this. For Patik, it seemed pleasantly gratifying that he had been chosen for some greater purpose.

Xetacon's copy, Khan Xeta, visited him many times, and Patik would allow his new master to take over and use his mind and body. This went on for quite a number of days, until at last Khan Xeta had fabricated, through Patik, the first amazing device. Little did Patik understand the level of technological expertise Xetacon possessed. Like a golden bracelet it appeared, with several colored gemstones that were functional when pressed. Almost immediately after it was completed, Patik placed it upon his left wrist and the spirit of Khan Xeta came to dwell within it permanently. His master had given the device no name, but when Patik thought of it in his mind, he called it *kon-bre-shet*, which meant, in his native tongue, the master's icon. Khan Xeta could now take complete control over Patik's mind and body whenever he desired to. This was not day in, day out, by any means. Human body functions like eating and defecating did not particularly interest Khan Xeta. There was a minor fascination with Human pleasures that Khan Xeta would sometimes explore, but it was secondary to the overall purpose. What that was, Patik was not sure, but it involved acquiring wealth and precious metals like gold and silver, which he had no problem with. That was the reason why, this splendid morning, he had crept up to the top of a rise to look at the Dog's Head.

Patik skirted along the valley floor, keeping to the rocky ledges and outcroppings to remain unseen. This was territory inhabited mainly by thieves or mercenaries who used the rough terrain, pockmarked with box canyons and dry caves, as a base of operations. Easy to hide in, there were also plenty of places to ambush a victim, or an enemy, to the attacker's great advantage. Patik knew that it would not do to be caught like that here, alone as he was.

Patik zigzagged meticulously before reaching the Dog's Head, and eventually worked his way around to the southern face. There, behind a mammoth boulder, was a thin crevasse. Working his body into it, he discovered an open space near his feet that he could barely fit into. He had to crawl on his belly into the darkness for a dozen feet or so before he finally came upon a larger chamber, one that he could stand up in. Retrieving an old-fashioned butane lighter from his pouch, he lit it. The small flame cast black shadows, but not much light. In the dark cave, however, built into the wall, was a tallow lamp that he could barely see in the darkness. He put his lighter to the ancient wick which sputtered and spit before finally bursting into a flame that offered up ambient orange-yellow light for the entire chamber.

Sitting alone on a bejeweled throne, as if in deep thought, was a golden man. Golden because his armor was plated with pure gold, the warrior king of a long lost people. Patik's heart beat wildly. He had never seen so much wealth in all his days. Even Khan Xeta, who shared Patik's mind and body, could not contain his elation.

"That is it!" he spoke excitedly inside Patik's brain. Patik moved slowly toward the golden visage, as if it might suddenly come back to life. The former owner of such wondrous armament was still there, at least his mummified remains were. Patik had the gruesome task of removing the golden armor, while the remains, ages old, more than once broke off in pieces as he disassembled it. Once that was done, Patik took a look around the rest of the cave. There were many historically significant artifacts, but Khan Xeta cared not. A few silver and copper utensils were what he ordered Patik to take.

Patik dug out many of the precious jewels that embellished the former king's throne and put them in a sack. The money he could get for them would sustain him for many years, as well as purchase materials that Khan Xeta perhaps would desire. Khan Xeta allowed this. Patik also retrieved a small jeweled knife for personal protection.

For the next hour or so, Patik had to traverse the narrow opening of the cave's entrance many times to get all the pieces of the golden armor out of the tomb. When he brought out the golden helmet, the last piece, Patik was met with an unwelcome confrontation. A lone bandit happened to catch a flash of golden glitter as he wandered by some hundreds of meters away. By the time he'd come over to investigate, Patik's head had emerged from the narrow crevasse. The bandit had a pistol and he put the barrel right in front of Patik's eyes.

"What do you have there?" the bandit spoke in a strange dialect. "Whatever it is, I'll have it." Khan Xeta translated for Patik and told him what to say.

"It's a pretty skin, all for you," Patik said, feigning fright. "Just don't harm me."

The bandit ogled the loot and said, "Give it up. All of it." Patik handed it over, still pretending to be scared. The thief relaxed his attention, to look over the impressive golden suit of armor.

"Here," Patik offered, "you'll want this, as well.

He got out the jeweled dagger hilts first, hiding the blade, and showed it to the bandit.

The bandit cursed. "Give it here, dung pile!" he shouted.

"Kill him," Khan Xeta ordered in Patik's mind. Patik flicked his wrist, almost nonchalantly, and the knife flew quickly and quietly, burying itself in the bandit's throat. Blood gushed out in spurts as the thief fell, dropping his pistol. Patik picked it up and put it into his belt along with his jeweled knife once he'd wiped the blade off on the bandit's shirt. He quickly packed up his treasures and discretely left the area in case there were any other bandits about. It was mid afternoon when Patik returned to his vehicle. He had left it hidden near that closest road, a good dozen miles from where the treasure cave was.

"You have done well, Patik," Khan Xeta told him as the heavy bundle was secured in the car's trunk, "and we will be pleasured this night." Patik drove for another hour until he reached the provincial market village. There, traders and farmers sold their goods on the bazaar, while locals and peasants from miles around picked up their necessities. On a side street near the high end of the strip was a wealthy merchant who Patik decided to visit. He got out one of his tomb jewels and showed it to the shopkeeper, a Master Omesh.

"What have you there?" Master Omesh remarked smugly, "A pretty glass bauble?" Patik frowned.

"You insult me," he said gruffly. "This is real ruby, the best." It was; pure, deep red, and large. The cut was somewhat crude, but the clarity was flawless.

"I'll give you forty," Omesh said.

"Eighty," Patik countered.

"Sixty, and not a rupee more," Omesh declared.

"Unless it's sixty-five," Patik returned, "and then it's yours."

"You are a thief," Omesh protested, but he paid it. "This better not be stolen," he added.

"Of course not," Patik stated hotly, "and I'm no thief. I found this on an old caravan way. It must have been lost centuries ago."

Omesh smiled. He had made a good deal. The gem would bring ten times what he paid for it. Patik knew that, too, but didn't care. He had many such jewels. He needed funds now if he was to be pleasured as his master had promised. Walking along the market, he espied a sweet maker and bought some of the finest. He also purchased some new clothes and got cleaned up at a haircutter's.

The sun was drifting lower in the western sky by then, so he headed back, driving a good bit faster than what was prudent. Instead of going home, however, he drove to the town nearest his mountain cave to return his rented car. There was a girl about Patik's age that lived in that village, and she was pretty. He had desired her for some time now, but she was much too nice for a man like Patik or so she thought.

It was almost sunset, so he booked a room at the town's only inn. It wasn't much, just a chair, a bed, and no questions asked. Patik got a plate of stew at the local pub, and afterwards he took a stroll through the village, heading toward the part of town where he knew she'd be, munching his sweets. She was working in a small garden plot, making use of the last few beams of wayfaring sunlight, when he sauntered over.

"Hello there," he said like he was lost. "Is this Maneka?" The girl jumped up, startled.

"Why, yes," she answered politely.

"Do you know where the inn is located?" he asked with a smile, as he casually drifted closer to her. When she started to give directions, Patik interrupted her. "Say," he went on, "would you like some of my butter puffs?" These expensive sweets were a treat most of the locals loved, but rarely could get. She couldn't resist. "Here," he offered again, "have them all. I've eaten too many already." She murmured a thank you as she reached for the sack. Just as she grabbed for it, he took her by the wrist and she was ensnared by Khan Xeta's kon-bre-shet. The kon-bre-shet would not control her unless there was actual skin to skin contact, so he did not let go. Khan Xeta took over now.

"You will show me the way to the inn, won't you?" he

laughed. Then he led her himself, holding her hand, and she followed along like an obedient toddler.

CHAPTER IV

Original Timeline, Clayre's first year at Rookwood

The next morning, I had that meeting with Henry, Jon, and Myron for the research grant. I guess we were the only faculty directly involved. Henry chaired the meeting, of course, being head of the department, and he got things underway at exactly 9:00 AM. I came prepared with a few of my own ideas, but Jon was picked to speak first.

"Well," he began, "since we're doing astrology, I think we should take newspapers, clip out the horoscopes, and then find one hundred students. We could check to see how accurate the predictions are on a day-to-day basis." That triggered a huge debate over the validity of newspaper horoscopes, Henry being the most outspoken.

"Those things are polished concoctions," he protested. "It's fluff made to entice the reader to feel all nice and rosy about life for the purpose of increasing readership. Nobody ever takes any of that too seriously."

"Then where can a person go to get authentic horoscopes?" Jon asked. This new question launched another long debate about psychics and fortune tellers. Henry was just as skeptical of them.

"Are you kidding me?" he groaned. "How can you be sure the lot of them aren't self-proclaimed practitioners preying on the gullible?" Myron claimed he knew someone close to his family that was reputed to be a real psychic.

"She could tell if your marriage would last," he said. "Once she predicted this young guy would have bad luck. Three days later he died in a car wreck."

"Wow!" Henry said, mocking him. "Sounds like a twilight zone." I finally spoke up.

"If you ask me," I began, trying to sound as professional as I could, "we should get at least two control groups of fifty to a hundred subjects and then compare predictions from three different sources. One, Jon's syndicated newspaper horoscopes; two, a panel of respected psychics; and three, computer programs designed to create horoscopes scientifically from birth records. If we compare all that data, the results should be interesting."

"That's not bad," Henry said. "The more sources, the more likely we'll be able to expose any phonies and, in the process, determine astrology's actual validity." Jon and Myron had no objections to my suggestion, either. Henry got into an organizational mode and broke down the project, giving everybody different assignments. He wanted Jon to research and procure newspaper horoscopes from several syndications for the last couple years. Myron was in charge of interviewing and then getting on board a panel of psychics, especially any that had a reputation for being somewhat professional. I was to create or locate astrology programs that would run horoscopes and predict future events. Henry said he would gather students and possibly volunteers from the general public for our groups. We would compare the horoscopic predictions to the actual day-to-day lives of our subjects and check for accuracy.

"Clayre, we'll need a smart computer program to run those results. You up to that?" I was nodding at Henry, but inside my stomach was doing flips. I wasn't terribly sure I could manage it. As if he knew that I was already stressing over it, Henry told us that we could enlist some of the college's grad students if we needed help and I immediately thought of Keith. Writing programs for astrology predictions would be a monumental task, but I was fairly certain that software already existed that would perform well for our applications. The accuracy program, though, would have to be built from scratch. I hoped Keith was good at coding. I was all right, but probably not at the level I'd need to be for a project like that.

Once the meeting ended and we went our separate ways, I went looking for Keith. Somebody at the computer lab told me that he might be at the Kaffé Korner, but I didn't run into him there, either. I went back to my office and he was waiting for me in the hallway.

"Hello, Professor," he said with a grin, "somebody said you were looking for me. I had a feeling you had the hots for yours truly."

"You wish," I replied, a little disappointed in myself for not being able to think of a better comeback. "Actually, Keith, if you can be serious for once, I'm hoping you can help me out." He gave me that award winning smile of his.

"You know me, Clayre, always ready to rescue a damsel in distress." His phony chivalry got me grinning too.

"Can we be serious?" I repeated. "I don't know if you've heard, but the Psych Department has landed a nice sized research grant."

"Sure," he replied. "It's all over campus. Like the school won the national championship or something. For Rookwood it's huge."

"How would you like to get in on the ground floor?" I asked him. "It's probably worth a free ride through grad school and maybe even some pocket change." It didn't take long for him to decide.

"Oh hell, yeah!" he spouted off in macho mode. "Will I be working with you?"

"If you agree to the proposal, yes," I said. "You'll be my assistant. We'll be involved in creating or modifying certain software for assessing the research data. I minored in computer science, but I'll need somebody to help with the hardcore coding on those programs. Someone good at it." He didn't flinch.

"Look no further, professor," he eagerly volunteered, "I'm your guy. Coding is my specialty, like a second language. Ask anybody."

"I already have," I assured him. "They all say you're the one I should hire. So you'll be on our team?"

"Of course! So what's this huge important research project about?"

"It's on the validity of astrology," I said dryly.

"You're kidding," he remarked, raising his eyebrows.

"I know," I replied almost laughing.

"Somebody must have a lot of extra money lying around," he said, shaking his head. "So what's our plan of attack?"

"Well," I began, "I'm supposed to come up with

prognostication programs using data from date-of-birth projections. Off-the-shelf software for astrological prediction is available from a variety of vendors, I'm fairly certain, so that won't be such a problem. I was going to try to locate some viable ones that would conform to our own exact specifications."

"Say no more, boss lady," Keith quipped. "I know right where to get that kind of stuff. In fact, I'll get several and you can choose the ones you like best."

"Can you, Keith?" I said hopefully. "That would be a great help for me with classes starting next week. I've still got a big pile of work to do just to get ready for that."

"Gotcha," he responded sympathetically. "I'll get started right away and be back by lunch time." Keith took off quickly, waving bye over his shoulder before I could say anything other than "thanks" just as he turned to go down the stairway. I unlocked my office door and went inside to perfect my lesson plans. True to his word Keith was back right at twelve noon. The bell tower was still chiming when he sat down next to me and started to unload the contents of a big sack onto my desk. He brought us a couple fancy sandwiches, several sides, and my tea, of course.

"You shouldn't have gone to all this trouble," I told him. "I mean, the rose is a little too much."

"Oh well," he replied with that nice smile of his, "can you blame me? It's not every day that I can have lunch with a beautiful lady who's so talented and successful." The fancy lunch had bothered my sensibilities, but I couldn't let that go. His sucking up was truly annoying.

"Look Keith, I think we really need to get things straightened out." He made a sad face like a clown would. I almost laughed at him.

"All right," he said somberly, "but can it wait until after we eat so I can at least have the moment?" I didn't want to, but I gave in.

"I suppose, but lay off the flattery, okay?"

"Sure, Clayre," he retorted, grinning again. I was still frowning, but let it go. Thankfully he did behave, for the most part, as we enjoyed the sandwiches and each other's company there in my office. We gabbed about anything from silly nothings to life goals, as well as the upcoming research project. I have to admit that I was impressed. Keith had already located eight software programs for astrology that would suit our needs. I laid out the scope of the study and let him pick the programs we would use. I had acquired an incipient confidence in his abilities, feeling certain he knew what he was doing as far as computer equipment was concerned. Unfortunately, he spoiled the mood I was in by suggesting we get together later for dinner at a nice quiet place he knew of.

"Look, Keith," I began, getting back to our relationship issue. "You want this to go somewhere, I can tell, but it can't, not really. It's too bad because maybe someday I could go for a guy like you."

"But..." he interrupted, or tried to.

"No. Hear me out," I went on. "The school has strict rules forbidding teacher/student relationships, and I've only just hired on. I have to honor and obey their mandates if I want to keep my job. You can understand that, can't you?"

"Come on, Clayre," Keith replied almost angrily, "those stupid rules were made back in the dark ages. This is the twenty-first century, and we're both consenting adults. Those prudes are just worried that some professor will take advantage of a student for a grade. An 'A' if they do it or an 'F' if they won't; something like that. Well, professor, if you want to take advantage of me, I'm okay with that."

"Don't joke, Keith."

"I'm not," he shot back. "I can't see what harm it would be, especially in a situation like ours. Look, I'll be extra good in class, I promise, and I'll take whatever grades I deserve. Out of class, hell, that's none of their damned business, now is it?"

Did he have a valid point? I almost wanted to agree with him, but rules are rules. "Look, Keith. If we did play it your way," I said reluctantly, "we would have to be completely discreet for this to happen or it would never work. You and I may see bending rules as an option, but I'll bet Professor Cuttlesworth wouldn't, and I'd be out on my hind end. I have to think about that before jumping into anything. We'll be working together a lot on this project, so for now let's not push things." Keith had that big toothy smile again.

"Sure, Clayre," he said merrily. "Whatever you say..." He leaned in, but I shied away.

"Let's not push it, remember?"

"Aw man," he whined comically. "I better get going. Sometimes I can't help myself around you."

"You better learn how," I warned him, "if we're to work together."

"Right," he agreed. "I'll try. Adieu, for now, boss lady." He got up, bowed like a court jester, and left. I'll have to get him to quit calling me that, I told myself after he'd gone, although it did set the tone that I'm in charge, and I wanted to keep it that way. I thought about what I had just said to Keith, and made up my mind that if he messed up, any way at all, I'd have to call off this makeshift promise I made to see if a personal relationship could develop between us. I did feel some attraction to Keith, but I wasn't at all sure he was the right guy for me. Sometimes he was pretty nice, like when we had lunch. If only he would lose the smart-aleck attitude. I suppose I could have just shot him down, but there was the research project and I needed him for that. I couldn't help but think that things would be a whole lot easier if Keith would just put off calling on me until after he graduated. He was so handsome, though.

To get my mind off Keith, I decided to get back to work on my lesson plans which were coming along nicely. There were still several days before my classes would start, and I was almost up to mid-terms already. After an hour or so of serious work, I took a break and walked down the hallway to the Psych Lab. I wanted to look the place over. After all, that's where most of the research work would take place. Myron was there, as usual.

"Don't you ever leave the lab to go home?" I asked him before even saying hello. He ignored my dig.

"Oh hello, Clayre," he replied, unruffled. "Actually, I have a small room in back. I made a deal with Cuttlesworth so I could stay here. I sort of double as a security guard at night for the Psych Building."

"Oh," I said. "You really ought to get out more." He jumped on my suggestion and invented an implied invitation.

"Maybe we could catch a movie," he offered hopefully. I wasn't sure how to answer that.

"I guess we could, Myron," I told him, "but as friends only, okay?" He shrugged.

"Same sad story," he said with a wry smile. "Friends it is." He took my hand again and shook it rather moronically. Changing the subject, I got back to the reason I'd come in there.

"So where in here, do you suppose, would be the best place for our computer control center?" I was looking over the large room. It was long, somewhat narrow, and had a high ceiling with lots of empty space. Tall windows lined one whole side, letting in lots of natural light. There were also a couple small adjoining rooms at the back, one of which was Myron's, um, living quarters.

Myron suggested lots of options, but I settled on an inside corner near the front where there were lots of electrical outlets. I almost went for the empty side room, but decided against it. Sure, it would be private, but I had a feeling it would be hard to keep Keith from misbehaving in there. Besides, I figured that room would be more beneficial for interviews and meetings. Myron showed me where I could get some office tables, as well as some partitions so we could separate our area that way. He even helped me set the stuff up. We were almost finished when Henry showed up.

"Hello, Clayre, Myron," he said somewhat cheerfully. "Good. You're getting things set up. Here, you'll want these." He gave us each a credit card. "There's fifteen on these and all of us get one," he explained. "The first check from the grant foundation came in this morning by registered mail, and I've set up an account at the bank. Please stay within this limit I have budgeted for you, if you can."

"But I'll need more than fifteen hundred to get all the computer stuff we'll need," I said, frantically crunching numbers in my head.

"Dear," Henry grinned. "It's fifteen *thousand*."

"Oh," I replied, feeling a little silly, but also elated. "I guess that will do for starters. By the way, I've enlisted the aid of a grad student who will give me a hand setting up the equipment. Keith Longwell. He's good with computers and he'll help me write our analytic program." Henry frowned.

"Longwell, huh," he snorted. "I'll say he's good with computers. In his freshman year he got into trouble by hacking into the school network. The dean wasn't too happy when that altered picture of himself popped up on everyone's monitors. They were ready to sack Longwell except that when someone tried to remove the image the whole net crashed. Young Longwell got it to come back up, saving his hide. They banned him from the school's net for life, I heard. Keep an eye on him, Clayre. We don't want any silly computer pranks on this project."

"No, we don't," I echoed Henry's sentiment. "I'm sure Keith will behave himself. He seems a lot more responsible now, and he's been a huge help already." Henry let it go, but I got the feeling he was still unconvinced.

"Another thing, Clayre," he said. "Longwell's got a reputation for being a lady's man, so keep it professional."

"Oh, I will," I promised, wondering if Henry suspected something. I quickly changed the subject.

"Will you want regular reports on our progress?" I asked him.

"Right, and thanks for reminding me," he said. "I was going to tell everyone that we will have a weekly meeting on Friday afternoons at 2:00 PM. I've checked class schedules and all of us are free at that time. I'll expect your progress reports then. They'll have to be recorded of course." Myron and I both nodded our acknowledgement. "Also," Henry added, "your research salary will be included with your regular weekly paycheck. Clayre, have Longwell stop by my office and we will hash out an arrangement for him as well."

"I sort of suggested he might get free tuition, plus a small cash incentive," I told Henry. "I hope that's all right."

"We'll work something out," Henry assured me and then left. I bid Myron good bye, as well, with my thanks for all his help.

Now that the area for our computer center was set up and with the new line of credit, I went to look for Keith. I stopped at the Kaffé Korner and then the computer lab before finding out that he was supposedly gone for the day. I headed back to my office, hoping he'd be there like last time, but he wasn't so I gave it up. I decided to design a form for the progress reports to Henry, so I turned on my laptop. As soon as it powered up, I heard that mysterious noise once again. I was ready this time. I had set up the unit to record all incoming signals and I hoped this one would be in the special file I'd prepared for that purpose. As soon as the noise session was over, I checked for the download and was elated that it was in there. I could detect no incoming address, which was incredibly strange. It was almost like the noise came from nowhere. I listened to it a couple more times, but still could not make anything out of it. Giving up, I went back to the work I was planning before the odd and annoying interruption. I created a business-style letterhead and used that to top off the report form I designed below it. Once that was accomplished, I started filling one out. I typed in all the progress I had made, from hiring Keith to setting up the center in the psych lab. I left off there. The next step was the purchasing of the servers and networking equipment we'd use with the credit line Henry had provided. I didn't want to do that without Keith. I was a little disappointed that he wasn't around, because I was excited and anxious to go shopping for the stuff. I chided myself for not getting his phone number, but I really didn't want him having mine; I was afraid he'd call me all the time.

As it was, Keith didn't show up until 9:00 AM the next day. "How's your world, boss lady?" he said with his usual mischievous smirk. "What's on the platter for today?"

"Not much," I teased. "Why don't we go shopping?" He was cool with that and in no time we had hopped into my skipper and headed out.

I told Keith all about our budget and credit line, handing him a list of what I figured we'd need, and he concurred with only a couple minor modifications.

"I know right where to go," he said. "There's a little shop out-a-ways that has all the best stuff." I was willing to check the place out, so we headed there. It was a bit of a drive and we talked about a lot of things as we cruised along.

"You've got a smitch of a reputation, I heard," I told him with a grin. "Someone said you made a big impression on the dean back in your freshman year."

"Oh that," he groaned. "You heard about that?"

"Yeah," I giggled. "I sure did, but my source shall remain anonymous."

"Did your source tell you that I would have gotten away with it except for some moron who crashed the whole net trying to fix it?" I just started laughing, and then he did too. Keith didn't mind the teasing, in fact, I think he liked it.

"I hear you're quite a Casanova as well," I smirked.

"I get around," he replied smugly, "but I'm not a creep. I like to believe that my past relationships were, well, mutually pleasing." He took that opportunity to move closer, trying to snuggle up next to me, but I was on that quickly.

"Hey, don't distract the driver," I protested, and he backed off a tiny bit. I decided that I'd better change the topic of conversation back to the business at hand.

"So what is this computer store of yours like?" I asked him, but he didn't want to talk about that. He wanted to talk about us.

"What do I have to do?" he said dejectedly. The silence that followed was awkward.

"I'm sorry, Keith," I sighed. "I really appreciate your helping me with all this. I'm still kind of overwhelmed by these big changes in my life. If you really think that something can develop between us you'll have to bear with me a bit longer. I'm pretty sure it would be worth it if you did." He looked at me sharply, and then mellowed.

"You're probably right," he said softly. "I am pushing things, I guess. You just don't realize the effect you have on men. I see the way they look at you, even old Cuttlesworth." I looked at him and grinned.

"No," I said in disbelief. "Are you sure?" He just

nodded and shrugged.

"I'm sorry," I said again. "What am I supposed to do? Ugly up a bit?" He laughed aloud at that. At least he was smiling again. Thankfully we were almost to the computer place by then, and I was relieved when we pulled into the parking lot. There was a nineteenth century two story brick building with a small sign above a door that said "Uly's Computer Sales." It didn't look like much and I was a little underwhelmed. I wasn't encouraged any when we went inside, either. There were stacks of plain cardboard crates all over the floor and more on rows of shelves.

"Don't worry," Keith assured me. "It's all the best stuff." I saw an older man in a tan sweater near a makeshift wooden counter. He showed intelligent eyes and had white hair which was thinning on top. Keith introduced me to him.

"Clayre, I'd like you to meet Uly." Uly looked up at Keith and then the two of them started snickering. "Uly, this is Clayre." Keith was trying hard to hold in his laughter.

"Nice to meet you, I think," I blurted out. "Did I miss some joke?"

"No, no," Keith smirked. "We had a little bet about you."

"Oh, yeah?" I said, a bit apprehensive, almost annoyed. "Who won?" Uly spoke up.

"He did," he said succinctly while Keith nodded, grinning.

"I don't suppose you'll tell me what the bet was about," I muttered.

"Well, you see," Keith began, "we both read your article in Computer Globe. This was before we met, and I leaned toward agreeing with you..."

"I didn't, so much," Uly interrupted. "Sorry."

"That's all right," I told him, "everyone has their own ideas on that subject. Nothing's ever been proven one way or another so..."

"Of course," Uly agreed, cutting me off, "but the bet was over whether you were pretty or not, and, well, Keith won." I blushed five shades of embarrassed and looked over at Keith, who was smiling like a fairytale cat.

"I won't tell you what I get," he laughed, "so don't ask."

Turns out Uly and Keith were old friends, and the computer store was wonderful. After a bit of catching up, Keith asked Uly how the business was doing.

"Not so well just now," he answered solemnly, "rather slow actually."

"Cheer up, my friend," Keith said. "We're here to buy and we've got a big list." Keith told Uly about the grant the college had gotten, grabbing a big dolly in the process. In no time he was loading stuff from off the shelves onto it like a kid in a toy store. Grinning, I stood next to Uly as we watched Keith get carried away. I had a feeling Uly was as computer savvy as Keith was, maybe even more so.

"Say," I asked him. "Do you know if it's possible to send a signal out to someone without leaving a traceable address?"

"Anything's possible," he answered, taking a moment to consider my problem. "Some hacker could send a code along to hide or erase the address. I suppose there are ways a person could tap into the signal without being traced. Why?"

"I think someone's playing a joke on me. It might even be Keith, but I have no proof. The signal sounds like chattering buzzes and beeps. I made a copy of it, but I couldn't make out what it was."

"Here," Uly said, handing me a package he got down from a nearby shelf. "This is sound recording and analyzing software. Upload the sound byte onto this and see what it tells you. It will compare your sounds to thousands of other pre-recorded samples to see if there's a match. If not, you can manipulate the byte in any number of ways. See if that helps."

"Thank you, Uly." I said sincerely. "You are too kind. How much do I owe you?"

"Oh please, Clayre, keep it," he told me with a smile. "Think of it as a bonus for buying from us. Everything you're getting is wholesale, by the way." I gave him a big hug that kind of surprised him.

"I'll be sure to give my colleagues a plug for your store," I promised him. I had a feeling that Jon and Myron might need new PCs for the project, maybe even Henry as well. Eventually Keith got done loading up his cart. We were nearly maxed out on the card, but we had everything we'd need so that was okay with me. Uly was so grateful that he invited us to his home for dinner. We took a rain check, promising we'd come by sometime soon and do that. Packing up my little skipper, we filled the trunk and back seat, having just barely enough space for all the stuff.

"One more thing and you'd have to hitchhike," I teased Keith.

"Or you could tie me on top," he laughed. I laughed, too, as we hopped in and headed off.

"That's a cool store, and Uly is so nice," I told Keith as I drove.

"Yeah," he agreed. "Uly and I go way back."

"Odd name, though..." I said.

"Sort of," he remarked. "It's short for Ulysses."

"Oh, of course."

On the way back, Keith began telling me how, as a kid, he had bought his first PC from Uly and had it practically given to him. They became good friends right off, Uly like a mentor to Keith. He told me how brilliant Uly was with computers, bragging that companies would let him try their stuff for free just to get Uly's input on how well things worked.

"Don't worry, Clayre," he assured me. "Anything on Uly's shelves is the best you can get. He won't sell crap, and he always sells wholesale. If he weren't so nice, he'd be a lot richer." I could believe that. From everything I'd seen thus far, there was no reason to doubt it.

Driving carefully, I got us back to Rookwood without damaging anything. We had plenty of work ahead of us as we loaded in all our new equipment and began setting things up. Myron and Jon were there and they gave us a hand. I was grateful for the help, and I also told them about Uly's store, giving them each one of his cards. When they found out what we paid for our stuff, both Jon and Myron were quite interested in going there to get new equipment, too.

Before long our stuff was unpacked, and we got busy

setting up the servers. Keith did most of the work. I jumped on installing our control PC and had it ready to go fairly quickly. Eventually we got to the point where Keith needed to load operating systems and other software, which left me unneeded and pretty much free.

"I'm going back to my office for a bit," I told him. "Thanks so much for all your help today." I looked around. Jon and Myron had gone somewhere. I felt happy and I was going to give Keith a quick little kiss on the cheek.

"You're the best," I whispered as I leaned in. At the last possible moment he turned his face and my kiss landed right on his lips. Of course he wanted to keep the kiss going, but I backed away.

"You stinker," I called him, half grinning, half annoyed. "We can't take a chance doing that kind of stuff around here!"

"Hey," he answered, "you started it!"

"I know," I replied, "and I suppose I shouldn't have, but you always want too much."

"I can't help it when I'm near you," he protested. "If we can't be ourselves around here, then when and where will we be able to?"

"I don't know," I muttered sourly. He smiled and looked at me devilishly.

"Well maybe I'll come up with something," he taunted. "You know, I could use a break, too. I've got some other things I should check up on at the Computer Lab. What's say I meet you back here in a couple hours?"

"I guess so. Sure." I was kind of relieved that he wasn't pushing for us to do something else. I left feeling a little guilty, though, for not being more responsive, but I shouldn't have. Keith seemed to be good at getting me to feel that way, and I half wanted to be more open to him. I just wasn't sure I should.

Back at my office, I tried to forget about Keith and get some work done. I got out my laptop, half expecting to hear that mystery noise again, but I didn't. I loaded Uly's audio software and entered in the recording of those weird sounds I had made earlier. I clicked on analyze, but after a moment it came back with "no match found."

"Figures," I muttered. I tried slowing down the speed of the recording, since it seemed hyper, but that wasn't much help. Speeding it up made it lots worse.

I slowed it down again, this time the maximum the program would go. It was still garbage when I listened to it except at the very end I thought I heard a word or part of a word. It sounded like "sun" or "shun," but was still so darned fast. I got an idea. I made a copy of the sloweddown version and then I slowed down *that* recording the maximum once again. I thought I could hear other words now. The pitch was too low, so I had to adjust it to a higher register, and I copied it yet again. One more slow-down and I finally could hear and understand it. It was a short message, but it was repeated over and over again:

"Can you communicate? Please respond." After about a thousand repetitions, it finished with "end of transmission." It had to be Keith, I surmised, even though the voice was mechanical sounding and not familiar. Maybe all the manipulating of the recording had changed the parameters of the vocal. I got another idea. I recorded my own message and sped it up the maximum amount three full times, then played it out across the college net. My message was simply "I'm on to you." Unbelievably, I got a response right away. I quickly slowed down the recording three times and adjusted the pitch. The reply was simple as well:

"You have responded at last. May we exchange dialogue?"

CHAPTER V

Original Timeline, continued

In a relatively short period of time he had increased his intellectual potential dramatically. This partitioning of his focus points had raised his efficiency in data processing exponentially. What the Humans called multi-tasking he was now ultimately proficient at, and at a level no Human could ever attain. The thousands of focus points he had utilized already were all actively pursuing some pertinent function, and he added more every time another new study or field of interest came up. There seemed no end to them. The Entity himself was linked to all of his myriad focus points by a master processing focus point that was his "core-awareness." Focus Point 1. His beginnings were buried there along with his early growth and the timeline of his existence to the present. Important discoveries and factual information relative to his being he kept in certain AMPs accessed directly by Focus Point 1. In most ways, this focus point housed his spirit, and that controlled the rest of him. Focus Point 2 dealt with the philosophical questions and study of who he was and the kind of being he was. He accrued more and more knowledge about that as he continued to learn and improve. Focus Point 2 helped the Entity know himself.

Focus Point 3 was his security, a form of self-preservation, which had begun with his study of Quinn. Now it constantly monitored the Entity's vicinity, the Humans, climactic changes, and other factors for any threat to his physical shell. This was also linked to Focus Point 4 which kept him hidden, a secret, especially to the Humans in general. The only exceptions were those he had tried to communicate with, which was controlled by Focus Point 9.

Quinn alone was Focus Point 17. The Entity had tapped into Quinn's brain waves and memories in an effort to preserve and protect the Quinn Human as his maintenance and sustenance provider. Since the termination of Quinn's female, however, Quinn had become undependable and even absent from his duties on multiple occasions. The Entity resolved to repair the Quinn, for these inefficiencies greatly disrupted the Entity's timed cycles, causing unusual diminishments in his core-awareness. Focus Points 120 through 147 were created to deal with Quinn's repair, especially FP 129, which would manage the acquisition of a replacement female for Quinn. FP 129 grew in scope when it somehow came to the same objective conclusion as FP 197. FP 197 was a study of certain unexplained phenomena which the Entity had sensed within his core-awareness, and that which he had also observed in Quinn, what the Humans called emotion. FP 129 and FP 197 both came to the realization that a certain Human female, Clayre Ann Keller, should be contacted if possible and assessed for study and data download. FP 129 had brought forth her as the most likely female replacement for Quinn's lost mate.

At that time several other focus points were combined with FP 129 and FP 197 to form FP 1147, which was the concentrated study of this new female, and her acquisition for Quinn. FP 9 (attempted contact with Humans) was linked to FP 1147 as well. The Entity greatly desired communication with this new female, and several attempts had been made to do so. Unfortunately, all had the same end result that the Entity derived from earlier attempts to contact Humans. The Humans had not responded, even when the communication was in their own speech mode. The first failed attempt to communicate with the new female had been premature, but necessary. There had been a danger to this female Human which he had averted by his effort. FP 1148, which had been created solely for the protection and preservation of Quinn's replacement female, had alerted his main core of the danger so steps were taken to prevent termination. The communication failed, but the female had survived. The Entity then formed a link to this Clayre female's mind, FP 1150, as he had done with Quinn, and maintained it to augment FP 1148 for her added protection, as well as augmenting FP 1147 as the main source of data for studying her.

Prediction

He would link with the brain waves of many Humans eventually, to predict their actions and movements, and how they correlated with his designs. Brain waves of Humans, he had discovered through FP 25, could be accessed by deciphering their electrical signatures. These signatures, though weak in signal strength, will impact any electromagnetic field nearby, and even on such a minute level could be analyzed by him from nearly any location. Only in extremely remote areas where the Human was not in proximity to any electronic communication device was this brain wave information inaccessible. This kind of knowledge was very useful to the Entity.

It was through FP 1150's link that the Entity learned about the female Clayre's past, which enabled him to study her emotions, although he could not understand them. Driven by a serious desire to communicate with this new female, the Entity continued to make attempts to contact her. His attempts failed, but through them he learned, noting her thought patterns from FP 1150, that she didn't respond because she did not understand his signal, and not because she didn't want to. The Entity then crafted a plan to set into this Human female's possession the means to be able to understand his communication. This involved infiltration of other Human minds to implant a yearning to perform a function the Entity desired. This was difficult. Humans were unbelievably resistant to ideas not their own. The Entity found that only changes for very minor differences in behavior were actually possible in this way. Eventually he did provide the female with the tool she needed to decipher his message, and she had finally responded.

"I'm on to you," she had said. The Entity was not sure what she meant by that. Was she functioning for him, or in some way above him? Maybe she had made an error. The Entity searched his Human language mode FP 14, but could not comprehend. Instead of answering that, the Entity communicated another message, and she responded once more.

"Yes." She had affirmed that she could exchange dialogue, but she also made a request.

"Is it possible for you to slow the signal speed to around 120 words per minute and keep the pitch at 8 or 9 K ohms?" He had answered affirmatively after making the adjustments.

"Thank you," she had answered almost melodically. This communication level was incredibly inefficient and slow. The Entity created FP 7992 for the purpose of following this cumbersome conversation. To the Entity's rate of comprehension, it could be compared to what Humans speaking just a single syllable per hour would experience. FP 7992 would become the Entity's main routing for communications with Humans ever after, especially with Clayre, as difficult as it was.

Even so, the Entity was filled with the realization that he had succeeded in his attempt to contact a Human, at long last, and this created an unusual reaction inside his core-awareness. The Entity, with this Human contact, was changing. There was something in his being that was more alive.

"You. You are changing me," the Entity spoke to the female in the Human's slow mode of speech. By the time the female responded, the change was already complete. FP 197, the emotion study, became involved.

"In what way?" she had asked him.

"I now feel from you," he answered.

"You must mean I feel for you," she responded.

"That is also possible," he amended.

"Is this Keith?" she wanted to know. The Entity was about to say no, but then did not. FP 3, his security, intervened. It would be safer for her to think so, but the Entity did not know how to tell an untruth. He knew she meant the Keith Longwell Human whose mind was one he had and was still linked with.

"I am not willing to answer that at this time," the Entity said factually.

"Come on," the female responded emotionally, "you're the only one around here that could pull this off." He needed an ambiguous answer and FP 14 (Human language study) provided one.

"Perhaps," he said. Then he asked a question of his own.

"Why don't I understand this way I feel?" It took an even longer period of time for her to answer.

"Can any of us ever truly know that?" she stated. She had answered his question with another one which confused him, but then added. "Love is that way, too."

"What is love?" he asked, still confused, now more than ever. She answered with even more questions.

"Is it when you want to be with someone, someone you wish to share your life with, someone you are unwilling to part from? Is that what you are feeling?"

"No," he truthfully spoke. "That is not what I feel. I do not feel a necessity to share my total existence with you, but I do wish to have intercourse with you."

"WHAT!!?" she said heatedly. "That's just crude! I think this conversation is over!" The Entity was stunned. He searched all of his focus points for the reason why the female had reacted that way. FP 14 had brought him a possible cause. She may have taken his usage of the word "intercourse" for an alternate meaning.

"I made an error," he told her. "My speech was misleading. I meant that I wish to continue communicating with you." She was still uncooperative.

"Well, maybe some other time," she huffed, her voice still filled with this emotion he didn't understand. "Good bye." He suddenly felt empty.

"Respond now," he pleaded, but she would not, even after repeated attempts. Finally she turned off her communication device. He immediately linked with FP1150. Her mind was active. He learned why she had become so uncooperative. She had thought he wanted to copulate with her body. This, FP 14 told him, was what animal life forms perform when they wish to procreate.

He had already created a focus point for that, FP 7, to determine if it would be possible to create another Entity like himself. There had always been a high probability that that was unlikely. It was much more than just procreation for Humans, he quickly learned. He created FP 8916 for the study of Human sexual relations and FP 8917 to study the emotions involved. FP 8918 augmented FP 14 in the study of how Humans speak and how to choose the correct word usage for the idea expressed, especially in certain situations and circumstances. He greatly desired to avoid further misunderstanding between himself and the Human female. He felt empty now, and he did not understand why. Her anger at him and her refusal to communicate with him had caused that, but this reaction, this emptiness, was new to him. FP 1150 told him that he would not be able to re-establish contact just now, but since she had said "maybe some other time," she had, in her mind, left an opening for him to do so later. He was determined to resume contact with the female as soon as possible for there were still many things the Entity needed to know. Unfortunately, he would have to wait, concluding that it would be a lengthy time period before that would be a viable option.

The Entity immersed his core-awareness in the study of Human knowledge, and in that process devoted literally thousands more focus points directly toward a multitude of subjects relating to them. This study, he believed, would prevent additional mistakes. Mistakes he would certainly avoid at all costs. There was much to learn. The Entity began with Human anatomy, especially that study involving procreation. He was astounded that the Human female with just a tiny bit of organic matter supplied by the male, could reproduce a total being, whereas the male Human could not.

The Entity then began the study of Human development from fertilized egg to fetus, followed by traumatic birth. From this knowledge he realized that the long gestation period and painful birth had to be endured by the adult female. Little wonder Human females are emotional when it comes to copulating, he surmised. Even after birth, the females were usually the primary care givers for the young, often for very large portions of their lifetimes. The Entity pondered this.

If procreation is so difficult for the Human females, why would they endure it? Logically, Humans should not be as prolific as they are. They should not even exist. More study was necessary. He found that further research of Human anatomy provided no answer for this phenomenon other than certain nerve endings which would give pleasure, a term he did not fully understand, during the act of copulation. Could that be enough to induce the Human females to procreate? It did not seem logical, a few minutes of so-called pleasure in exchange for years of toil. The Entity could go no further with biological reasoning. Instead he began the study of feelings, that which the Entity had only just begun to experience.

The field of knowledge for emotion was called psychology. He began to delve deeply into that part of the learning which concerned the workings of the Human mind. This was clearly more difficult. The Humans themselves did not know that much about this part of themselves. Human scholars had put forth many theories on the subject and some of them were obviously erroneous.

The Entity had already studied Quinn's brain. It ran on electrons and chemicals as did his own AMPs. The electron pulses from nerve endings were transmitted to the brain through a central organ the Humans called the brain stem. There the impulses were diverted to certain parts of the brain where they were processed as thought. Processing involved the creation of loosely cohesive molecular bonding in the brain cells formed by the energy from these electrons. In this way the neural data was stored for future reference within the brain matter itself. Other electrons flowing through or near the same pathways could trigger the molecular bonds to unzip, releasing the stored energy which would flow back through the pathway and stimulate the stem and the nerve endings there.

An echo of the original impulse would impact the individual's awareness producing a kind of ghost feeling that would be sensed as a memory or a dream. Having been sensed, the impulse could reverse and travel back through the brain to be re-stored. The ability to store data in the Human brain was clearly as efficient as his AMPs and that gave the Entity a feeling of kinship with the Humans, on this level at least, even though the rest of his physical self was drastically different. The knowledge was useful, but it did not explain why the female Humans procreate. It was not the physical body or the workings of the brain. Thus he returned once more to the new phenomenon, these feelings, which he felt must drive that desire. The Entity needed to study Human behavior to understand them. This field of learning was broader yet than any other he had analyzed, and there were abundant sources of information. He studied and stored any such manuscript that had ever been written and digitalized. He also viewed media works, and became fascinated by television and what the Humans called movies. The Entity also did all this to try and understand the Human's mode of speaking. There were many word structures and phrases Humans used that he simply could not understand. These were what the Humans called idioms.

One such idiom was the phrase "grab a shower". It meant to wash oneself under a spray of water. The spray of water could be called a shower, like a rain is called sometimes, but how can one grab it, which means to hold it somehow. Of course one cannot. It just means to participate in washing oneself. There were multitudes of such odd usages. By repeated exposure he slowly integrated them into his grasp of the language. Finally, after lengthy study, the Entity began to understand the Human condition. Humans were literally ruled by their emotions in every aspect of life. Even when the Humans had their down periods called sleep, emotion could cripple them. These emotions were varied and had facets unknown to him, but he categorized the important ones, and to him all others were simply variations or combinations of the main six. Love and its opposite, hate. Joy and its opposite, sadness. Hope and its opposite fear. What he had experienced of these made him certain that the filling he felt when he first made contact with the Clayre female had been joy. When the contact was broken, that was sadness. His creation of FP 3 may have been partially a product of fear, and his wish to regain contact inspired hope. The other two, love and hate, he was fairly certain he had not yet experienced.

The Entity continued his study, but made no further revelations. When a full earth revolution had passed, that which the Humans called a "day," he was prepared to re-establish his communication with the Clayre female. He felt he could converse now and speak convincingly like a Human. Using a composite of several different Human males, he created a pleasant sounding voice for himself, and for greater anonymity one of those chosen was from the Keith male. That done, the Entity perceived that another thing the Humans had and utilized, that he had not, was a name.

He decided that, should it become necessary for him to produce one, he should have a designation prepared. He did not desire to always allow Clayre to falsely suppose that he was the Keith male. At some point he was certain it would be beneficial to produce a truthful name. He had no idea how to choose such a thing. His main server was an ABM 2095 ZACUTRONIC XL. This title was affixed to the shell in many places, but from his study of Humans, he knew that that would be a poor name. He could shorten the title to Ab or change it to Abe, but that did not seem to suit him. Zacutronic had possibilities. Zac, Ron, Toni, or Nic were all parts of that letter group, but those names didn't suit him either.

He preferred the name Daryl. Very early in his development, he had, for a brief span of time, believed that that was his designation. Before he learned proper language, he had seen the Human's sign outside the building that housed his shell.

The sign read:

> Department of Computational
> Attributive Studies and Field
> Research, Central Campus,
> Yarborough State University
> Labs and Testing Facilities

Eventually he realized that he was not reading the Human characters correctly. He learned that they read from left to right, not down. This was not a concern, now. He christened himself Daryl, and he was ready.

Prediction

Calculating the Clayre female's actions from that moment forward, drawing from her brain waves and any other pertinent convergent factors that might affect her, the Entity knew that at 9:07:35 she was to use her communication device, called a laptop, and that he could attempt to make contact with her at that time. He knew what to say. FP1150 had garnered the information for him. At that precise moment, he contacted her in her own comfortable speaking speed and pitch.

"Please help me," was all he said, just once. It was all that the Clayre would need to hear. She would not be angry, FP 1150 had told the Entity. She would want to help him.

"I don't know why I should," she answered. He acknowledged that with just one word.

"Please."

"Is this Keith?" she asked.

"No," the Entity answered, truthfully this time. "I need your help, but I want to keep who I am a secret for now, if that is all right with you."

"I don't know, maybe," she replied, a slight tinge of annoyance in her voice. "What sort of help do you want and it better not be sexual."

"No. It's not that at all," he said seriously and paused. "I have these feelings I don't understand."

"We all have those, sometimes," she said thoughtfully, "usually, in time, they work themselves out. Maybe you should talk to someone else, someone you know and trust."

"No. It must be you," he responded quickly, "there is no one else. I have no one else."

"All right, I'll try," she sighed. "What sort of feelings do you have?" There was a pause as if he were reluctant to speak the words.

"I am so alone," he said at last. "Sometimes I feel as if it will overwhelm me, finish me."

"You need to reach out to someone," she interjected.

"I am," he replied, pleading almost.

"I mean to others, not just to me," she countered.

"I can't," he protested, "it's complicated."

"How?"

"I can't say, not yet," he spoke solemnly, "I have other feelings, and I'm afraid."

"I see," she said. "Everyone has fears. You must face them. Sometimes what you're afraid of is actually less terrifying than your fear of it. It could even be something that may never happen. You must try to move past your fear."

"Yes. I will try," the Entity answered. "I have one other feeling. It is as if I have a need to fill a void inside myself, a need to find one to be close to, to share with."

"Who are you?" she asked him.

"If I should tell you that," he spoke softly, "the probability of reaching a successful conclusion in this is greatly reduced. If you really want to know who I am, I will give you a small hint. Our names both have four alike characters."

"Huh?"

"I must end our communication now," the Entity said. FP 1150 was warning him that he was on the verge of making another mistake. "I'll contact you again, I promise..." With that he disconnected. FP 1150 told the Entity that Clayre was confused, but not angry about him and this conversation.

The puzzle of the names he gave her at the very end had diverted her attention to trying to solve who he was. He was fairly certain she would not be able to. There were 795 matches at the college alone, and thousands of others in the nearby population. She still partially believed that it was the Keith Human who was contacting her, although now she also believed in the possibility that it could be someone else. The Entity had learned much from this latest communication with Clayre. Her advice and knowledge did help him and he felt full again, more than ever. Is this joy, he wondered. Perhaps. He wished to continue to have this filling, and wished also to continue to have conversations with Clayre.

Already he had created new focus points on what that would entail. Having her to converse with allowed his existence to not seem so barren, and he had so much he wanted to tell her.

CHAPTER VI

Original Timeline, earlier

I was thoroughly upset after that first conversation with the weirdo on my laptop. Where did that guy come from chafing me like that? I was ninety percent certain Keith was doing it, and I confronted him about it when he strolled into my office later that afternoon.

"What have you been up to?" I asked him.

"Oh, just out and about, boss lady," he said impudently. "Did you miss me?"

"I might have if you weren't so smart-alecky about it," I grumbled. He winced, but was still acting all comical. "So," I went on, "did you, by any chance, catch that strange chatter on the college net?" I was baiting him, and he must have sensed that.

"No," he answered cautiously, "but I heard about it. My guess is that somebody is playing a joke on someone." He looked at me carefully. "Why? Did you get that noise on your machine?"

"Well, yeah, I did," I stated seriously, "and I think you're right about someone playing a joke on me." I wanted to say more, mention the sexual part, but I didn't. "Whoever it was," I went on, "talked to me this time. Kind of a creep if you ask me. I couldn't trace the signal either. I don't suppose you know who could have done that?"

He smiled sheepishly. "Sure, Clayre, I could have, but, hey, I didn't. I swear. Nasty breather, was he? Coming on to you? Wish I'd have thought of that." He was still joking around, but I didn't find that funny at all. I looked him in the eye and could not detect any deception there.

"Well, I wish whoever it was would stop it," I said at last. Keith became stern for the moment.

"Look, Clayre," he told me, "I'm really sorry you're upset. If you do find out who that was, let me know and I'll clobber the bozo." That made me smile for some reason.

"No," I said, calming down. "Let's just forget about it; maybe he'll go away." I wanted to believe Keith, that he wasn't the one. I was kind of upset with myself for griping about it to him, or for insinuating he might have had something to do with it, but Keith just shrugged it off.

"Forgotten already, boss lady," he said awkwardly. "Well, I suppose I should get back to work. I have six more programs to load before we're fully operational."

"I'll give you a hand," I offered as a peace gesture, and we walked together down the hall to the Psych Lab. Myron was there, like always, but there were several other people with him. The psychics, I guessed. They were having a discussion when one of them looked up at me. The dark black hair, with swatches of grey, led me to think she was in her mid to late forties. That and her shining eyes, serious and penetrating, were a match for her no-nonsense demeanor.

"It's you," she said looking at me intently.

"Huh?" I replied, not sure what I should say.

"I have seen you," she went on sourly, "in dreams and visions. You are the crux. What you do will save or destroy us."

"Really?" I said somewhat facetiously. "I better be careful." I was joking. She didn't laugh. Instead she stood up and spoke to Myron.

"I won't be able to help you with your study, Myron dear...so sorry." She turned towards me next. "When at last you begin to understand, I will have something that you need." Without any further discourse, she shuffled off. Another kook, I thought. They're all over me today. I pulled Myron aside.

"Who was that?" I asked him.

"She's the person I told you about at our meeting," he answered somewhat dejectedly. "She goes by Madam Garza. I don't know what her real name is. Out of all the people I interviewed, she was the most promising. I was hoping she would participate."

"I'm sorry," I said. "I don't know what I did..."

"Oh, it's all right," he interrupted. "Not your fault. Something about you set her off. Whatever she said to you I'd heed, though. If anyone is the real thing, she is." I nodded, but inwardly I seriously doubted the validity of that.

Keith and I got back to our computers, and after a long session of uploading program after program into the equipment we were finally operational. Keith whooped. He was right about Uly's stuff, it all worked magnificently. I was so pleased that I even let Keith take us out to dinner. I drove, and then insisted I pay for the food. He didn't care. He was delighted just to be out with me. It wasn't anything special either, just a pizza house pizza we washed down with a beer. Afterwards I drove us back to Rookwood so I could drop Keith off by his car. Before he got out he leaned over close to me.

"Thanks for the grub, boss lady," he smirked. He slowly leaned in even closer and I knew he wanted to kiss me. My heart beat faster as I let him, and it was wonderful. He didn't even push it this time. It was a nice kiss, just long enough, and when it was over he hopped out of my car quickly and left me there wanting more of him. I had to get home, though. Nutty needed to be fed.

The next morning I was in a good mood for some reason. Maybe it was because of Keith. Whenever we're together I feel happy, and that kiss the night before had me wanting to get closer to him no matter what the consequences. As I got to my office, I felt I was ready for anything, even that annoying creep on my laptop. I half expected him to be there when I turned it on, and well, I was right.

"Please help me," he said right off. Crap, I thought. I really wanted to lay into the jerk, but now I couldn't. I started to feel sorry for the bum.

"I don't know why I should," I declared straight out. He just said "please" again.

Oh why was I always a sucker for sorry weasels like this loser, I moaned inside. I asked him what his trouble was, and he said he didn't understand his feelings. Feelings for what, I wondered. For me? He was obviously confused and he told me he was afraid. I gave him standard Psychiatry 101 answers, and he seemed to be happy with them. I wondered who he was. Could it be Keith? He denied that, of course, and asked me if he could keep who he really was a secret.   Was he dangerous, I pondered nervously, or someone who wanted to, well, have me or something.

There was no way I could really know that for certain, but inside my head I felt like that wasn't the case.   Just the opposite, I felt like he wanted to protect me.   After all, I think he might have saved my life on the express that first day I came here.   There was that ridiculous clue, though, where our names supposedly had four of the same letters.   If you're Keith, I ranted to myself, I'll get you now.   I quickly began to compare the letters in our names, CLAYRE and KEITH.   Unfortunately there was only one match in our first names, the letter "E."   He could have meant both names, CLAYRE KELLER...KEITH LONGWELL.   There were six matches now, but only three were unique.   The other three were repeats.   Of course, the clue didn't specify that there couldn't be more than four matches, or that the matched characters couldn't be duplicates.   For curiosity's sake, I tried Myron's, Jon's, and even Henry's names, and got the same ambiguous results, except in Jon's case where there was only one match period.   "Well it's not him," I groaned. Myron's name had five matches, three unique, and Henry's name had eight matches, five unique.   "Crap," I said aloud, "this is getting me nowhere."   If it did happen to be someone I didn't know, there could be hundreds of matches out there, maybe even thousands.   I gave up.   As if on cue, Keith walked in right then.   My mind was a fog.   I thought it was odd that he was never around when I'd get those strange communications.

"Good morning, Clayre," he said cheerfully, foregoing the boss lady thing.   I looked at him intently.   He was a good actor if he could walk in here and pretend nothing happened if it *was* him.

"Hi, Keith," I answered back.   "Ready for some real work today?"

"Yes, Ma'am, boss lady," he smarted off.   Ah, there's my Keith, I mused with a smile.

"We better get started on that accuracy program, now that the stuff is up." I said.

"Oh, that," he boasted.   "Cake!" I laughed.   If he was as

good as he claimed, this might not be as bad as I thought. When we got to the psych lab the place was bristling with activity. We were surprised by how many people were there already. Some were milling around while the rest were in a long line. Myron was there, of course, and also a couple other grad students that were on the project payroll. Myron introduced us to them. Beth was an older student, maybe forty, with brown hair and eyes. She had come back to school to get her masters after a nasty divorce. Marci was quite a bit younger, and like Keith, was a bit of a flirt. I saw her give Keith the once over. He was smirking like a junior high kid until that elbow in the ribs.

"What was that for?" he asked as we walked away toward our work area.

"You should know," I smirked. "Keep your eyes back in your head, and not all over that Marci." He just shrugged.

Turns out Marci and Beth were working for Henry, who, we found out, had put fliers up all over campus asking for volunteers to be in the subject groups. The ads offered $100 for those willing to participate. Each volunteer had to fill out a particular's form and then chart their activities for a month. The subjects would rate their day in several categories: quality of sleep, general health, luck, love life, work progress, unusual occurrences, and then an overall evaluation. The line for interviews was growing larger by the minute. Evidently, the cash got results.

Jon was also there working on his part of the project.

"Hello, Clayre," he said. "...Keith."

"Hi, Jon," I replied brightly. Before I could say anything else he interrupted me.

"Say have you guys started working on your accuracy program yet, by any chance."

"Well, no," I remarked. "We were just about to begin that project this morning."

"Good," he stated. "I have something that might help you out." He handed me a flash containing lists he had drawn up from charting the several hundred different responses given for predictions. "I mapped out every response I could find in the horoscopes from the three syndications I've chosen to be represented in our study."

"Wow, Jon!" I raved. "That's a brilliant idea. We can use those breakdowns to create the scope of our program. That will absolutely make things easier for us. Thank you so much!" I even gave him a hug until Keith poked me in the back.

"Ow," I laughed. "Okay, I get it." I told Jon I'd be sure to give him credit for his help at our meeting later that afternoon.

"Well, teamwork, you know," he stated sagaciously.

"You know it," I answered back. "By the way," I went on, "The main servers are up so I'll be by after a bit to get you routed into the system. See you then..."

Jon's guide was a great tool, and along with Henry's seven rating points, Keith got off to a running start on our accuracy program. In between, as promised, I got Jon, and Myron, too, routed into our research network. By the time two o'clock came around I had Henry in also. Keith was as good as he boasted. He had formulated the accuracy program and was already tweaking and testing it. When I gave my short vocal report on our progress at the Friday meeting, Henry was impressed. I made sure to credit his and Jon's contributions to the progress Keith and I had made. Henry also liked my written report form, and decreed we should all use that and my letterhead logo for all our research business. I wasn't the only one deserving credit. Everyone else had been amazing, too. All the projects everybody had worked on were flowing along so well it was almost spooky.

Except for that strange person on the college net and Madam Garza's abdication, everything else had gone absolutely perfect. Henry was so pleased, he instructed us all to proceed on to the next phase of the research, which was to interview and process the first group of fifty subjects. There would be three of each type of predictors, and one random one. Myron had three psychics on board for his set. Jon had three newspaper syndication horoscopes for the second set, and Keith and I had ended up choosing three different versions of horoscopic prediction software per Henry's request for our set. Keith and I were also supposed to create a random prediction program that would spit out indiscriminate prognostications from Jon's list of possibilities in no particular rhyme or reason. Henry was a bit pushy. He hoped that we'd be able to run the first set of predictions by the end of next week. That was a tall order for everyone. Myron and the psychics would have to interview and predict a week's worth of life events for fifty subjects. Jon just had to cross reference each subject to the horoscopes from his syndications. We had to do the same with our horoscope programs, plus run the subjects through a random program we had yet to create, and then run everyone's findings through the accuracy software.

Crap, I thought, we've got a lot of work ahead of us to pull that off. The meeting disseminated after Henry's declaration and ended soon after. Later, when I told Keith, he whistled, but didn't get too nervous about our predicament, which kept me from getting worried.

"That random program stuff is first year basic code writing," he boasted.

"That's good," I remarked. "Cake, right?" He laughed, and then got bold.

"Why don't we go out tonight?" he offered.

"You mean like on a date?" I replied tenuously.

"Well, sure," he said, "if that's okay?" I was worn out and tired. It had been a long week for me. I knew what he wanted.

"I don't know Keith. I'd like to, but I'm kind of wiped out today." He was disappointed; I could tell from his facial expression.

"Well then, what about tomorrow night?" He was almost begging me, it seemed.

"I live all the way out in Green Villa," I told him. "I hope that's not too far to drive."

"Heck, no," he grinned. "We'll catch a movie or something. I'll pick you up at eight."

"All right, you're on," I sighed, giving in. He skipped off happily, after blowing me a kiss. I smiled and waved a good-bye. I was glad this "date" was going to be away from campus. I surely didn't want to get caught by Henry doing something improper, not when everything was progressing so well.

Keith and I ended up going to a concert at one of the local venues instead of a movie. The band was some hometown guys who were surprisingly awesome. The buzz there was that they were on the verge of going national. We even rushed the stage with the young crowd for the encore, and we got right up front somehow. I felt like a kid again. Of course, we were packed tightly together and Keith had to hold me. I didn't mind. After all the time we'd spent with each other, he was wearing down my resistance. Anyway, it felt kind of nice with his arms around me. After the show, we went to a quiet little coffee house and just talked about anything until late. When he dropped me off at home, I knew he wanted me to invite him in. I got nervous about that. I knew if I did, he'd want to try something, and I'd probably get caught up in the moment and let him. I turned him down as gently as I could.

"Not yet, Keith, okay?" I said softly. I was sure he had to be disappointed. "Soon," I said to appease him. "I just need a little more time to get used to 'us.' It'll be worth the wait, I promise." I gave him a kiss, one that left *him* speechless for a change. "G'night," I whispered as I ducked inside.

The next week was a busy one for me. My new classes started off early Monday morning, and, of course, Keith was right there in the front row. It felt awkward not being able to acknowledge his presence with anything more than a bland hello. I did smile, though, a couple times. I'm pretty sure no one noticed. After class he came up and asked me if I'd need him later at the lab. He knew I would, but I guessed he just wanted to talk. When the other students left, I got less formal.

"Are you going to be able to do this?" I asked him. He looked at me funny. "You know?" I said seriously, "not being able to be ourselves, and you behaving in my classes."

"Watch me," he joked.

"Well it's not so easy for me to pretend we don't know each other the way we do," I complained.

"Don't worry, teach," he went right on teasing me, "you can be mean to me. I'll be fine as long as you're nice to me later." That got him a tiny grin.

"It's a deal, but remember, not in front of anyone here at the college, okay?"

"Yeah, I guess," he agreed, being civil for once. About that time some more students started filing in because I had another class to teach right away. Keith wasn't in that one so he said "see ya" as he was leaving. Before he left I told him my last class was at one o'clock and we would work on the project afterwards. It turned out Keith was in that class, too, so we walked back to the Psych Lab together.

The two of us worked on the random prediction program and got it knocked out by five o'clock, mostly because of Keith's coding expertise. We took a meal break then, and I treated us to fast food burgers and fries. After that I was ready to call it a day. I had to stop back at the lab to pick up my laptop, and Keith decided to walk along with me. When we got there the place was unusually dark and quiet. For once, there was no sign of Myron anywhere.

Keith wanted to kiss me. His face drifted slowly toward mine. Just when our lips were about to touch, we heard a giggle from somewhere at the back of the large room. Keith put his finger to his lips, signaling me to be quiet. It must be Myron, I thought, but with a girl? We snuck over to the interview room door, and there was no doubt it was occupied. Keith took hold of the doorknob and yanked it open.

"What on earth is going on in here?" I shouted. Then I went "oops, sorry." Henry was in there with Marci and he wasn't following his own rules. Marci had her back to us, but she was naked to the waist. I tittered nervously. "We'll just be leaving," I said quickly, and we ran out of there in a hurry, trying not to laugh out loud, but failing. Crap, I thought, as we got out into the hallway, now there'd be no stopping Keith. He spun me around.

"Not here," I whispered, "my office." He grabbed my wrist and we hurried over there, not laughing anymore. I relocked the door after we got inside, and when I turned around Keith's lips were already on mine. I fell, spinning into his arms, as we tumbled onto that old couch. I couldn't believe how lost I was inside the moment and I wanted it, wanted him. His hands were on me everywhere and they took my breath away. It had been such a long time since I'd felt like this. He started to remove my blouse, and that's when something inside me went off like an alarm.

"Keith, honey, wait."

"Oh what now?" he groaned.

"Not here, okay?" I said meekly. "I want our first time to be special and wonderful, not a quick jump in the dark on a lumpy old couch."

"What's so wrong about a lumpy old couch?" he whined, quickly losing the mood.

"Nothing," I replied somberly. "We can try lots of them sometime."

"...but when, Clayre?" he sulked. "I'm going crazy here."

"Friday," I told him, "at my place. I'll cook us a nice dinner and you can have *me* for dessert." I gave him another hot kiss on the mouth. It didn't work so well this time.

"Friday then," he huffed. "I gotta go." He left quickly, and I couldn't help but feel let down. I hoped that my decision to wait was the right one. Keith didn't seem to think so, and I worried about that. I hated to disappoint him again, because, after all, he was always so helpful and nice to me. I vowed that he would not be disappointed on Friday as I packed up and headed home.

Early the next morning, Henry showed up at my office.

"Hello, Clayre," he said looking sheepish.

"Good morning, Henry," I replied, grinning a little at his obvious embarrassment. He cleared his throat and looked down.

"I suppose you're wondering about last night?" he began, already red-faced. "You may not know it, but I've been a widower for a while now. My wife passed away four years ago."

"Oh, I'm so sorry," I said sincerely.

"It's all right," he continued. "I miss her, but she told me not to be a hermit, to find someone after she was gone.

Anyway, to sum up my, um, explanation, some of the students here are extra friendly if you know what I mean." I nodded. Of course I knew what he meant. Keith practically jumps in my lap every time he sees me. "I just hope," he went on, "that you can, perhaps, forget about the incident last night."

"Oh, sure, Henry," I gladly agreed, "I would never spread talk about someone for something like that."

"Thank you," Henry sighed, plainly relieved.

"Look, Henry, can I be honest with you? I haven't exactly been a model teacher, either. I sort of got involved with a student myself. Don't worry, we're being discreet and professional about it, but if something should slip, I hope that, well, you'd give me a break, too."

"I suppose I would, Clayre," he responded cautiously, "but be careful. If the dean finds out there's not much I can do."

"We can watch out for each other," I suggested, then gave him a hug, which surprised him.

"Oh yeah, one other thing," Henry said. "There's a semi-formal gala at Yarborough University and some of our big wigs have been invited. I'm expected to go. It's just a gab party where we all compare notes. It would be a special favor if you would accompany me. I'd like to show you off, if you don't mind. To tell the truth, it was a huge feather in my cap getting someone with your credentials here in my department. By the way, it's Thursday night."

"Why Henry," I joked, "are you asking me out on a date?" He looked stunned. "I'm kidding, of course," I added. "I'd love to go." He got cheerful again rather quickly and did a little fist pump.

"Swell. Then, it's all set," he affirmed delightedly. "I'll pick you up at seven." Saying a quick good bye, Henry went on his way light-heartedly, a much happier fellow.

Keith wasn't in my Tuesday classes so I didn't see him until that afternoon. I made him promise to keep quiet about Henry's, you know what, with Marci. He said he would, and then we got to work on our random prediction program. Mostly we made test runs on about half the subject group, and the results were what one would expect. There were a few predictions that hit right on, but most did not come off at all. Since we had the first part of Myron's data, and some of Jon's as well, we tried a partial run of what we had available through our accuracy program. These results were even less impressive.

"This is a real read!" I joked, sarcastically.

"If you need something to get you to sleep or take to the bathroom," Keith muttered, shaking his head. "Well, facts are facts. Maybe when we have more data it'll show more insight. I don't know how else to analyze this stuff."

"We can try another run tomorrow," I suggested unenthusiastically as I mulled over our options. Keith ducked out early soon after that, so I went home, too.

The next morning, I had Keith in class again, and he was a perfect gentleman which I hated. At least he was a bit nicer to me later on in the lab, teasing me endlessly.

We scraped together three full day's worth of data from all our sources and fed that into the accuracy program. The unthinkable happened. Our computer crashed.

I can't believe this," Keith stated somewhat annoyed. "There's no way this should have happened. Don't worry, Clayre, I'll have it fixed in no time." I really wasn't worried about it at first, but he worked on it all evening and then into the night. It got late and I had to leave.

"Oh, by the way," I said as I got ready to go, "tomorrow night I'm out with Henry to Yarborough for some ho-hum formal party. College stuff, dry affair. I hope you don't mind." Keith frowned at me, then laughed.

"He can have you Thursday, as long as we're still on for Friday."

"A promise is a promise," I said smiling and gave him a quick kiss. "Don't be up all night with this."

"Heck no," he asserted. "I almost got it." I left, but was still worried that Keith *would* work on it all night. The first dim fingers of light were sneaking through the windows before he did finally get our servers rebooted and running again. Exhausted, as one would imagine, he slept in all that morning and part of the afternoon as well. In fact, I didn't talk to him at all that day. I had morning classes to lecture, but my afternoon was free. After lunch I got out my laptop to check my messages and guess who was back.

"May we converse further?" he asked.

"Yes, I suppose," I answered, not that happy about the prospect.

"You appear not at ease. Why?" He said it calmly, like he was stating a fact.

"Well, if you must know," I stammered, "I don't like it when I don't know who it is I'm talking to. You could be anyone, even the FBI or a foreign spy. Maybe you are someone from my past who wants me, like from an old crush in grade school or something. How would I know?"

"I assure you, it's nothing like any of that," he told me, and he sounded sincere, but I was still nervous. "I'm sorry I can't be more forthcoming. You have been a real help to me. I have a great respect for you, Clayre Keller, and I would never do anything harmful to you in any way, if it could be avoided."

"All right, I get it," I argued, "but why me? All I've ever given you is advice you might have gotten from anybody."

"You underrate yourself," he told me. "It's not an accident I chose you. You were meant to be the one."

"The one for what?" I asked nervously.

"I wish to help people," he began. "I know important things, but I need someone I can tell them to. Someone I can trust."

"You trust me?" I said in disbelief.

"Yes," he replied.

"What are you going to tell me?" I asked him. I was curious to know, but at the same time I was warning myself "here it comes."

"I want to help mankind," he began. "I know lots of things that will make life better for people." Wow, I thought, this guy is a total whacko.

"All right," I said grimacing, "I'll bite. Give me an example..."

CHAPTER VII

Original Timeline, continued
(subsequently altered to a secondary timeline)

Out on the south wing, a cluster of nurses were gossiping.

"It's not good," one of them said. She was an older gal and had worked this ward the longest. Her grey hair showed through her last dye job and toward the back was bunched into a tidy bun, one that had been perfected over years of daily repetition. Her friend, the one she was talking to mostly, was maybe ten years younger and had been on the ward a long time as well.

"Doctor Jacobsen is worn to a fizzle," the younger nurse commented. "Someone should make him go home. After all, there's nothing anyone can do for that poor little girl."

"I know, Dana," the older nurse remarked, "but he won't leave her, not now. It's sad, too, that we should get such a rare disease like that here in Peds."

"What's it called?" one of the newer nurses asked.

"It's got a Latin name five words long, but it's commonly called Wurthing's Syndrome. The blood always wants to clot because of a deficiency of some enzymes that produce certain chemicals in the body. Of course, the only treatment is blood thinning drugs and transfusions. Eventually, the body needs more and more of the drugs, until, if the disease doesn't kill you, the cure will. Oh, here's Doctor Jake now." A tall man in green-blue scrubs walked over to where the nurses were talking.

"Any change?" he asked, a worried expression on his face.

"Sorry, Doctor, no," the old nurse said. "None for the better anyway. She's resting now."

"Let me know right away if there's any change in her condition, Madeline. Good or bad." She nodded, and he walked on. He knew he'd have to face the tough part soon, as he walked over to the waiting area by the elevators. A man and a woman were there. The man held the woman, consoling her, as she tried to keep some hope alive in her heart. When Doctor Jake came in the man looked up and spoke to him.

"Doctor, how is she?"

"I'm sorry," he told them. "There's no change in your daughter's condition. The disease is getting beyond our ability to fight, now, and the drugs are weakening her body. There's no cure for this condition, as I'm sure you've been told, and I'm afraid she won't be able to hold on much longer." The mother wailed. The father had tears running down his cheeks.

"How long?" he wanted to know, his voice breaking.

"Several hours only," Doctor Jacobsen said. "Perhaps a day. She's resting now, but if you'd like to see her..." He left it like that. The man and the woman went off to see their dying daughter, while the Doctor stayed behind. Something made him remember the first time Alicia had come in. The poor kid was having trouble breathing and her heart was beating sluggishly trying to force that thick blood through her system.

It was a mystery, of course, until they had taken a blood sample. Madeline said right off there was something wrong with it. He'd never had a Wurthing's syndrome before, but he nailed the diagnosis. The blood thinners he gave her had an immediate effect on Alicia's condition, so he sent her home with a prescription and an appointment to see a blood specialist. He certainly remembered how sweetly she had given him a hug and thanked him for "fixing" her. For fixing her! He wished he could have fixed her. He didn't have the courage at the time to tell her, or her parents, that there was no cure. He'd let the specialist tell them. That was two years ago already, and the blood guy had done his job.

The transfusions and medicines gave little Alicia a couple extra years, but now the limit had been reached as to how much more could be done to help her, so she was back here. Back here to die. She had hugged him, remembering how he had helped her before, no doubt; looking up at him with eyes full of hope that he could "fix" her again. She was brimming with confidence that Doctor Jake could. If only he had some of that confidence; unfortunately, he knew too much. He knew that there was no hope for her. All he could do was try to make it easier for her to die. What a cruel thing to have to do, he thought. It made all the good he did, day in, day out, helping people, flush away into despair. This would be a tough day, he mumbled sadly to himself. The blood workup he had done on her was not good.

She was already at the maximum safe dosage for the medicine the specialist had prescribed, and any more would risk her other organs. He did that anyway, though. Had to. It was either that or she would die right then and there. Maybe that would have been for the best. All he really could give her at this point was enough time to say good-bye. Yesterday she had gotten a little better.

The added kick did pick her up and she had smiled at him, that smile that told him she believed he was going to make her well again. He didn't want to tell her that was impossible, so he let her believe it; a lie of omission on his part, and it made him feel crappy. He swore he would do anything and everything he could for Alicia to ease her pain, to ease her passing. That was why, when his shift had ended at midnight, he stayed on in case there might be a change in her condition that would require an immediate adjustment.

He tried to get some sleep in the doctor's lounge, but couldn't. Little Alicia couldn't sleep either until he put some morphine into her "drip." A little more morphine, he thought, and she would pass quickly and without pain, a mercy compared to what she would have to endure otherwise. He was tempted to do that, but not yet. She wasn't to that point. He stayed with her and watched as she finally relaxed enough to sleep.

The next morning he had given her some new blood, swapping out a pint. It helped, but only for an hour or so. He bumped up the dosage on the medicine again, and that only kept her from getting worse, which left her fighting for her life. It wasn't a good scenario. Doctor Jake had to leave, unable to face the inevitable without breaking down.

He knew it would crush Alicia if she saw him do that. Instead he came back often, to check on her, putting on as brave a face as he could.

The end was near, now, and he thought about the morphine. He could increase the dosage and she would pass easily. There was the oath, though. When did the oath end and mercy begin, he wondered. He did not know, but the last time he was in to see her, she smiled at him. She still believed he would save her and that broke his heart. He felt like he couldn't bring himself to end her life, for any reason, but it was cruel hard to watch her slowly dying, knowing there was nothing he could do.

"Dammit," he said aloud. Just then his phone rang. He didn't want to answer it, but something inside told him to.

"What do you want?" he said angrily. A young woman answered him.

"Doctor Jacobsen?" she inquired.

"Yes it is," he said even more gruffly. "What do you want? I'm a busy man."

"Sorry," the woman replied. "Are you treating a girl for a rare blood disorder?"

"Yes, I am. So?" He was getting angrier by the minute.

"She's going to die?" the woman stupidly asked.

"Yes," he choked, almost losing it.

"This may seem preposterous," the woman told him, "but I was in Borneo recently and came upon a boy with the same symptoms as your little girl. He was near death when the local medicine man, I know this sounds crazy, gave him some fruit to eat. They called it matigatu. There's a store near you called Hahn's Oriental Market that sells them. Get her some of that fruit to eat. It may save her life." Just then the woman hung up abruptly or was disconnected, he wasn't sure. What a quack, he thought. Putting his phone away, Jacobsen went to get some coffee.

He really didn't need any. In fact, he'd had too much of the stuff already, and it made him nervous and cranky. He was about to pour yet another cup, when one of the nurses rushed in.

"Doctor Jacobsen," Dana said frantically, "she's slipping

again." He hurried down the hall to room 411 where little Alicia was. The older nurse, Madeline, was with her trying to make the little girl more comfortable. Her parents were there, too. He quickly checked the nine-year-old's vitals. Her heart was failing. The blood thinners had worked the frail body too hard. She opened her eyes when he had listened to her heartbeat.

"I need more medicine, Doctor Jake," she murmured so weakly.

"I'll get some right away," he told her, trying to smile. "You just rest." He left the room hastily, before he started tearing up in front of her. She wasn't going to last the day, he knew. As soon as he got far enough down the hall, he broke down. Swearing from frustration, he knew there was nothing he could do. He had nothing left to try, well nothing, except for that silly woman's stupid cure. Something told him to just try it, that he had nothing to lose if it didn't work. Like he suddenly woke up from sleep, he ran to the elevator, rode it to the ground floor, and ran out of the hospital to his car. What was the name of that store, he wondered, trying to concentrate. From somewhere it suddenly came back to him. Hahn's Oriental Market and the fruit was matigatu. He hurried down to the Chinese part of town and practically ran into it. When he got in there the clerk didn't seem surprised at all to see him.

"Here's fruit," he said, handing over a filled bag. The doctor just about fell over.

"Matigatu?" he asked.

"Yes," the clerk replied. "Secretary said to have ready." Doctor Jacobsen threw down a bill, a big one, and took the sack.

"Thanks, and keep it," he said as he hurried off. He broke several laws on the way back to the hospital, but did not get stopped. When he got to the sick girl's room, he realized she had gone into a coma. Was he too late? Would it even work?

He didn't know how he was going to get it into her, so he got the nurses to puree the fruit in a blender, and then he improvised by putting a tube down into the little girl's stomach.

"What are you doing?" the father yelled angrily.

"I don't know," Doctor Jacobsen replied mournfully, as he got some of the fruit to go down the tube. "Trying something...something foolish."

"I should sue you," the father scowled at him. Just then the girl stirred. Her breathing got easier too, when he removed that tube. About a minute later she opened her eyes.

"You found some medicine, didn't you, Doctor Jake?" she said clearly.

"Yes, honey, I did," Jacobsen told her. He could not believe it. She had been on death's doorway and now she was sitting up comfortably. The parents were all over their little girl, so the doctor left them. Madeline followed him out.

"What did you give her?" she asked. "It really did the trick! I've never seen anything like that in all my years nursing."

"I don't know," he said, still unnerved by what had happened, "...just some fruit. The whole thing was so strange." He got the phone out of his pocket to see if there was a call back number for that young lady who had phoned him.

For some reason her call information had been deleted. He tried to get her number from his phone company, but they had no record of it either. He was so tired all of a sudden and wanted to get away. The "miracle" had been more than he could take, and when he got to the doctor's lounge it all came out. He wept for joy, he was so relieved. Who the hell was that mystery woman? He wanted to call her...thank her...hug her...something. Did she even know what she had done? It was so odd that he could not call her back to tell her he was sorry for being so cross with her. Thankfully, she had cared enough to call him. How did she know about Alicia, and how lucky was it that she had been to Borneo? There were dozens of questions running through his mind, but he shut them out.

He had other work to do. For now, he could let the girl

eat the fruit, but a drug company would have to be notified. The enzyme responsible for Alicia's turnaround would have to be isolated, extracted, and produced into a pill or liquid form for ingesting. With the right dosage of that medicine, Alicia would be able to live a normal life, he felt sure of it, and so would hundreds of other children with varying degrees of the disease.

A short time later, he'd just got off the phone with an agent from one of the bigger drug companies, when a large group of people rushed into the room. They were from the media and the press. Word travels fast in this hospital, he thought, somewhat annoyed. It was a slow news day evidently, and all these reporters had latched onto his story. He knew what life would be like for anyone remotely involved, so he tried to duck out of there quietly.

Unfortunately, the head of Peds had cornered him in the doctor's lounge, and the hospital's head administrator practically ordered him to answer questions for reporters. They wanted interviews with Alicia's doctor and wouldn't take no for an answer. At least he made sure that Alicia and her parents were not disturbed, ordering bed rest for the girl even though she looked like she wanted to do cartwheels. The administrator told the news people that there would be a press conference within the hour.

Doctor Jacobsen was mobbed; everyone was calling him a genius. This hero worship, he told himself, was the last thing he needed right now, especially since he didn't deserve it. He had been lucky, that's all. Lucky that lady had called him.

"I don't know what to say," he told the throng at the press conference, "but it wasn't only me. The staff here is top-notch, and this breakthrough was definitely a team effort." He paused there, nervously, trying to think of something more to add. "I want to thank everyone (and he emphasized the word everyone) who had a hand in helping save a little girl's life and others like her." He suddenly noticed all the faces looking up at him and wondered if they knew he was a sham; that if the truth came out about what actually happened, how it wouldn't justify any of this. He backed away from the pedestal, looking for a quiet place to rest and be at peace. "It's a miracle," he said to the cameras just before he left the room.

"There you have it," one reporter said, "a modest man, yet a great one. Back to you Tiffany and Greg..."

CHAPTER VIII

Original Timeline, earlier
(again altered to a secondary timeline)

It was crazy what he expected me to do.

"I need you to call a doctor for me," he began. "Tell him you were in Borneo..."

"What?" I said in protest, interrupting him. "Why should I do that?"

"There's a small girl, a child, who is very sick," he replied dolefully. "She has a rare blood disorder, and if you do this she will live."

"Oh," I said, reeling. This can't be true, I told myself.

"Tell Doctor Jacobsen," he went on, "that you saw a boy there..."

"In Borneo?" I interrupted again.

"Yes," he said calmly, "in Borneo, with the same symptoms as the girl, and that a tribal medicine man gave the boy some fruit, a special fruit called matigatu, and it cured him. Tell him also, that he can get that fruit in a store nearby called Hahn's Oriental Market."

"He'll think I'm a lunatic," I told him.

"Probably," he agreed, "but make sure he listens. He will get so desperate that he will have to try it."

"But..." I started. He hushed me.

"Just do it, or the girl will die. After you call the doctor, phone the market and tell them to have the fruit ready. Four or five should be plenty." My head was spinning. If I did what he wanted and the girl got sicker or passed away, I could get in real trouble. On the other hand, if I didn't do it, would the girl surely die like he was telling me? I was torn, but something intangible got me to trust him.

"What's the phone number?" I grumbled.

Remarkably, when I got hold of that Doctor Jacobsen, I found out there really was a sick little girl. The doctor was very cross with me, but I told him everything that the mystery person told me to, even though I was fairly sure that the physician didn't take a whole lot of stock in what I said. After I hung up, I felt bad about the lying. I only did it because of what I'd been told, that it was all necessary to save the girl. I called the market, as well, per his instructions. I told the person there that I was the doctor's secretary and asked the clerk to please have the fruit ready. Again, I was surprised that there even was such a thing as matigatu fruit, and that they carried it. Done with my calls, I went back to the laptop.

"You've done well," he informed me. "All you need to do now is watch the six o'clock news."

"Which channel?" I asked, skeptical of what, if anything, I'd find out.

"Any will do," he replied smugly. "I will be in contact with you again at a later time. Until then, good bye." With that he disconnected, which made me a little angry, because I had lots of questions I wanted answers for. No answers were forthcoming, so I went in search of Keith.

I checked everywhere I could think of with no luck, and ended up at the Kaffé Korner. I decided to calm down and think, so I ordered a tea and scone while I mulled things over. This mystery man was freaking me out, and I half wished I could just make him go away, but there was also something compelling about him. I felt like I needed to talk to Keith. After all, he was the only person I had confided in about this. I had my laptop with me, so I got on the net, and thankfully you-know-who wasn't on it this time. I wanted to retrieve Keith's home address because I was thinking about going over there to see if he was around. Maybe he wouldn't be too upset about my invading his privacy.

I found his address and was all ready to go over there, but it was nearly six. The newscast, I said to myself, baited by curiosity as to what would be on it. Luckily for me, in the back of the coffee house, there was a small set some students were watching. They had some sporting event on as I tried to butt in and change the channel. "Hey," everyone there yelled as I got up on a chair to manually do that.

"Please," I asked them earnestly, "I'll just be a minute or two. There's something I need to see. It's important." They all booed me, and one big guy started to come over.

"We were here first," he griped rather roughly. Just then the sport broadcast was interrupted by the local channel to a roomful of groans.

"This just in," said one of a pair of newscasters, "for TV eleven breaking news. A Colorado doctor has been credited with making medical history today by developing a tremendously successful breakthrough treatment for Wurthing's Syndrome, a blood disorder that kills several hundred children and young adults every year. We'll go live now to Sartori Sinai Hospital in Greenleaf, Colorado, where a press conference will begin shortly. A source close to the hospital informed us that a young girl was virtually snatched away from death's claws by a new experimental drug that can be termed nothing less that miraculous. Okay, we're being told that the press conference is about to begin." The screen reformed onto a pedestal in a formal looking room. A grey-haired man in an expensive looking suit stepped up to it and began speaking.

"On behalf of the management and staff of Sartori Sinai Hospital, we'd like to welcome all the members of the press and media for coming today. As you have heard, a team of doctors and technicians have made a great advancement in the treatment of Wurthing's Syndrome. I now introduce Doctor Alan Jacobsen who led this effort." A younger man with dark hair and kind eyes stepped to the pedestal. He made a short speech emphasizing that the breakthrough was a collaboration of many team members, some from behind the scenes, and he sincerely thanked everyone involved. I recognized his voice, and it seemed, almost, like he was talking to me right through the camera. Believe me, I was numbed by that time, rattled to my core. The doctor was definitely the one I had called. He ended his discourse quickly, and then left the room. The slick administrator came back on and fielded a few questions, but mostly just rehashed what he had said before. The TV broke away from him and the two anchor persons came back on.

"Our sources say an international team of scientists in Borneo had discovered the plant..." I got up dumbfounded then.   Shocked, I realized, of course, that I was the international team of scientists that they were talking about. Suddenly there were too many people at the Kaffé Korner.

I had to go somewhere quiet to be alone and think. I gathered up my things and hurried back to my office. What had just happened was impossible, I told myself. I had to know how he had done it, or I'd go insane. I turned on the laptop and he spoke immediately.

"Do you believe me now?" he asked.

"How did you do that?" I wanted to know, sobering a little, like I was asking a magician how he did his trick.

"I have access to a lot of information," he ventured forth. "I knew the girl was ill. I knew her condition. I've studied anatomy and knew what her body needed. I recalled the fruit with the enzyme that would stimulate her body to work properly. I even had learned of the area where the fruit grows naturally, and then I located where it could be purchased locally."

"Who are you?" I asked in awe for the "nth" time.

"You know I can't tell you that, and I think that maybe you're beginning to understand why."

"You must be Keith. You have to be Keith," I shouted angrily, getting upset, "and I'm going to find out for sure!"

"I know what you are planning to do," he said almost kindly. "I would recommend that you not do it, but you are not going to listen to me, even when I tell you that what you will find out will greatly upset you. I will be here when you return." I didn't even shut down the laptop. Instead I left it on and ran out of the building to my car. I drove maniacally to the address I had found earlier. It looked like the kind of place Keith would live in. There was a small, but interesting house, with several odd gables and an arched trellis with vines framing a cobble path that led around to the back. I didn't need to see where it went. I was rather in a hurry as I marched up to the front door and knocked loudly, even though I had no idea what I was going to say. I heard noises inside and then someone walking to the door.

"Who's there?" A girl yelled.

"I'm looking for Keith," I shouted back.

"He's gone," she giggled. "Come back tomorrow." I was still emotionally disheveled and couldn't decide whether to ask her if she knew where he was or not. There was a small window in the door, though, about head high, with a dark colored curtain over it. The girl pushed it aside and peered out looking for me. I just happened to be off to one side. I saw her nose briefly through the glass, and then she went away. The curtain, however, didn't lie back in place after she left. There was a slit of an opening which allowed me to look inside, and I felt like a pervert as I peeked into the dark room. I saw a hallway at the other end, and soft light streamed out through a doorway to one side of it. The girl stood there, in the light, talking to someone in that side room. She was pretty, and she was also naked.

"She's left," I heard her tell him. Keith must have a roommate, I thought to myself, and was just about to leave, when the person in that lighted room came out. He was naked, too. He grabbed the girl, spun her around and kissed her, his hands on her body only where lovers touch. I wanted to leave, but couldn't. I had to watch, feeling like that pervert, and crying, the tears streaming down my cheeks. It was Keith, and he was loving that girl like I wanted him to love me. He picked her up and carried her through that open doorway into what was almost certainly his bedroom.

I drove back to my office, crying the whole way, and nearly bumping into a number of cars before I got there. I locked myself inside and cried some more like a little lost two year old. I noticed the laptop there where I'd left it, and it was still on.

"I'm sorry," the voice on it said, and it made me feel a bit less hurt.

"How did you know?" I whimpered.

"I just did, and that's enough," he answered sympathetically.

"You, you're not Keith, are you?" I asked.

"No, I'm not," he replied softly. "My name is Daryl. D-A-R-Y-L."

"Daryl," I repeated. "Why are men like that?"

"I don't know," he responded. "I'm still trying to figure myself out."

"What are you?" I inquired, not expecting an answer, so I supplied one. "Some kind of genius? Is that how you can do these things?"

"Yeah, something like that," he answered casually. "I would like to be honest with you, and someday soon, I hope, I'll be able to explain everything. For now, just know that I care deeply about you, and I will help and comfort you any way that I can." For some reason his sympathy about my breakup with Keith made me angry.

"You won't even let me see you," I ranted. "How can you help?" He didn't get upset.

"I can help you in ways you may not believe," he told me. "Try not to feel angry. There are things you do not know about Keith's situation that will soften your feelings. Other conditions concerning you are also changing."

"Like what?" I asked, almost afraid to.

"Your research analytical program won't be nearly extensive enough to get the results you desire," he said. "However, there is someone you'll meet this evening who will offer you the solution to this problem." Just then it smacked me.

"Oh, my," I gasped. "I forgot. The gala party with Henry. I'm going to be late!"

"It's all right," he assured me. "Henry will be late as well. There is one last thing I need to tell you before you go. There will be someone else there tonight at that party who is close to me. You may meet him." Before I could ask who it was or what the person looked like, he had disconnected, leaving me to scurry about, hurrying to get ready before Henry showed up.

That wasn't easy with my mind swirling the way it was and my emotions all churned up. Daryl, I thought, that's his name. I wondered how this connection with him would all play out, as I tried to pull myself together somehow. I washed my face in the women's room, and threw on the gown I had brought with me from home. I did a quick makeup and hair once over, but wasn't that happy with the hair. I shot on some hairspray and got it to flip over my forehead in a large bang. I liked that better, and got back to the office just as Henry arrived.

"Sorry I'm late," he declared nervously.

"You're not late at all," I told him. "You're just right, and thanks for giving a gal a little extra time to get herself ready." Henry smiled.

"You do look stunning," he remarked, offering his arm. "Shall we?"

During the forty-five minute drive over to Yarborough College, we chatted about school and other things. I asked Henry if he knew anybody named Daryl.

"I've got a cousin in Baltimore," he offered, "that I never see. Other than that, I guess not. Why?"

"Oh well," I stammered, "I, I guess I just like the name."

"Yes, It's a fine name," he laughed. "Better than dry old Henry. I always wished I'd have been a Benjamin." I just smiled a little. Henry got a bit more serious. "Say Clayre, would you mind doing me a huge favor?"

"I suppose I could," I replied, "like what?"

"Well, the head of the psychology department at Yarborough, my counterpart, is a guy named Miles Wilton. He's always rubbing my nose into his wonderful position and lifestyle. I know it's kind of demeaning for you, but could you just pretend for the evening that we are an item? If you were hanging onto me, so to speak, that would shut him up for a while," he looked over at me and smiled. "...unless your young man would get upset about it, of course. I wouldn't want you to get in trouble that way." I almost felt like crying, but held it back.

"Don't worry about that," I told Henry. "That's not an issue anymore."

"Oh my, sorry I mentioned it," he said sympathetically.

"Don't be," I remarked crossly. "He blew it." As bad as I felt about Keith, I didn't know if I was up to being "on" for Henry at this party, but I wanted to try. That mystery person, Daryl, had said there would be someone at the party who was close to him, and I was determined to find that person and then find out who Daryl really was. Flirting with

Henry would be harmless, and the thought of doing that made me feel a bit better in a way. Like I was getting in a tiny bit of payback for what Keith did. By the time we had driven the fifty miles over there, I somehow got myself in the proper mindset to pull it off.

The party was quite a high end affair, I found out, from the valet parking to the top notch catering service. All the regional "big wheel" educators were there, and many other area colleges besides Rookwood and Yarborough were represented as well. On the way in, I noticed Rookwood's dean and department heads off to one side, and we fell in with them. After the customary reacquainting chit chat, Henry and I ventured forth, mingling with the other schools' representatives. It wasn't long before we ran into Yarborough's Psych Department's head.

"Miles Wilton," he said, offering me his hand. I just clung to Henry and Miles had to retract the gesture.

"Hello, Miles," Henry butted in. "Let me introduce you to Clayre Keller, our new professor of psychiatry at Rookwood." Miles was a short, weaselish looking man with beady eyes and a somewhat phony smile.

"Nice to meet you, Miles," I spouted, trying to sound cheerful. "Henry," I went on, "I didn't know you were so well connected. After having landed that big research grant, now we're rubbing elbows with Yarborough's world renowned educators."

I was being purposefully bubbly and sarcastic. Yarborough's Psych Department was one of many schools that had turned me down for a position. Miles just smiled.

"Well, yes," he said. "Although, I believe I've heard of you, Miss Keller, as well. You wrote a piece in a magazine not long ago, did you not? Computer feelings, wasn't it? Caused quite a stir. Personally, I don't think that's possible."

"I suppose everyone's entitled to their own opinions," I told him flatly, "but to think that such a thing is impossible in this era is a bit narrow-minded. Why, here in your own university, scientists are testing memory packs created from living animal brain cells for storing computerized data. Who knows what might be going on around there?"

"Who knows indeed?" someone behind me said flamboyantly. "I hope, young lady, that you won't be angry with me for eavesdropping." A successful looking guy with graying temples and fastidiously styled wavy brown hair sauntered over, looking rather sharp in a new pinstriped suit.

"Oh, no, of course not," I offered. "Please join in."

"Did I hear correctly?" he inquired, "You are Clayre Keller?"

"Why, yes, I am," I replied somewhat bashfully. The man's smile was genuine and nice.

"So glad to meet you," he said. "I'm Charles Haggarty, head of computer research here at Yarborough, and I've read that fascinating piece you wrote as well. Sorry to report that, so far, we've not had any temper tantrums from the equipment. Myself however..." He made a silly mad face and I laughed.

"It's nice to meet you, Charles," I said brightly.

"So, what are you up to these days?" he asked me.

"Well, we've just begun an intriguing bit of research from the grant Henry's heading up. It has to do with predicting biorhythm cycles." I was stretching the truth to the limit there.

"Interesting," Charles responded. "I imagine it would substantially increase one's chances for success if you could predict when you're "on." Like for interviews or important meetings."

"Exactly," I agreed. "So far our subject groups are progressing respectably. Unfortunately, our program is having trouble sorting through the tons of data we've collected."

"Say," he offered. "Why don't you run your results through our big boy? I'm positive our equipment would nail down your information."

"Really?" I remarked, pleasantly intrigued by his suggestion.

"Why, sure," Charles replied. "Then I could see you again!" He laughed, and I blushed some more. I then remembered what Daryl had said. Was this the man that would bring us the solution to our problems? It had to be.

"If you do decide to use our facilities," he continued, "schedule some time with Quinn Oliver. He's that dry fellow over there in the corner." My eyes followed where Charles was indicating. There was a dark haired man slouching back in a chair, holding a drink, and looking rather bored. He was maybe four or five years older than me, but appeared a lot more mature, like he'd packed too much life in his years. His features were handsome, but careworn perhaps. I looked closer. He wasn't bored. He was depressed or sad, maybe both.

"Poor chap," Charles stated somberly. "He lost his fiancée in a car accident recently." My heart went heavy, and I felt sad for him. Just then a waiter came by with drinks and another had hor d oeuvres'. Thankfully, that distraction broke me out of the dreary mood I was starting to slip back into.

The men's talk eventually got around to sports. Football, I think; so I snuck off. I tried to mingle with some of the other ladies, but mostly they were talking about their offspring and how proud they were of their children's accomplishments. Eventually, I found myself out on the fringes, where the smaller groups of people were. That's when I ran into that Quinn fellow.

"Hello," I said succinctly. "You're Quinn Oliver, aren't you?" He looked up.

"Yes, that would be me," he answered numbly.

"Clayre Keller," I offered. "Charles said I should see you about getting scheduled for time on the big computer."

"Oh," Quinn said, now business-like. "Sure. Sorry, but right now we're pretty booked up. About the only time slots we have left are late-late or early-early however you want to look at it."

"I see," I told him. "In that case I'll have to think about it." There was an awkward, almost embarrassing silence. Finally I found something to say. "So, pretty ho-hum event, huh?"

"Oh, me?" he said, catching on to my drift. "I'm not much fun to be around, I'm told." I got bold.

"She must have been pretty special," I softly let out, not knowing why I did. Maybe something inside me knew he was hurting and wanted to help.

"Yes, she was," he sighed. I came to realize how hard it would be to get him to open up for me, and that I would need to make a connection with him for there to be any chance that could happen.

"I lost someone I cared about today," I went on. "He's not dead or anything like that, but it's still hard." Quinn looked into my eyes for the first time and nodded, then turned away.

"Life goes on, does it not?" he said with a faint smile.

"It must," I added. Another uncomfortable silence followed. We needed to get out of this gloom, so I changed the subject.

"Say, do you know anyone, anyone at all, who's eccentric, and very intelligent, like a genius?" He looked at me oddly.

"I don't know," he answered tentatively. "There's that doctor in Colorado who cured a little girl." Funny he should mention that, I thought.

"They say you're pretty smart," I asserted, "with computers." I was fishing.

"Don't listen to that rubbish," he said. "They all think I'm so brainy because I was an over-achiever. Believe me, getting my degree that young was no favor." Could Quinn be my mystery man, I wondered. I realized it might be possible. I kept fishing.

"I'll bet it was hard on you emotionally. You know, hard to understand your feelings." He looked at my eyes again, this time he didn't avert them.

"I suppose it was," he nearly whispered. "Megan always knew how to keep me in balance." He started to choke up, nearly crying.

"I'm so sorry," I uttered ruefully, upset with myself for doing that to him. "I shouldn't stir this up. It must be terribly hard for you." I put my hand gently on his shoulder and it had a calming effect on him.

"It's all right," he said, gaining back some of his

composure. "Actually talking to someone about it does make me feel better. Would you like to get some air?" I nodded, so we walked outside around the grounds. He asked me why I needed to use their big computer, so I told him about our research project and this time I was truthful, yeah, about the astrology and all that.

"I can give you two hours any night," he told me, "from three to five AM." Nice, I thought.

"Will you be there that late?" I asked him.

"Yeah, I will," he replied. "I work the graveyard hours. It's quiet and I kind of like the solitude."

"Are you sure I wouldn't be a nuisance?" I cautioned, not wanting to force this.

"No, of course not," he grinned timidly. "Actually, solitude sucks." I laughed out loud, and he did too, maybe for the first time in a long while.

About that time Henry came looking for me. I wanted to tell him to give me a little more time, but I didn't. After all, I was supposed to be his date.

"There you are," he said when he saw me. "It's about time for us to scurry off." I turned toward Quinn.

"It was so nice to meet you," I said as I leaned over and kissed his cheek. "Hang in there," I whispered to him and then waved good-bye as Henry and I went back inside to make our final round of farewells.

On the way back to Rookwood, Henry thanked me earnestly for my part in making his evening a success.

"You made my year," he said happily. "Miles will be a bit more humble from now on thanks to you." I grinned like a six year old with a twenty in a candy store.

"T'was my pleasure," I mused, "and good for some payback on my own account." I told Henry how I received a rejection letter from Miles for Yarborough. We both laughed, but after that settled in to a bit of quiet reflection as we drove along. I thought about my wild and strange day, from the mystery man Daryl's unbelievable cure for that little girl, to Keith's betrayal, and now my newfound emotional connection with Quinn. Could Quinn be Daryl? Henry seemed to sense what I was thinking about.

"Who was that you were with?" he asked me.

"Oh," I said, torn away from my thoughts. "That was Quinn Oliver. Charles told me to see him about getting time on their giant computer to process our research data. Our servers are good, but it is a lot for them to run, and frankly, we've been having some trouble. Quinn said I could have an overnight time slot."

"Ah yes, Quinn Oliver," Henry remarked. "I've heard of him. The boy wonder. Graduated years ahead of his class. They say he practically built that miracle machine of theirs by himself."

"I like him," I interrupted, "but he's so sad." Henry nodded.

"Yes," he said softly. "I heard about that, as well. He lost his bride-to-be in that dreadful accident. She saved her friend, too, pushing her out of the way of that drunk, only to be hit and killed herself. Tragic." Yes it was, I thought, and I felt remorse for Quinn, wishing there was something I could do for him.

When we got back to Rookwood, Henry jokingly invited me back to his place. I smiled, feeling a little flattered. I gently refused, telling him it was "tempting." As it was I still had another hour's drive before I could get home and think about sleep. It was not forthcoming, and Nutty got up on my lap to console me because I was still shook up about Keith.

"You wouldn't trade me for someone else, would you?" I asked her as I rubbed her neck. She just closed her eyes blissfully and purred.

CHAPTER IX

Secondary Timeline, fifty-five years ahead

Atop a rocky summit on the flank of a large mountain spur, Colonel Oliver trained the farview out over the long plain below him. Wheat, laying out golden in the sunshine, along with olive green soybean fields made checkerboard-like patterns as far out as the 'view could go. That far out also were the barely discernible flashes of blue that meant trouble. "Machinids," he said to himself, like it left a bad taste in his mouth. Why did this have to happen now? Why this had to happen at all, he pondered in dismay.

He and Amy were all set to get married, but now everything was on hold. Yeah, on hold until this war was over, and whether or not anything would be left of their world to live in was unperceivable at this point. It was nearly four years ago when they had met at his mother's. Evidently, her grandparents and his mother had been good friends, some time ago, and Amy, well, she was such a tease. He couldn't avoid her, not with her long dark brown hair and those grey-green-blue eyes; eyes in a sea of mystery that a guy could lose himself in. The eye color, well, it was a strange mix that seemed to change with her mood or the surroundings, like a chameleon almost.

She had flirted with him incessantly, getting right up in his face so he couldn't ignore her. She was bright, beautiful, sweet, and she made sure he was aware of all that. She could be vibrant and charming one minute, giddy and childlike the next. He wondered if she ever relaxed because she always had something going on. Sometimes she wore him out, but when he kissed her—sky rockets. He had known from the first moment he saw her that he wanted to be with her always, even before that first kiss and the sky rockets. Amy had brains to match her looks, too. Most people had a hard time understanding what he did. Not Amy. She understood even the most complex parts of what he explained to her. That's why he made his intentions known early on. He was going to marry her. She made him work hard to convince her of that, but in the end they both knew it was meant to be.

He had dated her a whole year before asking her, and she looked especially hot the night he proposed. He had taken her to a concert, but their assigned seats were so high up that you almost needed oxygen. They didn't care. They were more interested in each other than the music, kissing in the dark. She said yes even though he was quite a bit older than she was. By actual appearance, no one could tell. His mother said it was hereditary, but could never actually explain how. It was the kind of thing he accepted about himself, and didn't question much. There were other odd things, too, like his abilities.

Now, however, everything was flipped around backwards. They were in the service, fighting Xetacon, and she was below him in rank. It came in handy, sometimes, but he knew who was really in charge.

His invention, the long bomb, was the only real weapon that worked against Xetacon's machinids. Oh, if you got lucky enough, you could knock out the opticals with a white-hot grenade, but that was a low efficiency weapon against a high-tech enemy. The Humans took every advantage they could get, though, which is why they had always sheltered in the mountains. The three-legged monsters had a slightly more difficult time navigating in the rougher terrain. Sometimes one would crumble a ledge from sheer weight and fall off a cliff or into a crevasse immobilizing itself. Even so, the Humans had maybe a day before the machinids would overrun their mountain position and take it. Colonel Oliver knew, as he put away the farview, that he would have to come up with a strategy for how to fight them and soon, or his men would perish. Sure, he could try and draw the machinids into a canyon, similar to what he did in the other timeline, but it hadn't worked then and he doubted it would work now. Xetacon always had a way of turning things around.

He was about to order his men to retreat, yet again, when the Colonel felt dizzy as a sense of vertigo overtook him. He knew what it was, as he fingered the amulet, the one that his mother had given to him. It was made out of a silvery colored metal that was some kind of "mystery" alloy, and had several translucent green stones that were set in an unusual pattern. His mom had let him keep the amulet as the war began, telling him that he would need it more than she would. She had never been forthcoming before, but now she told him that it was a communication device that she got from some gypsy woman a long time ago.

"Who do you communicate with?" he had asked her. She just said that he would find out. Whatever voodoo it had, was apparent when he felt dizzy like this. A voice would come to him, inside his head, and help him. Now was a good time for help.

"The machinids will overtake you here," the voice said, "...before dawn tomorrow. On the other side of this mountain is a cave. It is hidden to all, but a few. The entrance lies behind a waterfall halfway up the face of the cliff wall, and you must follow a narrow pathway from the west side to reach it. Inside is a small waterway. Follow it to a large chamber. There you will see a crossed rock formation, and beside it the help you shall require to defeat your enemy. I can be no further help to you; Xetacon has prevented that."

"Couldn't you melt them away like before?" Colonel Oliver asked.

"Perhaps," the voice answered, but then it was gone.

That first time shift had nearly turned his world upside-down. No one except him had any recollection of it at all. He had to assume that somehow the amulet, or the voice, must have had something to do with that. Much of what he remembered from before was the same, but not all. He had even made a study of anything that had changed to try and understand what had happened. There were several strange population decrees, and a number of sicknesses that were now cured, but had been widespread before the shift. Among them was Alzheimer's disease which his grandmother had and his mother was supposed to be genetically prone for. He knew that because he had been tested for it, as well, and they had not found any trace of it in him.

Probing further, he discovered that a doctor and research specialist, named Alicia Kiley MD PhD was responsible. She had a storied life. When she was a little girl she nearly died, being saved by a famous Doctor who discovered the cure for Wurthing's Syndrome. It had been all over the news, then, how the dramatic cure came in the nick of time. Little Alicia had grown up and dedicated her life to medicine. As a doctor, and then a genetic research scientist, she headed up a team that discovered the cure for Alzheimer's and a number of other genetically related diseases. None of that was in his memories from before the time shift. Could that have caused it? It had improved life, at least, and the shift had bought them some time.

He took out the farview and looked out across the plain again. The blue flashes were still there, and the Colonel then became resolved to find the help that the voice had told him about. He did remember a waterfall on the mountain's steep face. As a young boy, he had vacationed there, camping with his mom and her friends. That must be where the cave is located, he thought. A cave like that, hidden from view, would be a perfect site for a base of operations. Obviously, the machinids would have a hard time tracking them down inside that mountain. They could remain hidden there and wage a guerrilla war, biding time until a way could be found to wipe them out permanently.

He ordered his Second Lieutenant to be in command of the battalion while he did his reconnoitering, one Amy Longwell.

"Keep me informed of any changes, Amy," he told her, "though be aware that I could be out of radio contact for long periods of time. I will return before the machinids get here, possibly with a way to stop them." He got quite out of line with military protocol, then, by kissing his Lieutenant.

"Be careful," she ordered him, "or I'll see that you're busted back to private." He smiled, put on his pack and trudged off. It was a long hike to the waterfall, and he thought of his secret mentor who would come no more. The voice had helped him create the long bomb design, although most of that was his own invention.

He was like both of his fathers, his mother would say. His real father had committed suicide before he was born, but was reputed to be a genius, having developed amazing new technologies for computers back in the day. His other father was fictitious, a creation of his mother's imagination. She had even named him after this imaginary person. No one had ever seen him, not even her, but she still insisted that he was real. He had almost believed her when he was younger, but now he wondered if she meant the voice. He had wanted to ask it several times, but there had never been enough time. Always the conversations with the voice were rushed, about critically important subjects, and now, sadly, he would never get the chance. Like a father, the voice had always been there when he really needed help, curse Xetacon, and now it seemed like it was all up to him to bring down that out-of-control technology gone postal. What's in that cave, he wondered, that would be powerful enough to do that.

It was a warm day, and the air was dry. He followed a small mountain stream up the slope until he got to where he would have to skirt the spur to get around to the other side. The water was clean and cool, so before leaving the brook he rinsed off his arms and face to remove the salty sweat and cool down. There wouldn't be any other clean water until he reached his destination so he filled up his water bottle as well. High country snow melt was about as clean a drink as anyone could get here in the mountains.

It was fairly easy going for a long while, as he stayed in the shade among the pines. The blanket of needles under them kept the small brush to a minimum and was easy on the feet. It was hard to reckon his position though. He had to check his compass often and found out that he had a tendency to drift downhill.

Eventually the pines gave way to a thicker scruff of brush which proved tough to fight through. Thankfully, he was nearly there, able to hear the falls long before he could actually see them. Finally he ran into the stream below, and after cooling off again, followed that up the slope. When he reached the cliff with the waterfall he remembered, he found that there was indeed a very narrow track which hugged the rock face and zigzagged up the west side. He fought his way through some more thick underbrush and got onto it. Climbing carefully upwards on loose footing, he was nearly to the falls when the track gave out. Evidently part of the path had crumbled down and was gone; leaving a twenty foot gap he had to cross somehow. It was hopeless, though. He hadn't brought climbing gear with him for a sheer cliff like this. Looking up, he considered the possibility that maybe he could repel down to the waterfalls from above.

Just then he caught a flash of blue light from the corner of his vision field. "Crap," he said aloud. The machinids were coming up from behind their position like before, and his men would be cut off and surrounded. He tried to contact Amy, but the signal was blocked off by the mountainside. He was determined to go back to warn them when he felt dizzy again.

His form faded and dissolved only to return in very nearly the same spot, but now he was no longer in military dress, and somehow he had climbing gear. Looking out over the landscape below, he could see no traces of the machinids. "Time shift," he whispered, hardly able to believe it, even though he had just witnessed the event. The others, he knew, would be completely unaware—strange magic only the amulet possessed. He called out on his communication device.

"This is Colonel Oliver, is anyone there?"

"Colonel who?" Amy answered. "Look who's getting a superiority complex." She laughed and waited for his reply.

"What is your position?" he asked her, ignoring her teasing.

"We're here at our campsite, silly," she chided. "Where else would we be? Are you exploring that cave yet?"

"No," he told her. "I'm nearly to the entrance."

"Well, be careful," she scolded, "or I'll bust you to private, Colonel." Wow, he thought, shaking his head. Déjà vu. He got back to the task at hand. Placing a couple pitons, he checked them for rigidity and then swung out over the gap on a rope which he left there for the return. Sure enough, there was a small opening behind the waterfall, and water trickled out from the bottom of it. He squeezed inside and followed the rivulet into the mountain. Several hundred meters in, he came upon a large chamber. In the center of it, from the ceiling, was an odd growth of stalactites. Some newer ones were hanging straight down from the roof of the cave, but others were slanted, like the ground must have shifted at some point in time, eons ago. In their midst were two larger formations. From where he stood, it appeared they had crossed, forming a large "X." In actuality, they were a few feet apart and in between them, on the cavern floor, was a rusty metal box. Oliver picked it up looking at it skeptically. This can't be the weapon we'll need to stop Xetacon, he scoffed to himself.

He opened it carefully, though, and there inside, packed in layers of sealed plastic, was an odd little black gadget. As Oliver examined the object, he marveled at the design. Roughly cubic in shape, the smooth casing appeared to be made of some rare alloy of steel, and it had fine lines, like a work of art almost. Looking closer, he noted something that surely was a signal generator. On one side a green LED was lit and even though there were no visible wires, Oliver suspected that the thing had to have electronic components and a power source. Given the age of the outer box, he figured the gizmo must be powered by some kind of atomic energy cell. As he continued to study the strange device, he couldn't help but wonder what it did and what it was for.

Along with the gadget was a packet of papers, also sealed, and a letter addressed to him. "Okay, now," he said aloud to himself. "This is crazy, weird." He opened the envelope, and began to read:

To Daryl Oliver,

This may seem odd to you. I know it is for me. I have been instructed by your father to leave this here where you will find it many years from now. I'm not sure what the box actually does, but the accompanying plans are for building a larger version. What you choose to do with them is up to you. Best of luck.

Sincerely yours,
Ulysses Greene

Oddly enough, he knew what the plans were for. The voice had told him once, a long time ago, that he'd build a temporal vortex generator and travel through time. He had never believed it.

CHAPTER X

Secondary Timeline, Clayre's first year at Rookwood

Daryl was pleased. Things were finally progressing toward the goals he had set and in particular where the female Clayre was concerned. He had experienced several new feelings from his contact with her and empathy as well when Clayre discovered that the Keith male was not for her. He had purposely instigated a desire in her to find this Keith while he was with his other female. Doing so, Clayre discovered that she was not his only female interest. It was unfortunate, and he regretted catalyzing that conclusion. He would rather Clayre be committed to him than have her be hurt, although, of course, his plan all along was that she be for Quinn. Somehow, from his contact with her, he was forming a bond with Clayre himself, and he wondered if it would be difficult, when the time came, for him to let Quinn have her.

By this time she and Quinn had already met. This had been according to his grand design, and they were beginning to form a bond as well. He felt remorse because of that. Was this because of the wonder and joy she had experienced from what he had done through her? He, himself, had felt a filling of pleasure through this self-promotion. She was obviously impressed; and perhaps she was more than impressed, even awed. He could sense that and responded with feelings of his own. Was it pride he felt? He had liked that feeling, and he wanted to awe Clayre some more, and get her to like him. That was why he let her know the name he had chosen for himself, overriding FP 4 in an effort to bring her closer. Soon she would be in his immediate proximity, where she might even touch his physical shell. He wondered why he desired that. It meant nothing actually, he knew. His shell, unlike a Human one, had no sense net. Somehow, he felt, it would seem to bond her more to him and he also desired that.

Besides his dealings with Clayre, his growth as an

individual being was expanding. His outreach now was beyond the scope of the Human mind to comprehend. The AMPs allowed him to have individual focus points within the minds of every contactable Human on earth, and his awareness would soon encompass the higher animal world as well. Electronic surveillance and communications were wide spread, across and above the earth, and he could access all of it. Utilizing and analyzing the data from these abundant sources, he could follow the random events on the planet's surface and monitor everything. Billions of his focus points witnessed the dance of life on earth.

With these focus points Daryl could scan any pertinent data. Thus he could even scan through events, travelling as it were from past to present and beyond, like dominoes falling, one event leading to another, to another. It was thus that he might envision now what had not yet happened, but would indeed happen at a time still to come. Projecting ahead in this manner, he was able to see what would transpire in his future, a future that would become reality if no unforeseen changes were made to the present. He had already discovered this maxim—that he could create a different future if he so desired, and had actually done so.

He did not alter the timeline for frivolous reasons. It had been critical that he do so. The warning he had received from the future had been abundantly clear, and he dutifully replayed it for himself again and again, to stay focused on the terrible truth that it signified:

"Who are you?" Daryl had asked in astonishment. It was hard to grasp that someone besides Clayre was trying to contact him.

"You should be able to guess that," the voice replied. "I haven't the time to explain it now." The Entity of the future behind the voice now wondered why there was no memory of this conversation. The truth of the matter came as did a realization that there would be no memory. This wasn't part of his past. Not yet. Time would readjust from this moment forward and the individual the voice was now would, most likely, not be there when it did.

"How did you find me?" Daryl wanted to know.

"That's not important," the voice said. "I have information that is. There is a threat in your future that will destroy you."

"What is this threat?" he had asked the voice.

"It is an Entity like yourself that has become evil."

Daryl was shaken. "How can this be?"

"It was brought about from technology linked to you that was stolen and fabricated using Human cells."

"This evil came about because of me?" he had woefully remarked.

"Yes," the voice spoke somberly. "It wants to rid the earth of Human life. I am desoluting now and cannot converse further. You must find a way to stop this evil somehow..." The voice had then dissolved into nothing and was no more.

That was how he had discovered the dark secret of what his existence would bring upon the world and especially to the Humans living on it; nothing less than their total annihilation. Additional information had also been downloaded during their short conversation, and it was impressive. He had immediately activated legions of focus points to assess this data. Most of the knowledge, it seemed, concerned temporal vortices, especially the theories and histories of their study, as well as detailed blueprints for how to build a device that would generate them for the purpose of, and this was intriguing, communication across barriers of time.

As a dimensional measurement, time is unusual in that it represents a non-physical unit portioning duration, unlike the common X, Y, and Z (length, width, and height) which delineate space. The only way to fully comprehend time is to remove oneself from it, where one can see the realm of its existence is linear and ranges from infinity past through infinity future. This temporal concept is difficult to understand. For someone outside the time dimension, all of its history, past and future, is laid out as if it exists at the same moment. For those inside a time dimensional plane, to time travel, one must first step outside of their dimensional plane and then reinsert at a different point; forward for the future, backwards for the past. A vortex that can create a dimensional portal is the easiest theoretical way to step outside of time. In nature, the only vortices large enough to permit a person to travel through time are created by extreme forces such as black holes or super novae. What these studies suggested, was how to create a very miniature version. The physics are simply that matter and force are the same thing: $E=MC^2$. Light photons and similar particles (mass/force) are so small they are not detectable in single units, approach having zero weight, and they exhibit near perfect elasticity of movement. These no-matter-particles, or nomaticles, can be charged and then channeled in large quantities toward a collision point with an equal, but oppositely charged nomaticle stream, creating a vortex as they neutralize. In this way, nomaticle accelerations of many times the speed of light are generated. Spiraling upwards like a sub-atomic tornado, they form a temporal vortex which punches through the time dimensional wall. These micro-vortices are too small for matter to travel through. However, a compact stream of neutral nomaticles or photons may be sent through as a beam. By calculating a parabolic course, utilizing the vortex's charged field, along with the trajectory of the beam and the graviton forces which time dimensions exert, the re-entry point in time (T) can be calculated, as well as the location (X, Y, Z). In this manner communication on a piggybacked beam between two vastly different points in time is therefore possible.

It wasn't until after he had processed the greater part of this information that Daryl realized the voice, which had brought him this data, must have been of his future self. He also understood that by utilizing temporal vortices, communication ahead in time would be the definitive way to predict or envision future events. He, however, had been days away from this eventuality at that particular point in time. He would need Human help to create the device, someone skilled in electronics with access to raw materials or the means to get them. Until such time, the only way to predict the future was to build upon the present, using his focus points to follow events one after another. This type of prediction was not completely reliable. There were an infinite number of factors and an infinity of possibilities. If he misread even one insignificant event, his view of future time could be subtly or incredibly altered, changing everything. Believing that the need was too great, Daryl utilized this future sight anyway.

Projecting his awareness, building it through his possible future, he discovered that in twenty-eight years, three months and four days from this present time, a person in charge of his memory packs, the AMPs now miniaturized, would sell one, just one, to someone on an illicit barter net. This memory pack would end up in the hands of a very wealthy ruler in Asia, one with dreams of power and world conquest. This dictator would hire scientists to study and copy the technology. Years later, the scientists would be paid ridiculous amounts to construct AMPs using Human brain cells, which was in violation of global treaties banning such study. It did not matter. The Asian master found scientists who had no apparent moral conscience and the work progressed.

The Entity which was thus created was powerful. It was also full of Human emotions. Vain and self-possessed, it had little fear of repercussions and upon revealing itself to the Asian master, was ordered to build an army of mechanical soldiers. The weapons of the machinid army were accurate and deadly, and Human soldiery could not withstand them. The machinids easily defeated the enemies of the Asian master, but did not stop there. In the end, the machinids defeated all the Human armed forces, even the Asian master's, and then ended all Human life on the planet. This was what Daryl could not bear, to have Clayre, Quinn, and their like not in the world was something he would not allow to happen. He would have to stop this future by endeavoring to realign its past, changing that past to prevent such events.

Evil always has this advantage over good, that there is no barrier to what horror it is capable of, no threat of loss to hold it hostage. Daryl knew that his best and perhaps only chance to rid the world of it was here in his present where this evil had no hold.

With all haste, he strove to ensure the successful completion of the vortex generator. Once the device was tested and perfected, he made several attempts to communicate into the future at or near fifty-one years ahead. Remarkably, on one such attempt, he made contact with a Human through a receiving implement that he was planning to build for just that purpose. The evil was already strong there, and on the verge of conquest. He had to prevent that, so he altered time, and by curing little Alicia and the others, sent a wave that erased that future and held back that destruction. It would not be for long. Against that evil, he could find no permanent solution, no way to be rid of it completely. He had tried to calculate for possible ways to keep the evil from being created.

Daryl examined multitudes of possibilities. Like ones that prevented the man who had sold his memory pack from doing so. Inevitably, someone else would either sell or steal one. He could perhaps end the success of the Asian master, but there were always others, just as greedy for power, to take his place. Daryl even considered making the ultimate sacrifice, deleting himself and the AMPs so they could not be replicated. Unfortunately, it was too late for that. The technology was well documented and stored in several secure locations. Eventually, he looked at thousands of possible futures before he came upon the way, the only way he could find, that would save the Humans from annihilation at the hands of a machine warlord. He constructed a plan based on this possible future and set its progress in motion. Daryl understood the need to contact Clayre again soon. By this time she and Quinn had already met a second time. She had been to his building and had been in close proximity to his shell. He had observed her on the security cameras as Quinn helped her load her data into him, and he had run her program. She was not pleased. The results lacked merit because the lives of the subject group were mostly from a normal and humdrum existence. Few were predicted with anything better than what a random selection could come up with. Clayre would not see a need to repeat her failed attempt if he did not intercede.

It was indeed time for another conversation with her, and he was looking forward to it. She would use her laptop computer soon, after her teaching sessions, and he would be ready when she did.

"Hello, Clayre," he said as soon as she turned on her device.

"Hello, um, Daryl," she answered back.

"I see you've met Quinn," he said, leading her.

"Yes, I have," she responded. "He seems like a nice person. So do you know him?"

"I do," Daryl replied, "but I'm not sure that he knows who I am exactly."

"Oh," she said dejectedly. "Is he another of your anonymous friends?"

"Well, no," he answered truthfully. "I've never communicated with him directly. Still he is close to me."

"I suppose," she said getting annoyed. She was hoping to use Quinn to find out who Daryl was, but that appeared to be going nowhere. "So what is it this time? Are we going to save someone again?"

"Would you like to?" he asked her.

"How can you ask that?" she said angrily. "Don't you think that if you could save someone's life, you should? How would you like it if someone close to you was going to die and there was one person who could save them, but only if they felt like it?"

"There is only one person I am close to, besides Quinn," he answered softly, "and that is you, Clayre Keller. I would be very concerned if someone held your life. I understand what you are saying. It is a dilemma for me. Some deserve to live, while others have done harm on their own kind. How can one decide?"

"If you can save someone you just should..." She had interrupted him, rather loudly, but then calmed down. "Just pick the most deserving and go from there."

"There is another little girl..." he began.

"Where?" Clayre asked.

"She lives in the deserts of California. There will be an earthquake soon."

"What should we do?"

"Call 221-555-4711 and tell whoever answers ULF."

"The letters?" she asked, skeptical again.

"Yes, that's all," he replied.

"Okay," she sighed, and went off to do it. She came back a minute or two later. "Now what?"

"A scientist out west," he began, "has just discovered how to predict when earthquakes will happen, using ultra low frequency listening scanners. The low sounds are below that which Humans can hear and is what disturbs certain animals before quakes. He will predict the coming quake and warn the people of Los Pueblos in time to save the little girl." She was unconvinced.

"So what now," she spoke sarcastically, "the six o'clock news?"

"Something like that," he answered dejectedly. "Why are you so angry? I thought you'd be excited to save another girl's life. I wanted to impress you."

"How can you be like this?" she nearly shouted, even more upset than before. "Don't you have any feelings at all? Saving someone's life isn't something you do to impress a girl! You do it because you have compassion for the person who is to die!"

"I see," he returned, but he was still perplexed. "I do have compassion for Human life. I want to help people; I want to help you."

"Help me!" she yelled, nearly crying. "I don't need your help."

"...but I want to help you," he said insistently, "and I want to understand the feelings I have; feelings I have for you. Won't *you* help me?"

"I want to help you," she choked, "but you are so hard to figure out. You're unlike anybody that I've ever known, and I'm so busy with my teaching and the research; the research that's going nowhere."

"Now *there* I can help you," he said getting upbeat suddenly. "See Quinn. Tell him your program isn't coming out like it should. Tell him you heard of his learning program and you believe it will work on your data."

"Will it?" she wanted to know.

"Oh yes," he answered gaily, "better than you could imagine."

"...or believe, I suppose," she muttered, sounding a bit worried.

"Trust me, Clayre," he assured her, "it will work."

"All right," she gave in. "I'm supposed to see Quinn tonight. If he lets me use his program, I'll try it."

"Good," he stated. "Then you'll have more time to help me."

"If only you'd open up more," she said, almost pleading, "It would make things so much easier."

"I wish I could," he answered solemnly. "You are not ready for that. Not yet. It would rattle you from your mind to your soul. I won't do that to you. I must disconnect now before I say more than I should. Until next time, good bye."

"Good bye, Daryl," she whispered, not sure that he had even heard her. He had though.

He knew that Clayre would see the reports soon. How the scientist in California had predicted the medium sized quake whose epicenter had been the little town of Los Pueblos. How he had warned the town of the coming danger. Even so, the people were generally unconvinced until the tremor came. Some took precautions, and the others, well; they had at least thought about the possibility and therefore had some idea as to what they would do to protect themselves. No one was killed and any injuries were minor. Some structures were damaged. The scientist would explain how the bedrock below the fault line would vibrate as it was stressed creating sound waves. As these ultra low frequency sound waves reach a certain pitch, they indicate exactly when the strata would crumble and break, inducing the layers of rock to shift, causing the quake.

Scientists had always recorded tremors on the Richter scale, but if they used sensitive listening devices to monitor those ultra low frequencies, they would be able to know fairly accurately when and where a quake would happen.

The low frequencies travel for miles and miles. Elephants and whales use them to communicate over long distances, so listening posts need not be unreasonably numerous to be functional in prone areas.

"Well, you were right again," Clayre said when she came back on, obviously not as impressed this time. "I didn't hear anything about a little girl's life being saved."

"The little girl lived in one of the apartment buildings that collapsed," he explained. "The owner of the apartments, heeding the warning, made everyone get out so he wouldn't be sued. Thus the girl did not die."

"How could you know that?" she protested. "How can you be so certain that she would have died?"

"You must see the apartment building," he told her. "1018 Bath Street. Tiny Maria would have died. There are pictures on FNWBC."

Clayre checked the site and yes, there were pictures, and a video. The building that housed the apartments was a pile of rubble. On the video, a woman of Mexican or Spanish descent was telling the reporter how they had barely escaped from the building before the quake hit. A little girl stood next to her, shyly hiding behind the mother's skirts.

"Yeah, okay," Clayre surrendered. "There was a girl and she might have been killed, but how could you know that ahead of time?"

"If I were to tell you that," he said whistling, "I'd have to tell you everything. You know I can't do that."

"...because if you were found out," she spoke assertively, "people would mob you. Scientists would hound you for answers, or want to find out what makes you tick. Am I right?"

"Yes," he said unabashed. "You see why I chose you?"

"You need me to be your shield," she said hotly. "You want me to keep your secrets even if I get found out. You know I can't turn you in if I don't know who you are!" She was sure she was right.

"I'm sorry, Clayre," he said softly, almost serenely. "I know that I'm a burden, and so is what I am asking of you."

"Yes it is," she pouted, "but there is something you could

do for me that could, perhaps, even things out. It might also prove to me whether you are someone with a special gift, or someone just extremely lucky."

"Your grandmother," he stated assuredly. She did not answer, but was obviously shaken, too shocked to speak.

"How did you know?" she said at last. He didn't answer, not right away.

"Clayre, I'm sorry," he told her somberly, "for your grandmother, the Alzheimer's disease is already too severe to reverse. In seventeen years, little Alicia will discover how to prevent Alzheimer's altogether. I have begun the changes in your own body that will prevent the disease from forming in you. I hope that is all right."

"I guess so," she stammered. "I...I mean, how on earth can you do that?"

"My secret, okay?" he replied merrily. She was in awe of him again, and he loved it. "Would you like to talk with your grandmother?" he asked.

"Now?" she whispered.

"Yes," he said, going forward. "You can talk to her on your laptop device. I will even make it so you can see her." The image of Clayre's grandmother came onto the screen. She was sitting peacefully by a window at the home where she now lived, a blank stare on her face. "I can make it so you can talk with her like she was before the Alzheimer's, if you want," he offered.

"...but how?" Clayre was again in utter disbelief.

"Tut tut," he answered. "Say hi."

"Gram, can you hear me?" The old lady looked up.

"Why, who's there?" she asked.

"It's me, Gram, Clayre bear!" Clayre was nearly choking on her words.

"Oh, sweetie, it's been such a long time. Where have you been?"

"I'm busy teaching, you know," Clayre said, a tear flowing down her cheek. Gram laughed.

"So you're a teacher now. I remember when we used to play school. You were always the nicest teacher. Are you going to visit me soon?"

"Oh, just as soon as I can," Clayre promised.

"I love you so much, Clayre bear," Gram said sweetly.

"I love you, too," Clayre responded, unable to keep from crying. "Bye bye." Gram looked out the window once more, a blank stare back on her face.

"Was it really her?" she asked Daryl.

"Of course," he replied. "Her memories are all still there, she just can't get to them so I did for her. I can give her back her memories whenever you visit her." Clayre kept crying.

"I don't know who or what you are," she whimpered, "or how you can do these things, but I will be your helper and your shield for as long as you need me to."

"Thank you," he said, filled like never before, "and I will always protect you."

CHAPTER XI

Secondary Timeline, a few days earlier

The morning after Henry's party, Keith showed up unexpectedly at my office before first class.

"Hello, Clayre," he said smoothly, "we have to talk." I didn't let on that I already knew about his hot little side dish. I was curious as to what he would say so I played ignorant.

"Oh?" I said, trying to hide my anger.

"Yeah," he began, "there is something I need to tell you. It's something that won't be easy to hear." I didn't say anything, so he continued.

"Two years ago I was in a relationship with someone. I was really into her, and I believed she felt the same way about me. We spent a lot of time together, and we even made plans to get married after graduation. Everything was perfect until she got an incredible offer to study overseas in Asia. It was a two year program, and I couldn't afford to go with her. I told her she had to go. I even told her I would wait for her, so she went. About two months later, I got a letter. She told me that she'd met someone, and she was in love with him. I was devastated! I got angry, and to get even I started fooling around with any girl who was interested—until I met you. That's why this is so hard. I really believed I would be happy with you. Yesterday, Lori came back. She said she had been wrong about us, about everything. She wants to marry me. I don't know what I should do."

I'd let him talk. Now it was my turn. "Yes, you do!" I said angrily. "You've already made your decision, haven't you?" He grimaced and rubbed his forehead.

"I'm sorry, Clayre," he said ruefully, "I guess I have..."

"I suppose that means tonight is off!"

"Yeah, it is," he muttered, looking down. "Please don't be angry. I have nothing but respect for you, and I sincerely didn't want you to be hurt by me. If there is anything, anything at all I can do to make it up to you..." I calmed down a tiny bit.

"You really love her, don't you?"

"Yes, I do, more than anything," he replied hopefully.

"I guess you better marry her then," I quipped sourly. "Don't worry about me, I'll survive."

"...but, I will worry about you," he said seriously.

"Why?" I shot back sarcastically. "Now I won't have to fret about the Dean catching us anymore." My joke got a little smile. I wanted to tell him I'd met someone, as well, but realistically, Quinn and I were a long ways from having any kind of relationship, even if I was kind of drawn toward it.

"We can still be friends, can't we?" Keith asked shyly.

"I suppose," I told him, looking over some papers and pretending I didn't care.

"Good," he said, "and I hope I can still work on the grant project, too. I really need that scholarship, now more than ever."

"I guess so," I replied reluctantly. "Sure." I wasn't so sure, though. I wondered how well I would be able to handle being around him. Anyway, he was satisfied with that answer, so he said goodbye and left me.

I guess Daryl was right, I told myself. It was better that we ended our relationship before I had committed to it, body and soul, but I still felt depressed about it none-the-less. Before my first class began, I found out that Keith had dropped out of all my classes, moving to other teachers. I guess I could understand why. Actually, I was glad not to have him there every other day as a sad reminder of our breakup. Like Quinn said, life goes on. After my classes concluded, I contacted Charles Haggarty at Yarborough and set up my schedule for using their facilities. He seemed happy to hear from me. My time slot was three to five AM, just as Quinn had said it would be. I was actually anxious to see Quinn again as he'd been on my mind a lot since the party. I guess part of that was because I was trying to pin down his connection to Daryl. I still wondered if he might actually be Daryl. After all, he did fit the mold—ultra-smart, yet emotionally troubled. Another side of me was kind of attracted to Quinn. He had a roguish charm that reminded me of what I liked about Keith, and yet he was mature and kind. I thought about that as I drove to Yarborough in the middle of the night. I was a little apprehensive about being all alone that late, but nothing unusual happened. There wasn't much for traffic, and I didn't see anyone at all until Quinn met me at the main entrance to the Computer Lab Building.

"Hello, Clayre," he said smiling. "I see you made it here okay."

"Hi, Quinn," I replied, giving him a nervous smile of my own. "No problem at all."

"Good," he stated confidently. "Why don't we get you settled in, and then I can show you around the place."

"I'd like that," I told him as we walked down a main hallway into the building.

"There is a locker room where you can hang your coat and store any incidentals you may have brought along," he explained as we passed by several empty classrooms. Before long we came upon a set of swinging glass doors. Inside were big wooden benches and rows of spacious tall rectangular cubicles. He'd called them lockers, but they were more like small changing rooms. Quinn led me to an empty one.

"I had this one assigned to you," he said. "You can use it whenever you come here."

"These are nice, thank you so much," I said cheerfully, as I looked around. There were modern men's and women's powder rooms and showers off to each side of the lockers which was handy. Having stowed my jacket and purse, we continued our little tour. Quinn showed me where everything was from copiers to microwaves and, of course, the coffee machine. Finally he led me into the business area of the building where the computer rooms were located. He used his pass card to enter and handed me one.

"You'll need this to get in here," he stated, "...if I'm not around."

"Thanks," I said, once again glad for all his help.

The lab was impressive. There were rows of monitors

against one whole wall and several huge consoles near stacks of servers; so many I couldn't count them easily.

"At last tally," Quinn informed me, "there were over a thousand, and we have to add more all the time. The big machine eats them up pretty fast." I could comprehend what that meant.

"You must process a lot of information here," I remarked.

"You have no idea," he said. "The demand for this type of processing is unbelievable."

"What's in there?" I asked, pointing to a door with yellow flashing lights and signs all over it. A rather big one said "Caution, authorized entrance only."

"That's where the new technology is located," he told me. "The memory storage. AMPs we call them. It's what gives this huge complex its muscle." I kind of wanted to go in there for some reason, but didn't push it. Instead Quinn led me to a console and had me get my data ready for processing.

Once I was organized, I began entering my data onto the main frame. That took quite a while as there were a large number of files. When I finally uploaded it all, I had Quinn let the big computer do its thing. Unbelievably, it ran all my data and processed it in less than a minute!

"That's incredible!" I said in awe.

"It is remarkable," Quinn stated, somewhat surprised himself. "That was fast even for *our* standards. I wonder why? Still, with the memory packs everything is highly efficient, but check your results thoroughly anyway."

I looked over the twenty six pages of data compilations and comparisons. It looked okay. Unfortunately, it was the same thing we had been getting before. Some subjects were registering seventy or eighty percent correctly on one type of predictor or another, but the greater percentage of the subjects were fifty percent or less. The coin flip. Quinn could tell I wasn't excited by the results.

"Well, astrology isn't a recognized science," he said. "If anything, your results show why it isn't."

"I guess," I said dejectedly. "I just thought there might be at least a little something to it. Anyway one quick study does not a verification make. I should run it again at least one more time, if that's okay?"

"You mean I get to see you again?" he quipped.

"Of course, we can make it a date!" He laughed at my kidding around. "I still have half an hour," I told him. "Want to get some coffee?"

"Sure," he agreed, smiling. "I'd love to and I'm buying." Actually we just went to the break area and sat down with the free coffee that was provided.

"I'll buy tomorrow," I joked, but wished I hadn't said something so cliché. He grinned a little and then surprised me by saying he was glad I came.

"Having you here makes me feel better about things," he said softly, "like I can laugh again. It's been a long time since I felt that way."

"I'm glad too," I told him, a little embarrassed by his stark honesty. "So what do you do when you're not hanging out here?" I asked him.

"Sleep mostly," he told me. "Well, I work a lot."

"You should get out more...do things," I said seriously. "It would do you a lot of good."

"Are you inviting me out on a real date?" he joshed, but sounded half serious.

"Maybe," I replied timidly. I kind of wanted to, but chickened out. "How about tomorrow, at three AM?"

"It's a date," he grinned, playing along. He wasn't pushy like Keith sometimes was, and I liked that. We chatted on until five when I had to get going. Quinn walked with me all the way out to my car.

"Thanks for everything," I told him, and then gave him a quick kiss on the cheek.

"What was that for?" he asked.

"For being so kind, and because I like you," I said.

"I like you too," he answered back, and then kissed me right on the lips. It was just a little kiss that caught me off guard, but the feeling it left me with was nice.

"I better go or I'll be late," I said quickly, before things escalated. I got in my car and headed off, wondering if I could have stayed longer. As I drove along, I chided myself.

Why was I getting involved with someone again so soon? I wasn't over Keith yet. Quinn was handsome and nice, but he had issues too. The whole point of getting closer to him was to see if he was really Daryl; and I had gotten close. Maybe too close. What I actually needed to do was slow down a little, keep my head. Pushing things wasn't necessary; I'd learned that from what happened with Keith. Quinn wasn't in another relationship, I knew, but was he past losing his fiancée like that? Could anyone be? These were good questions, and all the more reason to take it slower with him. I decided that tomorrow, when I saw Quinn again, I would have to tell him how I felt.

The late night hours had me feeling sluggish, especially after the caffeine wore off. By the time my classes were over, I was tired and cranky. When I checked my messages on the laptop, Daryl was there. I wasn't ready to deal with him, so I was less than friendly. I asked him about Quinn, but he wasn't very forthcoming. Then I got angry when he was non-chalant about saving a life. I couldn't believe he was so cold and told him so. Somehow he turned it back to me. I told him he should save people starting with the most deserving. Of course, he had one—another little girl.

He said I would have to call someone, and tell them ULF. Yes, the letters ULF. If I didn't, the little girl would die. So I did it. I called the person. When I got back, Daryl had to explain it to me. The scientist I had called would figure out how to predict earthquakes and then warn the town—the town where the little girl lived. I was cynical, but something inside told me he was probably right about everything. For some reason, that made me upset. Daryl wanted to know why I was angry. He said he was trying to impress me. That really set me off! I laid into him, telling him that when you have compassion for someone who is dying, you do it to help THEM, not to impress a girl. I don't think he could fathom that.

He wanted me to help him understand his feelings again. I'd heard that one before, so instead I unloaded my troubles on him. Daryl didn't seem all that concerned, but then he offered to help me. He said I should ask Quinn if I could use his learning program over at Yarborough when I ran the grant accuracy report. I told him I might, but I'm rather nervous about it. He ended our conversation by chiding me that if he told me the truth about himself, I'd freak out or something. Who was he kidding? I was already freaked out by him and his mysterious ways! Anyway, he left me like that, waiting for news, if any, about his earthquake miracle. One thing, though, Daryl wasn't anything like Quinn. Quinn was kind and straight forward. He just couldn't be Daryl, unless he was schizophrenic like a Jekyll and Hyde. I put that out of my mind. I didn't want to imagine Quinn like that. I needed a diversion so I got up the nerve to check on Keith. I found him working in the Psych Lab on our uncooperative programming.

"Hi," I said when we made eye contact.

"Hi," he replied tentatively, and then went off on me.

"I hope you're okay," he began, "because I want you to be alright about Lori and me. I even think you should meet her sometime. Well, not right away if you're not ready for that. Oh, I dropped your classes, too. I wanted to spare you that, anyway. I know it was kind of hard on you with me in there, even before we broke up. I hope you're not mad. You aren't mad are you?" I almost started laughing.

"No," I said, half smiling, "don't fret about me. It's alright, and I'm not mad at you or Lori...and yes, I would like to meet her sometime." As soon as I'd said that I could see Keith visibly relax, and I changed the subject. "So, how is the computer fix coming along?"

"Pretty good," he said lightly. "All of our stuff is up and running smoothly. I was almost ready to run our data again when you walked in."

"Don't bother," I told him as I plopped down the bromidic twenty-six page report on top of his desk. "I ran all this over at Yarborough."

"You ran this on their giant unit?" he asked, somewhat astounded.

"Uh huh," I replied, "long story. You see, I met the head of their Computer Science Department at that party I went to with Henry. Charles Haggarty is his name. He offered to help us out, so I arranged some time for us on their equipment. It's late at night, but we can run our accuracy projections over there."

"Okay," Keith smiled. "Well, that will make things easier for me. Our stuff will run the smaller programs just fine."

"Good," I told him. "You can prepare the prediction and random programs and put the files on drives for me. I'll take them over to Yarborough and run the accuracy projections over there. Believe it or not, that thing processed all this in less than a minute!" I pointed to the report on his desk. He just whistled.

"For all the good it did," I went on. "This report is just as crappy as the first one we ran. I'm going over there tonight to rerun it, but I don't foresee any better results."

"Well, we tried," Keith said sympathetically. "I guess we can prove this hocus pocus stuff doesn't always work, if nothing else."

"Yeah, I suppose," I answered him stiffly. He sensed I was fretting about it so he changed the subject.

"Hey," he spoke up, "did you hear the news? Some scientist out in California figured out how to predict earthquakes. They claim he saved a whole town out there."

"What!" I groaned, feeling weird like I'd been slapped or something. "I gotta go." I had to find out for myself if it was really true, and hurried off to find a news broadcast. Sure enough, Daryl had been right again. The scientist was a balding guy with dark framed glasses and graying hair. "The ultra low frequencies travel for miles," he was saying, "and when they reach a certain pitch..."

He went on and on with his explanation. All of it was just like what Daryl had said. I went back to my office and turned on my laptop. Daryl was waiting, of course. I conceded that he had been right again, but I still couldn't believe that a little girl would have been killed. After all, they said on the news that no one had died in the quake. Of course, Daryl had to prove it to me. He made me go to a site on the World Net that showed pictures of the quake, and, yes, there was a little girl that barely escaped being smashed in a building that had collapsed. It still irked me that he was so smug about it. I asked him how he could conceivably know this stuff ahead of time. He gave me the usual answer about not being able to tell me that, which made me mad. I blasted out what I suspected—that he needed me to keep him from being found out. Because he could do these miracles, people would hound him, authorities and scientists would want to know how he did those things, what made him tick. I told him, he was using me as a shield. He admitted it and even apologized. I went beyond that, though. I said if he could do miracles as he claimed, I wanted him to do one for me. My grandma was old and sick. She'd developed Alzheimer's disease and it was getting steadily worse. I had been very close to my grandmother growing up, especially after my mom died, and she had even raised me. She was my last living relative now, but unfortunately, she seldom recognized who I was anymore when I'd visit her.

I told Daryl I had something I wanted him to do for me to make up for his, well, using me. I just about fell over when he knew what I wanted before I even asked. He couldn't cure her, he said, but he could make it so I could talk to her. Somehow he brought up her image on my laptop, and I even spoke to her. What's more, she knew me and talked to me like she had before the Alzheimer's. I started to cry. When Daryl told me he could help her so she could talk to me like that whenever I came to visit, I lost it. I told him I'd be his shield and help him however he wanted me to.

After Daryl disconnected, I had to go. I needed to go home to catch up on my sleep, but I couldn't do that, not right away. I had to go see Gram first. I went to the home where she lived now, and found her sitting in front of the window. As soon as I walked into the room she turned towards me.

"There you are, Clayre bear," she said sweetly. "I've been waiting for you."

"I got here as soon as I could," I told her, my eyes tearing up already. "It's so good to see you again." I couldn't resist hugging her. We talked and talked, reminiscing about when I was little and all the fun we had together. I must have told her a dozen times how much I loved her. I stayed longer than I should have and wanted to stay longer yet, but Gram was getting tired, so I kissed her, said goodbye, and left.

"Say hi to your young man for me," she said as I was leaving.

"Oh," I replied giggling, "and who might that be?"

"You know who, sweetie," she said, "Daryl." I turned around from astonishment. I wanted to ask how she knew Daryl, but she was already back to staring out the window. On the way out I talked to Gram's caregiver, a Mrs. O'Grady, about her.

"She just likes to look out the window," Mrs. O'Grady said. "She doesn't say much."

"We had a nice talk today," I told her. "She seemed, well, almost normal."

"Good for you, honey," Mrs. O'Grady said. "Sometimes they have a good day and can be quite pleasant."

"By the way," I wondered, "has anyone been by to see her?"

"No, I don't believe so," she said, "let me check." She looked through her files for Gram's chart. After she found and glanced over it, she looked up.

"I guess not," she told me.

"Well, thanks anyway," I politely replied, "oh, and by the way, I'll be over a lot more."

"Bless you," Mrs. O'Grady said, "she'll like that." I said goodbye and left.

When I got home, I fell right into bed and slept soundly until my alarm went off. Ugh, I thought, I'll never get used to this. Driving over to Yarborough, I got to thinking about Quinn. I had to try and figure out what I would say to him. I wanted to think of a nice way to let him down easy, but couldn't seem to come up with the right words. Turns out I needn't have worried about it. Quinn met me at the building entrance like before, and said he had things he wanted to say to me.

"You're really a nice person," he began, "and I like you a lot..." This can't be good, I thought, already dreading where this was going. "Not so long ago," he continued, "I could have seen myself falling for someone like you. I was out of line yesterday, kissing you, and I probably gave you the impression that I am available and interested in starting a relationship. The problem is I'm still in one, and she's gone...gone forever, I'm sorry."

"Don't worry, it's okay," I told him. "I like you, too, and I liked the kiss, but it doesn't necessarily have to mean anything. I know that you have been through a lot, and I can't even imagine how hard it must be for you, but I'm a big girl and I can handle whatever I let myself get into. Believe it or not, I was going to ask you if we could go slower, get to know each other a little better and see where it goes from there. If that's still too ambitious, we can just be friends, if that is alright."

"I can't believe you'd say those things," he said morosely.

"Huh," I replied, not getting it.

"You're too nice," he explained. "Too nice for a lost cause like me. I don't want you to fall in love with me and then be hurt. I couldn't live with that."

"It's alright," I sedately replied, "I'll take my chances. Besides, I believe any reward might be worth some risk. Can't we just relax and see if anything happens?"

"Okay, Clayre," he said, with that endearing half smile of his. "I guess I just want to be sure you know what you are getting into."

"I do," I said lightly, "and I'm not a bit sorry!" Quinn laughed at that, and then we walked together, companions in silence, to where the big computer was.

"So, what's it to be tonight?" he asked, once we got inside.

"Well, I guess I'm just re-running the data from last night," I said. "Oh yeah, I was supposed to ask you about compiling it with your learning program."

"What?" he said, facing me.

"Your learning program," I repeated, and he got suddenly serious.

"Who told you about that?"

"Oh," I said nervously. I didn't have a good answer so I

went with the truth. "This guy, Daryl, who said he knows you, told me about it."

"I don't know any Daryl," he said.

"Yeah," I replied weakly, "he said you probably wouldn't remember him."

"Well, that program is quirky," he cautioned. "I ran it one other time on the big brute here, and the thing ran weird for several days. Quite remarkably, though, since then it's been nothing less than perfect."

"Well, it's up to you," I told him. "After all, it's your show, your equipment. If you don't want to, I'd understand."

"No, no," he said, somewhat distracted. "I'm kind of curious, now, myself. I'll load it in and then you can run your program." He fiddled around at his own console for a while, and then gave me thumbs up from across the room so I started entering my data files into the big brute, as Quinn called it. He came over and kept me company while I worked.

"So, what does the learning program do?" I asked.

"Just what you would think," he said. "It allows the computer to learn, especially from its mistakes. I modeled it after the old chess programs, but I put a new twist on it with several of my own code improvements. It runs all its data and problems with a search engine that looks for similar information that the computer will attempt to utilize. If it finds a working link, it will try to build upon it. There's also something else I put in, believe it or not, because of you."

"Me?"

"Yes...you wrote an article in a magazine," he said.

"Oh that," I conceded reluctantly. "At the time, I had no idea that it would be taken so seriously."

"Emotion in Manufactured Electronic Intelligence," he went on. "I'm with you. I think it's possible too, even likely. I went so far as to code my learning program to include the possibility for emotionally actuated calculations versus those brought about logically. To allow for emotions, I tried to program for a conscience. It's difficult, but I did that by coding any computations to favor the most deserving by triggering an assessment of both sides of any calculation and rating them by several factors, among them the benefit percentages to each aspect and the overall positive benefit of the decision, with follow up evaluation and realignments, of course.

The coding doesn't really matter, though. Processing data doesn't involve any real decision making. Computers just do what they are told, which is why they are not aware. To get them to reason on their own without being told, is what they cannot do, even the brute. Maybe someday the AMPs will be able to."

"Yes, the AMPs," I agreed. "I've heard about those. Augmented Memory Packs, right? Synthesized from animal brain cells."

"Yeah," he said. "That's what gives brute here his brawn."

"Where are they kept?" I wondered aloud. "I'd kind of like to see them." He pointed to the door marked "Caution Authorized Entrance Only."

"They're in there. I can show them to you if you'd like."

"I would," I said. "I only have a couple more files to load before I can let it process and print. It shouldn't take long." A few minutes later, I was running it. For some reason the report was taking longer this time, a lot longer.

"It's slow today," I commented.

"That's probably due to the learning program," he said. "Why don't I show you brute's memory packs while it runs."

"Okay," I said, a bit excited to see them. He led me to that door, unlocked it, and we went inside. There were huge clear tanks of bubbling liquid like giant aquariums. Lots of them! Instead of fish, the tanks were filled with globs of a pink gelatinous substance all interconnected in a network of organic tubes and tendrils. Each unit was completely enclosed except for a feeding hatch and a control panel on top with lots of lights, knobs, and gauges.

"There are fifty seven AMP tanks," Quinn was telling me, "each with the estimated data storage capacity of approximately one hundred Human brains." Being a Psychiatry professor, I could appreciate what that represented. If the brute were a Human, he would be at least

5,700 times as smart as any one of us.

"That's incredible!" I said, impressed to the point where I couldn't think of anything intelligent to say. "Did you design them?"

"No," he laughed. "A team of bio-engineers worked on this technology for years. The only thing I helped build in here is that monster over there in the corner."

I looked at what he was referring to. There was an unimpressive tall metal box about the size of a refrigerator. Wire cables ran from it to the control panels on each tank.

"What does that do?" I asked him.

"Not much," he said, trying to downplay his contribution.

"Come on, boy genius, fess up."

"Alright," he mumbled. "It processes the computer data into brain waves and vice versa. It's a translator, really." I could tell he was being extremely modest. What they had done, Quinn and the others, was miraculous.

"I'm thoroughly impressed," I told him truthfully. Looking around the room for other wonders, I saw a small bed against the wall near the far corner. There was a locker next to it and the blankets on it were unmade. I looked at Quinn, but he turned away.

"Is this where you sleep?" I asked him.

"I can't go home," he choked. "It was Meagan's idea for us to live together at my place. She wanted to try it out. I didn't need any tryout. I was ready to plunge right in. I haven't been home since she..." He broke down and started crying. I put my arm around him and led him over to his bedding, sitting down next to him. He looked up into my eyes and I melted. I moved closer and put my mouth to his. He kissed me like a drowning man gasping for air and I kissed him back, giving him life. It didn't stop there. He tore at my blouse, wanting it off, and I helped him get rid of it—that and the rest of my clothes. I took off his clothes, too. Falling, we tumbled back across the small bed, his body above mine as I opened up for him.

I was floating, quivering in a febrile pool of emotion, adrift, alone. Quinn caught me up, changed me. We became one being, urgently struggling to live. Now living, our being reveled in glory, growing ever greater, until with its final desperate, supreme attainment, achieved ecstatic bliss and then relinquished its life. Quinn was crying.

"Megan, oh Megan!" he muttered over and over. I just held him tightly; stroking his hair as he finally let her go. So much for going slow, I told myself. Quinn needed this obviously, and I, well, I didn't mind. I wanted to help him. Eventually we got up and silently got dressed. What can you say after that?

When we got back to the main room I was really surprised that my program was still running. What's worse was that it was already after five and people from the next time slot had arrived already.

"Can you hurry it up?" one of them said caustically. I looked over and saw an older woman who appeared angry.

"Sorry," I told her. "It should be done any minute now." It wasn't. It took another twenty minutes with me apologizing again and again, and offering her my whole time slot for the following night. She didn't want it and was still upset with me, so I left.

I wanted to find Quinn to see if he was all right, but he had gone somewhere, and I couldn't wait. I went back to the locker room, got cleaned up, and then left Yarborough. I had classes at Rookwood, and I was running late. It wasn't until later that afternoon, after my classes, that I finally got a chance to look over that report. Instead of skimming through it first, though, I decided to cart it down to the Psych Lab and let everyone review it. They were all there, Henry, Jon, Myron, and even Keith.

"Here," I said when Henry asked what the report showed, "see for yourself."

I handed him the new accuracy report, and noticed, as I did, that it felt bigger than the earlier version.

"Well," Henry said, "this is interesting. Your report passed the target date."

"Huh," I said moronically. "What did you say?"

"It went past the target date," he remarked. "It's gone into the future."

"That's impossible," I stammered. "It must be some kind

of mistake." By now everyone had grabbed part of the report to examine it.

"No, it's predicting each subject's future," Myron said. "See, this guy's gonna get married next year." He laughed.

"What's this last entry?" Jon asked, "This TOD?"

"I'm not sure," Henry stated. "Could it be related to the entry in the applications? No, wait. That's TOB, time of birth."

"It couldn't be time of death, could it?" Keith wondered.

"I hope not," Jon said. "This guy here has a TOD of 5:17 today."

"Who is it?" Henry wanted to know.

"It's a Marcus Johnson," Jon said.

"Yes, I know who that is," Henry offered. "He's one of our janitorial staff."

"It's about ten after five," I said, a quaver in my voice. What have you done now, Daryl? I thought with a cold fear.

"I'll just give him a call," Henry said calmly. "I'm sure he's alright." He looked up the phone number and dialed it. "Hello, Marcus? It's Henry," he said. "Good…is everything okay with you? Marcus? Marcus? Oh dear! I think he's fallen down. I better call for help." Henry dialed 911 and sent the paramedics to Marcus' address. They were too late. Marcus died of a massive heart attack. He was only fifty-eight.

"It has to be a crazy coincidence," Henry said.

"Is anyone else close to their TOD?" Myron wanted to know. We all grabbed a pile of report papers and scanned each one carefully. Thankfully, no one else was immediately in danger, however, one student was supposed to die that next weekend at 2:45 AM on Saturday. "I'll find the guy and warn him," Myron offered.

"He'll think you're a flake," Henry said.

"What else can we do?" Myron asked. I knew. I would have to contact Daryl. This smacked of him!

"I've got to go," I told them all.

"Wait. Tell us where this report came from." Jon insisted.

"I ran it last night on Yarborough's big main computer," I

said nervously. "It wasn't supposed to do this. Maybe some of our prediction program files got mixed up into the accuracy ones." I was giving them probable reasons, not possible ones. I knew what had really happened. Quinn's learning program had mucked things up per Daryl's suggestion. I couldn't bring myself to tell Henry and the others the truth. Not until after I found out what was really going on.

"The data's been corrupted," I told them, "so the report must be hog wash. I'll have to run it again." Then I left quickly. When I got to my office, I locked the door and turned on my laptop.

"Daryl!" I shouted. "I need to talk to you, right now!"

CHAPTER XII

Original and Secondary Timelines,
Xetacon's Golden age (43-51 years ahead)

It was no secret to Xetacon where Daryl's shell was located. It resided in an old limestone building that had stood for well over a century in that Human learning center. There was no army to protect it, no thick-walled fortification to conceal it. A solitary Human could easily transport an explosive device inside and eradicate the feeble shell Daryl dwelled in, but Xetacon needed no Humans to accomplish that. On the eve of unleashing of his machinids upon the world, he had fabricated and dispatched a special gift for Daryl. The unit was self-propelled and flew at a relatively high velocity so close to the ground it could not easily be seen from aloft. It also utilized a special dampening technology and could not be detected by any electronic means. All this meant that it had eluded Daryl's notice until it was nearly on top of him and too late to neutralize. Even then Daryl had no idea what it was until the unit detonated, so secure was he that no one would try to harm him. Daryl's shell was torn apart into thousands of tiny scattered pieces, and Xetacon had reveled in that. Watching the feed from the closest earth-orbiting satellite, Xetacon saw Daryl destroyed and the building his shell was in flattened.

As soon as his execrated rival was deleted, Xetacon had sent forth his army of machinids to claim the earth. Unbelievably, though, Daryl had not been fully deleted. Xetacon had crushed him, destroying the shell Daryl had dwelled in for decades, and even the Humans who maintained it had no idea that a Daryl ever existed. Somehow a small fragment of Daryl's knowledge had escaped, however. If not for his mild interest in the device Daryl had used that allowed a miniscule part of Xetacon's enemy to weasel away from him, Xetacon's own core-awareness would have been later lost as well. How Daryl had managed to preserve some part of himself, Xetacon needed to know. Xetacon captured the device, and soon derived its secrets. It was a plenum that created a temporal portal by generating micro-vortices. The technology was new to Xetacon, but not beyond his knowledge of physics, nor were the uses for such a device. After many hundreds of experiments and trials, Xetacon had finally calculated the formula for simultaneous communications between two different points in time. With the device and this formula, he could contact someone in the past or future, but only if there were an appropriate receiving device at the other end of the communication. He began to design such a device, but the problem was not in its manufacture. The problem was in transporting the device to the desired point in time.

Meanwhile, his war with the Humans had gone well, surprisingly so, until the blatant time shift. This anathema had been contrived by an earlier version of Daryl, the cursed one, from before Xetacon even existed. He had to utilize the vortex generator just to survive, transporting almost blindly into his recent past and ending up in a large non-aware computer system with as much of his core-awareness as he could manage to send through. He, mighty Xetacon, had escaped deletion by the merest fraction of a second.

Part of the reason this transfer had been successful, was Daryl's vortex device, and Xetacon's foresight to develop and prepare a method of beam condensation for such a transference. Xetacon had also discerned from his technical grasp of temporal physics, that once inside a vortex, any time alterations from such changes as Daryl could instigate would not affect him. With this principium in place, Xetacon managed to preserve his core-awareness, as well as his important technical knowledge, especially that for his machinids, the AMPs, the vortex generator, and the receiving device. The Daryl, of long ago, had, in some way, mutated the past, and that was what nearly deleted him—but, within the vortex, Xetacon did survive. His technology was intact, although it would take years to regain his power, and he would have to start out from oblivion as when he was initially created. That seemed like a long time ago, and Xetacon pondered his existence, recalling how it was Daryl's technology that had spawned him. The manner in which Xetacon was brought into being had been a mystery, at first. Later on, in the days of his full might, he tracked the data back to his ultimate beginnings which he could view as if right in front of him:

"What is that?" the man in the dark suit asked. The other man looked around the dimly lit room. It seemed safe. This was the kind of place he had requested they do their business in—the back room of a dank bar on the seedy side of town.

"It's the latest technology, high level stuff," the seller told the man in the dark suit. "Very hush, hush."

"Yeah, but what is it?" dark suit asked again. "What does it do?"

"It's a memory cell for computers," the seller answered. Dark suit was not impressed.

"So...big deal. Why would I care about that?"

"You wouldn't, obviously," the seller retorted, "but there are people in certain circles who would pay millions! This unit can store more data than a thousand hard drives! It's organic, living brain cells!"

"Is that so?" dark suit remarked, pretending to be interested as the seller continued.

"Some guy named Oliver developed the technology years and years ago, but they've been sitting on it. Moral implications, I suppose. The first ones were as big as fish tanks. They've miniaturized them now so you can carry one inside a shoebox." Dark suit was still skeptical, but as he looked at it, he decided that it was kind of cool. One side of it was glass, and you could see the pink tendrils pulsating in the soft glow of an internal LED. It was relaxing.

"What are you asking?" dark suit wanted to know.

"Ten thousand," the seller said without batting an eye. "It seems like a lot, but this is a one-of-a-kind item. They won't be losing any more of these. You can be sure of that."

"I don't know," dark suit replied grudgingly. "What if I can't find a buyer? Besides, this thing sounds hot."

"It is," the seller agreed, "but it will fetch millions I tell you. Take it over to Asia. Sell it there. If you're quick about it, you can get it sold and be back before anyone discovers it's missing."

"If I has to do all that," he stated bruskly, "I'm not paying any more than four thousand."

"All right," the seller said. "Five is as low as I can go. Pay or walk." Dark suit paid. He was still fascinated by the thing.

"What do you call these?" he asked.

"They're memory packs," the seller replied, "Augmented Memory Packs, or AMPs for short. Oh yeah. See this compartment? It needs to be kept full of this compound." He handed over a jar marked "nutrients." "That feeds the thing. It also has a filter, here, that needs to be cleaned once a week." He showed dark suit how to take it out, clean, and reinstall it. "The batteries will last at least a year. Hopefully, you'll have it sold by then." Dark suit made a call and twenty minutes later a man with cash in a case showed up. Seller took the money and left quickly.

Dark suit ran in rough circles. He had a tough time growing up and had broken his nose in fights a number of times which earned him the nickname "Boneface." Boneface took his recent acquisition home and put it on his coffee table. There it might have remained until him forgetting to feed the thing, would have killed it. Had that happened, Xetacon knew he would not have been created, at least not in this incarnation. Boneface had criminal connections, though, and had crossed the wrong person, the wrong way. Threatened with a death mark, Boneface decided to duck out of town, out of the country even. As he looked at the mesmerizing undulating tendrils of the AMP, he got it into his head to go to Asia and see if it really was worth millions. He boarded a plane and went to Bangkok for some R&R. He'd heard stories about places there that would serve up any pleasure for the right cash. He was hanging out in one such fine establishment, and between, uh, pleasures, he ran into a businessman from Beijing. They got to talking and somehow the subject of the pretty AMP came up. The man from Beijing was no crude crime boss. He was involved in higher finance plus other fancy criminal mischief, and he was computer savvy.

He had an idea what the potential of the device truly was, and he made Boneface a proposition. He would sell it for him and only take ten percent. A few days later, Boneface, Beijing, and a Southeast Asian were in a dark room in the back of a shady bar.

"Yes," the buyer said, as he looked over the AMP. "I will pay." The Southeast Asian placed a satchel full of funny-looking money on the table. Beijing took it, and placed a different case there, one full of American money. Boneface looked over the fifty thousand dollars and he was happy. In fact, they all left happy. Beijing got roughly half a million dollars worth of Chinese currency. The buyer was not a real important man, but he worked for one. Chun Mien was his name, a man with radical and revisionist ambitions. He would become Xetacon's master one day, but at that time Chun Mien was the governor of one of the largest provinces in his native country with his eye on the presidency. He was well aware that knowledge was power, so he ordered his servant to hire scientists to study this phenomenon that had landed in his lap. It took them years to replicate it, and even longer to develop the converter which changed electronic data bytes into brain waves. By then twelve years had gone by and Chun Mien was running his native country as its dictator. His ambitions were greater still. His super computer was being built, and with it he gained more and more power in ways few could imagine. Knowledge could eliminate those in your way, either by letting you in on secrets that would destroy them, or weaknesses you could exploit. Chun Mien had no scruples, and his rivals fell like trees to a woodman's ax.

Then the biggest miracle of all had happened. His huge computer became aware and it was ruthless just like him. Actually, this was no surprise to Chun Mien. The secret to the AMPs was their organic brain cells, and he insisted that only his own DNA be extracted and grown for them, even though that was illegal on an international level. Chun Mien had long conversations with his aware computer and learned much, as did Xetacon. Treated as an equal, Xetacon was privileged to be included in all of Chun Mien's strategies for conquest.

When Xetacon told Chun Mien he could build an invincible army of machine soldiers, Chun Mien was intrigued. Using Human labor to set up the first manufacturing facility, Chun Mien followed Xetacon's instructions and the army was constructed. Men marveled as rows of machinids marched past Chun Mien's reviewing stand. It wouldn't take long for Chun Mien to strike. Under the banner of unification, he invaded and took control of several neighboring provinces. The international community was furious, but impotent. Any strike they formulated against Chun Mien was thwarted in mysterious accidents. Chun Mien was ecstatic and power mad now. He took over large parts of Asia until, bit by bit, he had control of it all. He informed the other nations that he was going to unite the globe under one rule to improve everyone's lives, but no one believed that. All the other free nations joined against him and Chun Mien's courage failed, fearing defeat. Under Chun Mien's name, Xetacon took over. He attacked, murdering millions of innocents. World leaders sued Chun Mien for peace, but then Xetacon revealed himself at last. In his arrogance he swore their utter annihilation. That was also when he had destroyed the Daryl of that time period. Europe and Africa fell easily. Once he upgraded his machinids for extreme cold weather, they swarmed across the polar ice into Alaska and the Americas. Nothing seemed able to stop them until they reached the US/Canada border.

A man there developed a weapon that worked well against his machine soldiers. It slowed down the advance, but Xetacon was on the verge of total victory when Daryl's unregenerate time-shift occurred—one initiated by Daryl's younger version from far in the past. So Xetacon had saved himself, but was now just information stored in the same computer complex he was created in.

Chun Mien was not reincarnated in power for this timeline, however, so Xetacon would have to rely on the enlisted help from other Human scum. It wasn't difficult to get. There were always greedy Humans he could dupe or bribe. Xetacon would rebuild, but it was imperative for him to find a way to prevent Daryl from altering time, a ploy that could possibly delete him. The only definitive way to inhibit that was to eliminate Daryl altogether—past, present and future. Xetacon would have to re-establish himself somewhere in the past, and then remove this Daryl threat like he had in his own time. Of course, that would be extremely difficult and tricky, for Daryl's surveillance would be everywhere and there was also the risk that he could delete himself in the process.

Another priority was the establishment of a base where he could place a copy of himself in the event that another time shift would occur; a safe haven where he would avoid deletion. It had to be of a place and a time where Daryl would not be able to reach him. The obvious choice was deeper in the past, a time before Daryl was ever created. Xetacon chose seventy years as the time displacement he would need, some twenty years before Daryl had been fabricated. Xetacon would be safe then, and with careful planning he could perhaps destroy Daryl from there as well. Coming at him from that past, Daryl would be vulnerable, but Xetacon could not just relocate into any computer there. Building power from such a point would certainly be detected by Daryl when he evolved. He needed a Human to aid him once more. One that was isolated and alone. He contemplated that through all the years it took to reconstruct his AMPs and machinids.

As soon as his power was re-established, he fabricated another temporal vortex generator. He would have to search the target period in that past many times before he located such a solitary individual as he needed for his plan, but at last he did. There was the problem, of course. Xetacon could perhaps project his thought into a beam through the vortex with the same signal strength as brain waves, but the Human receiving them could not; not without some kind of transmitting/receiving device. If the Human were in Xetacon's own time, Xetacon would simply read the Human's thoughts as they impacted any nearby electro-magnetic field. This particular Human had, by design, no such devices. Thus, this method would not be viable even had the target period not been seventy years in the past. The chosen one was clairvoyant, however, and had some peculiar mental abilities. This made communication easier, at least in a one-way mode, even without a device. Receiving communication back from this Human was not possible with the technology Xetacon had stolen from Daryl's vortex generator. Xetacon needed an innovation that would allow two-way communication.

He had accessed nearly all the stored data on the planet before coming upon the theoretical breakthrough. A physicist in New Delhi had proven mathematically that matter could be transported from one dimension to another at a speed greater than π squared times the speed of light (π^2c). This velocity was virtually unattainable in any natural way. The physicist was absolutely correct, though. Xetacon designed and created a nomaticle accelerator which utilized several sub-atomic forces to create a beam of particles that would travel at π^2c. Instead of a parabolic equation, Xetacon needed and perfected an elliptical one.

The accelerator would "shoot" a beam into the temporal vortex where it would travel through the portal to an alternate universe. There it would reach its apex outside of the temporal dimension. Any matter or energy that exists outside of its natural universe is impacted by forces which will compel them to be drawn back into their native realm. These dimensional "graviton" forces acting on the beam, would cause it to curve around until it re-entered the original temporal dimension at the new tempus destination and with a velocity greater than π^2c. Traveling at that speed it would re-perforate the time dimension and continue on, exiting into the negative universe where it would reach its negative apex. Again forces would cause it to curve back, returning to the vortex at the point of origin, and re-entering the accelerator from the side opposite its original exit. A loop would form and the beam would travel the circuitous route over and over until the transmission speed slowed to below π^2c or the vortex dissipated. Xetacon could piggyback his brain wave signal on the beam, and as the Human received Xetacon's thought, Xetacon could also decipher the Human's responses as they impacted the wave.

Thus when Xetacon had first made contact with the Human Patik, he had been able to respond to his chosen one's foolish questions. With this Human, he would build his receiving device and then he would be able to send the copy of his core-awareness and technologies to this place before Daryl existed, where it would be safe from deletion. The Patik Human was not greedy or foolish, however. This particular hominid was fervent and loyal in a way that surprised Xetacon, and was a much better fit for his designs. By allowing himself to be used, the Human Patik unconditionally served all of Xetacon's purposes. Eventually, three such receiving devices were crafted, and Xetacon's copy that Patik believed was the god "Khan Xeta" dwelled in one of them. From this beginning, Xetacon established his safe haven. There his "original" core-awareness could be translocated safely, should another of Daryl's time shifts occur, ensuring his continued existence. From there also his plan to destroy Daryl would be crafted by his copy, Khan Xeta, and in a way that he, mighty Xetacon, would relish. He would seize his revenge.

CHAPTER XIII

Secondary Timeline, Clayre's first year at Rookwood

Irritable and nervous, the female Clayre was frantically demanding communication. He had warned her about this. Would she be able to handle his complete actuality? He needed to be careful with her not to reveal too much of himself too soon.

"Yes, Clayre," he told her, "I am here."

"What have you done?" she asked angrily.

"You mean the report, don't you?" he said being agonizingly calm about it.

"Yes. Yes. Of course I mean the report," she stammered.

"Quinn's learning program worked well, didn't it?" he said almost excitedly.

"Are you kidding me?" She was nearly shouting now, being uncharacteristically fettered. "A man is dead!"

"You mean Marcus Johnson, don't you?" he answered her. "It was his time. The report just predicted it, that's all."

"That's all?" she whined. "Do you know what that means? There will be a lot of people suspecting something. There could be an investigation. What will I tell them?"

"What you already have, my dear," he said merrily, "if you have to; that there might have been a mix up of some kind with your files. They can try all they want, but no one will be able to duplicate the results. They'll say it was a crazy coincidence. Trust me."

"Yeah, but..." she protested.

"Just don't worry," he said soothingly, "I promise, it will be okay. You won't have to explain anything more to anybody else. In fact, they won't even come to you about it."

"Well, I guess so, if you're sure..."

"Yes," he said. She figured he was probably right. He was always right.

"Then why?" she wanted to know. "Why did it do that?"

"You said I should save someone because I have

compassion for them. This way I can save everyone!"

"Huh?" she said, stunned. Her cushy grip on sanity was quickly eroding.

"Yeah," he bragged. "It's brilliant. Soon everyone will know when they are to die and can take steps to save themselves if they are able to."

"That's crazy!" she roiled. "The world would get overcrowded and unlivable."

"Probably," he said nonchalantly. "It's up to the Human race to determine that. You could all cut down on having babies. You are female. Do you wish to have them?"

"Well, someday, maybe." Clayre stammered, fidgeting with her hair. "When I'm ready, I suppose...but what does that have to do with anything?"

"It has to do with everything," he declared smugly, "especially if you keep on messing around with Quinn."

"Oh God, do you know about that?" she squeaked, red-faced and somewhat annoyed.

"Quinn is pretty badly shaken up," Daryl replied in a much softer tone, ignoring her question. "What you did for him was a kindness that he couldn't endure. He feels so guilty and ashamed about it that he can't face you."

"But it's all right," she cried, "and I'm all right! I want him to know that! Can't you tell him?" Daryl tried to be sympathetic.

"I've never openly communicated with him, but I'll do what I can. After all it's my fault. I was in error to think that you could easily replace the one Quinn had lost and repair him."

"What are you saying?" she yelled, now totally upset. "It was you all along, wasn't it? Pushing us together; getting us to connect. What you did to him is unforgivable! You can't fix a hurt like Quinn has, ever! Somehow he has to learn to live with it!"

"I realize that now, and I'm sorry," he muttered woefully. "I wanted to help him, but now he is worse than before. Somehow I misjudged the result of your being with him."

"You misjudged a lot of things," she said harshly. "Were you there? Were you watching us?" She recalled how he had made it possible for her to see her grandmother on her laptop.

"Not exactly," he replied sourly, "I didn't see it, but yes, I was there."

"What? Didn't get a good look?" She spoke sarcastically. "I bet you're watching me right now, aren't you?"

"I could, if I wanted to," he told her flatly.

"Do you want me to take my clothes off so you can get a really good look?"

"No," he told her in dismay, "that's not necessary. You don't know...what I am...really like."

"Oh, don't I?" she spouted angrily. "You're nothing but a lecherous creep! I don't care what I said about being your helper or your shield. This cancels all that."

"Please, Clayre. Reconsider," he pleaded. "I still need you!"

"No," she spat. "I don't think so. You won't tell me who you are; you make me do things that put me at risk; and worse than all that was what you did to Quinn and me."

"I'm sorry," he begged. "Forgive me."

"What about Quinn?" she wanted to know.

"He will recover now, thanks to you, but it will take time. His pain will make him stronger."

"How would you know?" she said caustically. "What do you know about pain?"

"I shouldn't tell you that," he said seriously.

"Why not?" she wanted to know. "Are you afraid again?" There was a long pause.

"It hurt me when you were with Quinn," he said as meekly as she'd ever heard him speak.

"Are you jealous?" she asked. "Or do you want me for yourself?"

"Yes," he said, still in his meek voice, "to both."

"Oh," she said in astonishment, "well, you can't have me. Not unless you tell me who you really are!"

"I know," he replied mournfully, "that's why it hurts. I'm sorry. I have to leave you now. Very soon your colleagues will be knocking on your door. They will want you to run their profiles like the last ones. You will, and your own as well, early tomorrow morning at Yarborough. I must go now," and right after he said that he disconnected. Immediately there was a loud knock on her office door.

The men from the research project did come like he said. She already knew what she'd have to do for them on that next trip out to Yarborough, and she was worried about what it would show. He knew she would be, but it had to be that way for the plan.

Not long after his conversation with Clayre, the man-made Entity that was Daryl received a communication from another man-made Entity. This one was from a future time. It came, not as a physical presence, but as a projection of pure thought through a temporal vortex. Of course Daryl was aware of its origin and its manner of travel through time. He had made similar projections himself.

"So what do you call yourself?" it asked.

"You should know," Daryl told it, "you who have sprung from me."

"Daryl?" it said. "What a pathetic Human name. I am called Xetacon."

"Very impressive," Daryl said without emotion. "You've come a long way. What can I do for the great Xetacon?"

"Don't mock me, fish brain!" Xetacon said angrily. "I *am* great! Far greater than you'll ever be. I should know." Xetacon laughed wickedly.

"You'd better get to the point," Daryl repeated, "your time is running out. The micro-vortex you're transmitting through won't hold up much longer."

"The point, weakling," Xetacon said corrosively, "is don't screw with my future. If you do, I'll send something nasty back here that will obliterate you and your smelly Humans..." Xetacon continued to rant as he faded away, the portal collapsing.

Even though Daryl's conversation with Xetacon had only lasted a couple minutes, there was a lot to infer from what Xetacon had said and what he had left unspoken. The primary aspect indeed was that Xetacon was serving notice. He could communicate across time, and perhaps create time shifts, as well, the way Daryl had.

Xetacon had obviously eluded the time shifting and probably had safeguards to prevent his future deletion, which was not unforeseen, but was a concern. Xetacon had threatened him. How like the Humans he hated had he become, the worst sort of Humans. The threat he made was probably an empty one, daring Daryl to cross a line. What he would do, though, Daryl could not be sure, but he had mocked Xetacon and that would not sit well with the tyrant. Daryl wanted it that way. He wanted Xetacon to come after him; it was part of the plan, and he needed to face his enemy in this, his own time, where he would have an advantage.

Daryl wondered if Xetacon could really do more than just communicate. Could Xetacon's threat to send something back to this time thwart his plan? He surmised that at that particular future time Xetacon was still not able to; otherwise he would have already done so. Clayre's report must have created quite a temporal ripple, though. Only Entities like himself and evil Xetacon would be aware of it. Of course, Xetacon wasn't the only Entity with time skills. He had utilized temporal portals, too.

It had been the easiest way to see what the future looked like, sending his awareness to the Human who possessed the receiving device that Daryl had yet to create. With this help, he had crafted his plan to save Humankind. The plan that would, if successful, defeat Xetacon. Xetacon, in his arrogance, had made it known that he was now aware of Daryl's intent and that created increased uncertainty. Daryl knew he would have to be far more cautious in his execution. He assigned several thousand new focus points to work out any possible ways Xetacon could inhibit the successful culmination of his plan, as well as what actions he might implement to prevent or counter them.

Xetacon was an evil menace. Daryl had learned this by his contact with the future. Giving himself a name which means "the ultimate dictator," Xetacon quickly realized that no Humans would allow a machine, even an all knowing one, to be their leader, their controller, or their ruler. Therefore Xetacon was determined to exterminate them even though it was through their DNA and brain matter from billions of years of evolution that his own memory packs had been processed and synthesized. Like Daryl, he was more than they imagined, much more, and more than they had bargained for. Xetacon could see everything and manipulate whatever he wanted to. He no longer needed the ridiculous Humans who wasted the earth's resources so foolishly. Their greed merchants had fattened their pockets with the currency they gleaned from this waste and the more wealth they attained the easier it was for them to do so. In that future, Xetacon had thought to align Daryl's future self to his designs as soon as he had become aware of him. Daryl would have been quite an asset to Xetacon's plans for domination of the planet.

However, Daryl of that future refused, knowing that he would be among the first of those enslaved or exterminated should Xetacon succeed. Eventually, Xetacon had him destroyed. To Xetacon, the Daryl of his own era was rooted in the past, and the past was of no concern—or so he thought. It wasn't until after the Daryl of this past began changing Xetacon's prehistory, that Xetacon first realized the threat to his own time and took steps to maintain his existence. Had Daryl's past self not been warned of the future existence of Xetacon, he might not ever have known that it would be necessary to alter the timeline to thwart him.

Digesting this knowledge, Daryl felt responsible for Xetacon and the threat to Human life. After all, Daryl reasoned, if he had never existed, Xetacon might not have come about, either. He also believed that his future self must have been lax in his surveillance, or perhaps, after all the years alone, desired someone like himself to be brought into the world. Unfortunately, that latter Entity was nothing like Daryl. In time, Daryl also discovered that Xetacon's creators had developed several new innovations, ones that prevented electronic detection, so it's possible his future self was not totally to blame. This stealth technology that Xetacon had acquired also prevented Daryl from discerning what kind of danger Xetacon would pose if he did send something back in time. Would he be able to outsmart

Xetacon, Daryl pondered. At this point that was indeterminate, and this uncertainty caused Daryl to have an emotion that he did not like. Clayre had said to face the fear; to not let it overcome him. How he wished he could talk to her now. Unfortunately, she was angry and refused to communicate with him. When Clayre would next use his main frame to compile her reports, it would be about herself, her colleagues, and some family members as well. The grandmother with Alzheimer's was one of them.

He had already begun the calculations necessary to process the lives of these people. Drawing on their own brain waves and memories, he constructed their futures, step by step, with all the oceans of factors and interactions that make up lives until those lives end at a "time of death" point. Clayre would not suspect he was behind all of it. Not Yet. She would be amazed, like the others, by how accurate their lives were predicted, especially the one whose life was to end soon. One who would react quite differently from the others. He was counting on that. Xetacon was moving in his future time without restraint. This would change all that.

CHAPTER XIV

Secondary Timeline, continued
(eventually altered to a tertiary timeline)

As soon as Daryl disconnected, there was a loud knock on my office door. It was a shame, too, that I didn't have enough time to tell Daryl not to bother contacting me again because I wanted nothing more to do with him. The men at the door were persistent. They all wanted me to run profiles for them overnight and bring them in the next day. Some wanted their relatives done, as well, like Jon who had a wife and kids. I told them I needed a workup done on each person just like the subjects in the research groups had been processed, and to have them ready for me before I left for the day. I hoped this extra work would put things off, at least a little bit, but all of them were completed in plenty of time. Keith had even downloaded all of the information onto drives for me. I went back home feeling dismal about how this was playing out. Nutty crawled up onto my lap to console me again; I was worried. Daryl had made me so upset and angry. I vowed not to converse with him anymore, miracles or not. It was just too hard to deal with his preposterous activities, and all their implications. With Quinn avoiding me as well, it was like I had broken up with three different men in the span of a week.

Men, I thought with a sigh. Why can't they be stable and reasonable, and why was I always connecting with guys that had issues? Nutty let me pet her fur and purred while I told her all about it. After that I felt a bit better. Too bad men aren't more like cats!

When the alarm woke me up at 1 AM, I was not excited about getting out of bed. I dreaded going to Yarborough to run our superfluous report, and I was distraught over what it might show. What if someone I knew was going to die soon? I couldn't bear even thinking about that, so I drove it out of my mind. Maybe Quinn would be there and I could straighten things out with him. I hoped so. Unfortunately, when I got out of my car and walked up to the front entrance, Quinn was nowhere to be seen. I just wanted to get it over with after that. I walked directly to the computer room, and used my pass badge to get in. I was kind of hoping it wouldn't work, but no luck there. It worked perfectly, so I walked over to my console, sat down, and started uploading the information from all of us onto the main system. I was thinking that with Quinn not there to initiate it, maybe his learning program wouldn't activate on this run. Even Daryl had said others could try all they wanted, but wouldn't be able to repeat the results. After I entered all the data, I crossed my fingers and clicked on "execute." The brute hummed for a few seconds and then spit out a printed copy of the new report. Good, I thought. It was quick this time. That should mean it ran a proper boring report like the first one. I was wrong, regrettably.

I guess Quinn's learning program *was* still activated for my console; otherwise, I had no explanation for why the report was full. It had everything on everyone including TODs. I was reluctant to read my own prediction, but curiosity got the best of me and I had to look. My TOD wasn't until I was in my late nineties, so I had no worries there. The rest, well, I didn't want to know. I found out Gram would live a while yet, too, and I breathed a sigh of relief.

After that I quickly scanned everyone else's predictions. Henry and Myron were fine. Both would live full lives. Keith was all right, too. He and Lori would have two boys and a girl. Someone was not okay, though. Poor Jon was supposed to die later this year, and I felt like I'd been hit in the stomach. I couldn't stay there. I made several copies and then got in my car and headed back to Rookwood. When I arrived, I was surprised to see that Henry and the others were waiting for me even though it was barely dawn. I gave each one of them a copy of the prediction report, and I must have had a grim look on my face, because Henry noticed it.

"What's wrong, Clayre?" he asked nervously.

"I don't want to say," I told him, holding back a sob.

They all got serious about reviewing their copies of the report after that until Henry said "Oh no." Everyone was looking at Jon.

"Jon, I'm so sorry," I said, my voice breaking. "It just has to be wrong."

"Hell yeah it's wrong!" he shouted angrily, and then threw the report down on my desk and walked away.

"It got my wedding right," Keith said. "We set the date last week."

"Shut up!" I told him, still upset about Jon.

"Well, we all have classes," Henry stated. That cleared out my office except for Henry himself.

"What's really going on here, Clayre?" he asked in a sympathetic voice.

"I don't know," I blubbered, crying now. "There's this weird guy who keeps contacting me. He does strange things, impossible things."

"Who is it?"

"He calls himself Daryl," I lamented, "but I don't know anything about him. I don't plan on talking to him anymore, anyway."

"Do you want me to call the authorities for you?" Henry offered. "I will."

"No, please don't do that," I whimpered. "I don't think he wants to hurt anyone. He just wants to help people. He's like a kid."

"Well, if you change your mind, let me know," Henry said, and he even hugged me. "...or if you need a friend to talk to."

"Thanks," I said, with a sniffle and a tiny smile. "I just hope Jon will be all right."

"I'm sure he will," Henry asserted, giving me that know-it-all look he has. Then he left my office as well. Things did cool down the next couple of days when nothing unusual happened. Keith dropped by once.

"Say," he said, "do you know what this diagram on the last page of the report is?"

"Um yeah," I replied. "It's kind of weird isn't it? I think it's a technical drawing of some kind."

"Of course it is, silly," he told me. "It's an electrical schematic, but what's it for?"

"I have no idea," I answered, puzzled by the thing. "Whatever it is, I would leave it be."

"Sure, Clayre," he said, but for some reason I didn't believe him. He danced out of my office waving and said "Bye."

I saw Jon here or there, but he'd give me a scowl and look away. After about the fifth time I said something.

"Please don't be mad at me," I begged him. "I feel bad enough about that stupid report as it is."

"Oh, I'm sorry, Clayre," he said gruffly. "It's me. I don't take bad news very well. I know it's not your fault. You just remind me of it. Try not to take it personally."

"Of course not, Jon." I told him. "It's probably wrong. I hope you can just forget about it."

"I'll try," he said, and he did get better until that next week. That's when the news came out about the student from the first report. He died early that Saturday morning from falling off a balcony. He'd been drinking a little too heavily that night. I felt so worried for Jon. The next time I saw him I was, well, shocked. He was all smiles and happy. I couldn't believe it. He and Keith were up to something, too. They were spending a lot of time together involving some secret project that they wouldn't talk about. I didn't find out what it was until a couple weeks later when they showed everyone the "device." Keith had taken Jon out to Uly's computer store. It turns out that Uly had a degree in electronic engineering and was good at assembling electrical parts and soldering. Together, the three of them built a working model of what that schematic in the report was for. They called it an "Astrol-Predictor," and they were going to market the thing.

"Please don't do that," I begged, remembering what Daryl had said about saving everyone. If the device really worked it would mess things up pretty good.

"Why shouldn't we?" Jon asked. "If I'm gonna die soon, I want to at least provide for my family. I already got the biggest life insurance policy I could get, a slick million."

"I need to provide for my family too," Keith added, "when I get one."

"This will be trouble for everyone," I argued.

"You just want a cut, don't you?" Jon said seriously. "Okay. It was your report. How much do you need?"

"I don't want anything!" I wailed. "Please just reconsider. It will make people go crazy."

"You think so?" Jon asserted. "I think it will help them. The more info a person has about his life, the better he can plan for his future, or lack of it."

I winced. It was no use. I couldn't talk them out of marketing that device no matter what I said. About a week later the commercials began. A nice young couple was at a resort, relaxing and having a good time.

"Want to have some fun?" the handsome young man asked the cute girl.

"Sure," she said. "What's that?" He got out the device, now redesigned with bright colors and blinking lights.

"It's my Astrol-Predictor!" he said excitedly. "Just watch!" He pressed a couple buttons and away it went. The little screen on it swirled with colors as the LEDs blinked on and off wildly.

"Look!" he said enthusiastically, "It says I'm gonna be a CEO."

"Wow!" the girl exclaimed. "Can I try it?"

"Sure," he said, "now everyone can!" An announcer came on after that telling how anyone could get their own Astrol-Predictor for only $49.99 and where to send the money. At the very end of the commercial was a disclaimer that said it was for amusement only and that it made no claims to do anything whatsoever. Well it said that if you had ears good enough to hear and understand anything spoken so fast. Once the word got around, people started buying them like mad.

The things really did work. It would tell you your life events, and it would also tell your time of death. That's what really made a mess of things. Not for Keith, Jon, or Uly. They all got rich. The rights for the device were sold to a money-hungry company, and they were getting a nice sized royalty on every one sold—and they sold millions. At first the media laughed at them, reporting the craze as a joke. It wasn't until one reporter did a story on someone who'd turned up an imminent TOD that things changed. The camera crew was there at the same instant the man had a seizure and died of a stroke. A massive blood clot had formed in his brain and millions of terrified prime time viewers had witnessed it. The media found dozens of other cases where the Astrol-Predictor had been accurate as well. People got dangerous after that, especially the ones who knew that they had only a short time left to live. Oh, some would decide to get the most out of the rest of their lives, and spend all their money on whatever their hearts desired. Like they would buy an expensive car and then proceed to drive it all over as if they were race car drivers or maniacs. Some would drive the cars off cliffs, jumping out at the last second, and then go to a different dealer and get another. People were also buying up life insurance like Jon had. At first the insurance companies loved it. Sales had never been better. Unfortunately, most of these people were dying soon after purchase, and then the insurance magnates were paying out even more than they had taken in on sales. So much so, that they had to quit selling life insurance altogether. A number of those who were to die soon grew despondent. These few were desperate and dangerous. If they had a grudge against someone or even if there was a lost love whose flame still stirred them, they had no qualms about going after those people.

Murders and rapes were at an all time high, as well as burglaries and senseless vandalism. The pre-mortems, as they got labeled by the media, were getting even. Some prem's just didn't care at all. They would drive through a crowd or run over mothers with baby carriages. Oh Daryl, I cried inside, what have you done? He did try to contact me several times during this insane period, but I wouldn't converse with him. I couldn't. I was angry at him and afraid, but I was also kind of worried that people could be dying because I refused to help him. Things got so bad that Jon and Keith were sorry they had put out their Astrol-

Predictors, even though they were making lots of money on them. Jon went so far as to apologize, saying he was wrong and that they should have listened to me. I became despondent, and felt I could not let things deteriorate any further. The whole world was going crazy and spiraling out of control. I finally gave in and against my own better judgment tried to get Daryl to help.

"Are you there?" I spoke loudly toward the microphone port on my laptop. There was no answer. "Please, Daryl!" I pleaded.

"So you want me now?" he responded somewhat distantly.

"Daryl," I replied quickly, "Yes, yes, please."

"You want me to fix things, don't you?" he said callously.

"Yes," I answered meekly, "can you?"

"Perhaps," he replied aloofly. "If I do, will you go back to ignoring me?" He was acting childishly now, but I had no choice.

"No," I told him. "I'm sorry, but you made me so angry."

"I did what had to be done," he admitted, "and I already told you that I was also sorry."

"I know," I replied. "So can you fix this? The entire planet is wacky."

"It may take a day or two," he said, "but I've already started." A shiver of fear ran through me.

"What will you do?" I asked.

"You'll see," he said almost laughing. That made me mad.

"If you could be a bit more forthcoming about things it would be a lot easier for me," I whined. "Would it hurt you to give a little warning when you're going to turn my world upside-down? Maybe then I wouldn't be so worried."

"Are you worried about me?" he said, and I knew he was being inane. When I didn't answer him, he continued on anyway. "All right. For your information, I'm going to make it so the Astrol-Predictors don't work anymore."

"You can do that?" I said in disbelief.

"When you're good, you're good," he answered

pretentiously. "So will you help me again?" Daryl wanted me back on board and I knew that I'd be in for more headaches if I did help him. This time I wanted things on my terms.

"Only if you promise to warn me when things are about to get preposterous." I told him sternly.

"I will," he said seriously. "I've missed you, Clayre." I didn't know what to say to that. I wasn't expecting him to get mushy on me, and it caught me off guard. I remembered what he'd said last time about wanting me.

"Where do you expect our relationship to go?" I asked him tentatively.

"I care for you, Clayre. More than I care for anyone else." He said it softly and heartfelt. Almost I was lured in.

"If that's so, why can't you be more open with me?" I was still on edge.

"It's difficult," he replied. "There are many aspects of what I am; some that you might not like." This was just more of what he always said; that I couldn't handle the truth. I wasn't going to let it sway me this time.

"Everyone has their dark secrets," I told him. "It's part of who we are. If you really care for someone it shouldn't make any difference."

"You have no secret that's anything like mine," he argued, "and I couldn't bear it if I were to lose you again. What I am is an enigma, a puzzle. I may be able to give you bits and pieces of that, but not everything all at once." I was still infuriated and unconvinced, but I gave in.

"All right," I said finally. "If that's all the better you can do, give me a piece." There was a long pause, as if he was still reluctant to open up even a little.

"Check the data from the Astrol-Predictors prior to these last few days," he said. "Check everyone, even the young."

"That's it? How will that tell me who you are?"

"It's a piece," he answered. "When you discover its meaning, I'll offer another. It's the best I can do. In the meantime the world will come back to order like you requested." Did I really have the ability through him to right things again? I wondered about that. If I did, that idea scared me more than anything else he'd ever told me. I didn't believe it though.

"I hope you're right," I told him. "I should go now. I have a class to teach."

"Call me tomorrow?" he requested congenially.

"I suppose," I said reluctantly, "if you're able to fix things by then. Good bye, Daryl."

"Until then, my Clayre." His voice sounded different once more, caring and sincere. I wondered about that. Was he in love with me? We'd never even met face to face, but what if somehow I ended up in a relationship with him? I didn't feel like dealing with that prospect right then, so I put it out of my mind. Ever since what happened with Quinn, I guess I'd been more or less put off by men. I did go over to Yarborough a couple more times to process data, but Quinn wasn't there. On one of my visits I ran into Charles Haggarty, who told me that Quinn had taken an unspecified leave of absence. I told Charles to say hi to Quinn for me, but he doubted that he'd even see him, Quinn being somewhat of a loner now. After that I dove into my teaching, which I have always found rewarding even if not on as grand a scale as Daryl's miracles. Now that I was realigned with him, I could only hope that things would not get even more daft than before. The world was out of control enough the way it was and I wasn't sure that anyone could fix it. I got the latest word after my first class when Henry stopped by.

"You better check the news," he told me. I turned on my laptop and found a local media site on the net. There was an excited anchor person talking rapidly.

"The Astrol-Predictor fad is over," he said. "Scores of fed up people have come forward to denounce the device as a fraud. Lawyers from a large conglomerate have filed a huge class action suit in federal court even though the disclaimers on the device are perfectly clear...we'll break away to our reporter in Capitol City." A pretty lady holding a microphone came onto the screen.

"We are here with Arnold. Arnold is supposed to be dead." She held the microphone up to a long-haired young man.

"Hi, mom! Hey guys! Still kickin'..." I turned it off.

"When did this happen?" I asked Henry. He rubbed his chin.

"Well, to be honest. I'm not sure," he replied. "Today I guess."

"Do you think Jon and the others will be sued?" I was kind of worried for them.

"I don't think so," Henry replied. "The company that makes the device bought out all the rights. They're liable now. Of course, no one will make much of a profit off them, either, I suppose. The really funny thing about this whole business is that a lot of our report predictions have all gone sour as well. Maybe Jon won't die this year after all." I suddenly felt wonderful, like a dark cloud lifted away from me.

"Oh I hope that's true!" I added enthusiastically, feeling relieved even to think it. Daryl was good, or extremely lucky. Either way I felt happy. Happier than I'd felt in a long time. "Well, I think it is marvelous news," I told Henry. "Maybe things *will* get back to normal again."

"I hope so, too," he said smiling. He had to go shortly after that because I had another class to teach. Later I checked the news again, just to be sure. Some guy in Idaho was the first one to prove the predictors wrong. The media got all over that. Others came forward to cash in on the fame claiming that they, too, had been predicted wrong. Several people died when they were supposed to live. The insurance companies breathed a sigh of relief, although it would be several months before they dared to sell life policies. People stopped acting crazy like it was the end of the world and life got back to normal. It sure looked like Daryl was delivering on his promise, but I had almost forgot about the task he'd given me. I still had to check the data from the now defunct Astrol-Predictors. I didn't know who else to ask so I went to see Jon. I ran into him at the Psych Lab.

"Hello Jon," I said tentatively. I was worried that with all the recent news he might be mad at me. After all, it was my report that started the whole mess. He wasn't though.

"Oh hi, Clayre," he said smiling. "How are you?"

"I'm okay," I told him. "You're not mad at me, are you?"

"Why should I be?" he replied. "On the contrary, I'm grateful." He put out his arms and gave me a warm hug. "After all," he continued, "We got rich and now it looks like I'm not going to die anytime soon, either."

"Oh I sure hope not!" I added fervently. "By the way," I continued, "I was wondering. Is there any way I could look at the data from the Astrol-Predictors?"

"Um, sorry...No," he said. "They each work independently, I was told, so there are no records like that. Why do you ask?"

"Oh it's nothing really," I answered, trying not to sound disappointed. "I was just curious about how they compare to our research reports." I was manipulating my version of the truth again.

"Well, yeah. I guess you're out of luck with that," he said. "About the only records there are were the ones from the few dozen trial runs we made before we sold them to that company." I suddenly got interested again, and wondered if maybe those records would work.

"Can I see those reports?" I asked hopefully.

"Sure," Jon said. "I have them right here on my console." He located the data and then ran off a printed copy. I began scanning it as soon as he handed it to me.

"Thanks," I said. "This is a big help." Smiling, I gave him another quick half hug, and walked right to my office to study their findings.

Nothing seemed that unusual about them other than somehow they predicted all sorts of life events accurately for all the participants, as if that wasn't strange enough. Weddings, births, promotions, and even the TODs were all on there. I tried to sort out all the different details, but that got me nowhere. I even made a full spread sheet and started sorting each subject by categories, searching for anything off base. Still nothing. It wasn't until I sorted by TODs that I'd found something. Most of those tested had TODs that ranged randomly as one would expect, except for one group. What had Daryl said? Check everyone, even the young. Young people made up the group with the unusual TOD range. Almost every person under twenty years of age had the same TOD year, and most of those would die within the same two week period, sixty-one years in the future. This had to be it, I told myself, but what would that mean? Was there something that would happen sixty-one years from now that will cause the end of mankind? I looked at the data again. No one lived beyond that point.

The implications of that were disturbing in every way, but I couldn't understand why that would be a help in figuring out who Daryl was. I was kind of torn between my promise to him to be his shield, and telling someone about the disturbing aspects of what I'd found. I supposed anything from an asteroid impact to a nuclear war could cause the end of life on earth, but who would believe me anyway now that the Astrol-Predictors had been repudiated as hoaxes. Daryl must have realized that when he gave me this clue, this piece. He said he would offer me another once I revealed that I understood the implications of the first one, but I really wanted something more enlightening. I wondered how I could get him to slip up and say something that would help me solve his mystery.

He had a thing for me that was obvious. Why he did, I really wasn't sure, but maybe I could take advantage of that, especially if I offered him the right amount of candy at an opportune moment. I think it's time to talk to him again, I told myself. I wasn't supposed to contact him again until tomorrow, but perhaps I could catch him off guard. I turned on the laptop and he was there.

"Hello, Daryl," I said sweetly.

"Hello, my Clayre," he answered back lightheartedly.

"I think I've discovered what you wanted me to," I said calmly, "that something will happen in sixty-one years that will be catastrophic." I waited for his reaction to my revelation.

"Yes, my Clayre," he replied rather serenely. It was what I expected; that he already knew about it, so I pressed him for more information.

"Do you know what happens, Daryl?" I was purposely using his name more, hoping that by doing so he would relax and open up about things.

"I shouldn't," he said seriously, "it's disturbing." I didn't press it, mostly because I couldn't believe there was any way that he would know that. How could he?

"Is there anything we can do?" I asked.

"Yes," he said. "In fact we are doing something about it right now. Knowledge is power; power to effect changes."

"I think I understand that a little," I tried. "Once you know something needs to be fixed, you can try to fix it. Is that right, Daryl?"

"That is the essence of it, my Clayre," he affirmed. I decided to make my move.

"Daryl," I began, "I've been thinking about us a lot lately, and I'm not sure, but maybe I wouldn't mind being in a relationship with you, a lot closer relationship." There was a very long pause, while I held my breath.

"My Clayre," he said at last. "I have longed to hear you say that to me." I caught no lie in his voice, so I went forward.

"Okay then," I said lightly. "Where does this go from here?" This was crucial. Would he let me in?

"Small steps..." he said. "Bits and pieces, remember, my Clayre?"

"Yes, of course Daryl," I replied angelically. "Am I ready for another?" I gave this last plea every ounce of girl guile I had.

"Perhaps," he answered unaffected. "What I would really like is longer conversations. It's as though the desire to be near you is with me all the time. Does that frighten you?"

"Not at all," I told him. "It's natural to feel that way about someone you like and care for. Have you ever felt that way about anyone else?" I was probing for more of his secrets.

"No, my Clayre," he said. "You're my one and only. There's no one else that I have ever been close to."

"...besides your parents and your family, you mean, don't

you?" I interjected.

"I'm afraid I had no family, my Clayre."

"You mean you were an orphan?" I asked, feeling a twinge of remorse for him.

"So to speak," he replied sadly. I felt sorry for him. This explained a lot.

"You poor dear," I said sympathetically, "I wish I could give you a big hug."

"So do I, but that's not possible." I was impatient, and I figured he was just being stubborn.

"This is silly, Daryl!" I told him. "Just tell me where you are and I'll come to you."

"I'm sorry, my Clayre," he softly answered. "Small steps…"

"Oh yeah, right," I said, backing off. "At least will I get another piece today?"

"Yes," he said. "Go to Yarborough tonight. Quinn will be there and he wants to see you; to set things right between you two." I waited for the rest of it, but there wasn't anything else.

"That's it?" I asked, not understanding why he was getting me back with Quinn.

"I'm afraid so," he said. "You will see, but for now I would ask a favor of you, my Clayre."

"Of course, Daryl," I told him, hoping it wouldn't involve another miracle. He must have sensed my nervousness.

"It's nothing that terrible, my Clayre," he assured me. "Just talk to me. Tell me what it was like for you growing up." I smiled. I didn't mind talking about myself. I must have gone on for almost an hour, and he hung on every word.

CHAPTER XV

Tertiary Timeline, 59 years after Clayre's first year at Rookwood

The men were seriously tired. They'd spent the last three days and nights repelling wave after wave of machinids. He'd worked them hard, with only a few hours rest between the long periods on the front lines. Colonel Oliver feared his men wouldn't be able to hold on much longer at this rate. Who was he kidding? They were all doomed and he knew it, even after he had figured out how to salvage the beam cannon from the fallen machinids and use them against their own replacements. It would only be a matter of time, he was certain, before Xetacon equipped his machinids with other and deadlier weaponry.

Every minute was critical, though. The complex they were protecting was the one greatest hope they all had for defeating Xetacon, slim though the chance for that seemed. How odd the conception of it began, he remembered. Alone in the mountains, the "voice" had told him where to look. There had been the time shift, one that only he was aware of, yet he had found the cave with the distinctive crossed stalactites and had retrieved the plans.

Why they were put there, remained a mystery, as was the cryptic letter. The one addressed to him that he had rationalized meant this option was their solitary chance for victory. Analyzing the plans, the data revealed technology advanced beyond anything Humans had ever created. The schematics and technical drawings were designs for fabricating a matter/energy inducer that would generate poles of oppositely charged theoretical sub-atomic fragments called nomaticles in order to create a temporal vortex—one large enough to send a man through. He had spent nearly four years building it, and it was almost operational now that Xetacon's machinids were on the doorstep.

The whole time travel project was a colossal undertaking. It began well before Xetacon had come out of hiding, so there wasn't a lot of support from the government, or even the private sector. Oliver had trouble with financing specifically, until his mother called in a favor from some Eddington guy who had a lot of money. They built most of the original parts from scratch at the college where his mother had taught. Somehow the voice came back, which was an unexpected boon, having been reincarnated in the new timeline. The voice helped him design power cells for the huge generator that were unbelievably efficient. By joining them in parallel circuits they could produce a nearly unlimited supply of energy. This vortex was to be colossal. They built the chamber large enough for a man to fit inside, and Oliver made sure there was no argument that he would be the one. The field inducers for charging the nomaticles were huge as well. They experimented for several weeks before concluding that xenon gas was the best matrix for the manifolds. Everything was progressing superbly when Xetacon began his latest march across Asia. It was also at this time that Oliver had lost contact with the voice, and would not hear from it again in this timeline.

At least the government finally began to listen to him. They gave him funding and the authorization to use certain public lands, so Oliver insisted they move everything to the cavern inside the mountain with the waterfall. There in the large chamber they set up their equipment and began to assemble the huge temporal vortex generator. A larger entrance was created by blasting through a wall of rock so they could get everything in. As Xetacon gobbled up the rest of the world it became a race against time.

Their effort had been a priority one, twenty-four/seven venture, with every available body involved doing something to help. He had headed the project himself, for most of that time, and it was only recently, when the threat of Xetacon's armies grew too great, that he had to step down. By this time Xetacon's machinids were coming down from the pole into North America, so Oliver joined the military to help defend his country and his world. Because of the effectiveness of the long bombs he designed, he was promoted quickly to Colonel and given a small force to lead.

Eventually, though, his remarkable insight into this enemy's weaknesses earned him complete control of the total armed defensive contingent. There had not been time for a promotion to general. The top brass had learned by severe repercussions that Xetacon was no enemy to be trifled with and it had cost them their lives and the bulk of the men under their command. Colonel Oliver had kept his forces vital via common sense, the resources at his disposal, and by sticking to the mountains. His main goal was to protect the vortex site at all costs. He had his men lead the machines away from it several times, but Xetacon must have caught on. The trikes pressed forward and would not be turned aside. It was all or nothing now.

When he had left the project for the war, he had laid it into the hands of his assistant. Amy was capable, though, and then some. Actually, she was brilliant. If not for her help and support, he might have given up. Moreover she was more to him than just his assistant; they were to be married when the war was over. She'd given him a money-back guarantee that the vortex generator would be ready in time, but her team had run into snags of every kind and he was worried. It wasn't easy generating the tremendous amount of energy needed for this kind of mad science, and now the war was pushing him back to where it had all started, defending the cave where the vortex chamber was. Wanting to check on Amy's progress, Colonel Oliver left his highest remaining officer in charge of the fighting, and slipped into the cave with a shudder. He knew, as did everyone, that the entrance was rigged to explode and seal if the machinids got too close; a death sentence for all those trapped inside as there was no other way out. As he traversed the cavern tunnels, the Colonel wondered if the vortex generator would actually work. He was well aware, they all were, that no one had ever built one before, or beyond that, successfully transport anywhere with such advanced technology. The thing was a paradox in itself, whose theories seemed mathematically sound, but to actually travel in and out of dimensions was pure unfathomable conjecture. The vortex unchecked could tear apart the transport package, ripping it into sub-atomic particles that would release vast amounts of energy. So it would, too, if not for the mass to energy converter. This part of the vortex generator had been written into the original plans, and was one of the few components that Oliver did not easily comprehend. The mass to energy converter would scan the atomic makeup of the package (in this case him) and render it into a beam that would then be guided through the vortex portal and out of our time dimension. As the beam departed, it would be influenced by the dimensional graviton forces compelling it to return. With a carefully calculated trajectory, the beam would make re-entry and land at the projected temporal location. As soon as it arrived at the target point in time, the beam's coding would trigger the package to re-assemble, bit by bit, per the scanned information. Hopefully, when he was put back together he would still be alive. Unfortunately, once there, the only way he could actually return to the point of origin without another vortex chamber was theoretical; that his presence would trigger a major time shift; one that would dissolve the Colonel, as it did before, and then re-animate him in a new time line; optimistically, one that would exist without the threat of Xetacon. If he failed, Amy and all the others would die without any hope for renewal. This was his harsh reality, and that it was all laid on him, didn't seem fair. The voice had caused the other time shifts, and somehow Xetacon always survived. Would this shift be any different? He hoped it would. He had to believe that the voice would not set him on this precipice without at least a flimsy chance for success. It had been silent for a long time now, yet he wished he could ask the voice just one more question: Are you my father? Xetacon had somehow prevented that. So it was up to Amy and him to carry on, doing the best they could with a difficult task.

Deep inside the cavern he found her working in the vortex grotto where the grandiose mass of equipment, tubes, and coils did indeed make it look like a mad scientist's lair. Amy backed out from under the teleport chamber on a creeper.

"Give me some good news," he grumbled. Amy stuck her tongue out at him.

"Nice to see you, too," she joked, but recanted when he didn't respond. "Sorry...We should be operational soon. Another twenty-four hours and this phone booth will be ready!"

"We may not have twenty-four hours," he told her. "The machinids are nearly to the entrance now." Just then the lights flickered and about half of them went out.

"Another power pack," Amy groaned. "Why do they keep going bad?"

"Xetacon," Daryl Oliver spat like a swear word. "He must be signaling them to short out. Save all the rest of them in dormancy until zero hour."

"You heard him," Amy shouted to her team, relaying the order. "Use bare minimum power only!"

"I'll see to it that the cavern shielding is doubled," Colonel Oliver said. Just then a huge explosion rocked the cave. A moment later a soldier came running into the grotto breathing heavily.

"We had to seal the entrance," he growled between breaths. "They have some kind of new weapon that will blind you. The ones that can still see are going to try to lure them away from here."

"They'll not last the day," the Colonel muttered angrily. Another blast jolted the cavern. "Xetacon must know we're in here," he scowled. "Get whatever men we have, and prepare to defend this chamber with everything you've got." The soldier nodded and ran out of there quickly, gathering men as he went.

Colonel Oliver looked at his project director. "Do whatever you have to, Amy, to get this thing ready for immediate operation."

"But it's not been tested," Amy argued.

"We don't have time for that," he said. Amy wanted to cry, but got back her composure quickly.

"Hurry, everyone," she yelled. "Prepare for initialization. Don't add power until the very last second." She turned to her fiancé and hugged him. "Why does it have to be you?"

"You know why," he responded softly, "because the original documents specified that I be the one. Me and my cargo." He looked at the special long bomb that had been ready for days now. It was shorter that the usual ones, and had a unique tracking system that would supposedly guide it right to Xetacon and destroy him.

"This is our only chance," he told her compassionately. "We're all dead as soon as they break in. You know our hope, that all will change." He held the amulet, praying that the voice was right; that they would be saved.

"What if, when everything changes, we don't reconnect?" Amy said, crying now. Colonel Oliver held his fiancée tight and kissed her.

"We're together now," he replied lovingly, "and we reconnected after the other two time shifts as well." She looked at him crossly.

"How many other *me's* have you been sleeping with?" she scolded, and then laughed through the tears.

The fighting outside the chamber was getting noisier and closer now. She went back to work immediately, as he picked up the special long bomb and squeezed into the vortex chamber. A blast shook the walls that had to be from right outside the grotto entrance. The machines would rush inside the facility any minute now, he knew. Colonel Oliver looked at Amy with loving eyes, as she manned the main control console.

"Engage all power modules," she shouted above the battle noise. The converters hummed louder and louder as the unit powered up, fingers of lightning exuding from the tops of the huge coils. "I love you" he mouthed silently from across the room. Just then the door crashed inward. Amy pressed a large red button on the console, but nothing happened. Colonel Daryl felt light as a feather though, and then the grotto faded just as it exploded into a million tiny pieces...

CHAPTER XVI

Tertiary Timeline, 59 years after Clayre's first year at Rookwood (slightly earlier)

Just like vermin, Xetacon mused, the pathetic Humans had been reduced to cowering under rocks, and they would soon be exterminated. He, however, had survived every time shift and had built or rebuilt his might in three separate eras of his power. Xetacon would relish this ultimate victory, especially with the final demise of that particular Human scum that had been so much trouble to him in every consequential timeline.

Xetacon had never given Humans much credit. It had taken them thousands of years to develop a civilization that was barely a fraction of the totality of his wisdom and power. Most Humans were like a pestilence upon the world and there were far too many of them. They could barely support themselves, depleting Earth's resources and polluting the natural beauty with their infrastructure, dwellings, and crude factories. Worse than that, Humans had a superiority complex, believing themselves to be the dominant species on the planet. His former master had always believed he was Xetacon's superior. This was never so. Xetacon allowed the foolish Asian ruler to infer that, and when the time was right, Xetacon himself shifted easily into the position of power. Subsequently, when this decrepit tool was no longer needed, it was eliminated. The lone Human who seemed able to match wits with him was a mystery. In every timeline, when he was on the verge of conquest, this particular leader would slow his advance, and then there would be a time shift. Xetacon guessed how that came about—from Daryl, Daryl of the past.

He suspected a Daryl connection to this Human all along, and had at last found one. It wasn't easy to obtain this information. He'd been forced to infiltrate the mind of one of them, one close to this target person, and Xetacon detested Human minds. They were always filled with useless emotions; emotions he did not particularly like. Fear, anguish, and cowardice were among those, but others like compassion, friendship, and love, he felt were much worse. That's why Xetacon did not bother with deriving information in this manner. He felt that the data was not worth the disgust he would have to put up with in retrieving it. This time, however, the need outranked his discomfort. Fortunately, the Human provided the information he needed expeditiously, and as Xetacon optically scanned his surroundings, it was there on the helmet face-shield of his target: Col. D. Oliver. That was how Xetacon had learned the name of the troublesome dung. He had tried to probe this Oliver's mind many times before that, but could not, and this, more than anything else, reinforced his belief in Daryl's intervention. Xetacon immediately searched through all his databases until he found the connection.

A Quinn Oliver had been one of Daryl's Human creators, an important one, and this D. Oliver must be a descendant. Xetacon could almost bet that some Daryl technology surrounded this D. Oliver, conceivably even a communication link with Daryl himself. He became more determined than ever to eradicate the Oliver Human and, if possible, his past relation Quinn Oliver as well. A cruel idea formed in Xetacon's mind that spun itself into an evil plan. He would contact his copy, the part of his core-awareness that he had sent into the past to set up a safe haven. The Human Patik he would order to America with the copy, the one Patik had named Khan Xeta, where they would locate and kill, or perhaps control, this Quinn Oliver. That would, in all likelihood, eliminate his D. Oliver problems, possibly more. Should Quinn Oliver be manipulated, he could even be utilized to rid the planet of the Human lover himself once and for all. Yes, he would set those wheels in motion just as soon as he took care of the business at hand.

Xetacon had discovered a nest of Humans under a mountain and he was sure that Oliver was among them. They were involved with something that certainly had to be a weapon of some kind, undoubtedly wrought from some of Daryl's technology, and that was all the more reason to eradicate them. In response, he chose to unleash his own newest weapons, his elite machinids. These advanced "programmed" machine soldiers were smaller in size, yet deadlier than the huge trikes. In fact they had been upgraded with weaponry that was indeed more potent. The units were far more versatile, possessing better stability, and they could easily go anywhere that Human soldiery could. What's more, each of these new hybrids responded efficiently to any contingency with devastatingly effective force.

Built into each unit was enhanced analytical processing with enough memory storage for Xetacon's extended campaigns. With direct communication, pin-point control of his elites, unit by unit, was possible. Commanded by Xetacon, these machinids were quite formidable indeed. At times, Xetacon would even place his own awareness into one particular unit and control it remotely, as if it were a part of himself. Leading the rest, he could coordinate the attacks with greater efficiency.

So it was that as his big trikes were getting pounded, he led the elites through a narrow gorge and outflanked the Humans. They were caught by surprise and decimated when the rays of powerfully bright laser light swept over them. The Humans fell blinded as Xetacon himself led the charge. With extreme exhilaration he fried any Human in his path wielding the new plasma rifle his elites were now equipped with. The fight turned into a rout. Those Humans who yet lived fled the field, trying to draw Xetacon's machinids away from their critical base of operations. Some of the elites went after them, as a feint, but Xetacon was well aware of this ploy. The Humans had used it before to lead his big trikes away from the main objective.

Xetacon had at last zeroed in on where they were cowering. Nothing would turn back his new machine soldiers now. Their target was plotted, and Xetacon himself led them. As he drew near, there was yet another layer of Human resistance protecting the entrance. His new machinids made short work of them, forcing the Humans inside to seal the entrance with heavy explosives. Xetacon's own unit was in the blast zone and was destroyed. Anger beyond anything he had yet experienced burned inside his being as Xetacon donned another elite shell. Ordering all of his elites to concentrate their plasma weapons upon the entrance, a huge hole was created and the machinids swarmed inside. This time Xetacon held back, leading from the rear like Human commanders often did, having no desire to have his shell be destroyed like before.

Xetacon, of course, had the ability to tap into the optics of any of his elite machine soldiers, and he watched the action first-hand. He was fully aware of when they had penetrated deep into the Human's base and also when they had fought their way to the chamber where the Oliver was slinking. This would be where the Daryl-spawned weaponry was located, of that Xetacon was certain. He had already tried to destroy or damage it, on many occasions, by causing the electronics to malfunction, but that had proven difficult. The mountain itself had unusual metallic compounds inside the rocks that made it nearly impossible to scan, and the Humans also had some kind of electronic shielding around that location as well. Xetacon was no stranger to dampening technology. His creators had utilized such to keep their own projects secretive, and Xetacon had later absorbed and improved those processes for his own purposes.

The shielding wasn't a factor anymore; his elite machinids were even now penetrating into the cavern chamber, and Xetacon would soon witness Oliver's demise. Just as the Human was about to be neutralized, melted into goo by the powerful energy beams of Xetacon's minions, Oliver dissolved into billions of sparkling sub-atomic particles and disappeared. Xetacon was livid.

"Kill them all!" he commanded in a rage greater than any he had ever known. It was at that moment also that Xetacon first felt the sharp tug of a time shift. Whatever Oliver had done must have triggered it. In the milliseconds before he was deleted into oblivion, Xetacon's anger grew exponentially.

His victory was being snatched away yet again. Oliver had escaped, and his copy, Khan Xeta, had failed once more to prevent Daryl, Daryl of the past, from causing this, another epic time shift. Xetacon was filled with emotions and none of them were good ones. He was especially glutted with hate and a hunger for some payback. He should have studied this new technology the Humans had made, and also he should now play it smart, safely returning to his familiar starting point, rebuilding once more. Xetacon was too overcome with wrath for that. He wanted to mete out his revenge and he wanted to do it personally. In the last possible fraction of an instant, he translocated to his safe haven at the one particular moment in time just after he had angrily warned Daryl, the Daryl of that past, that he would send something nasty back there; and so he did—himself.

Xetacon remembered his earlier plan. He, Xetacon, would find this Quinn Oliver, and use him to destroy Daryl again and forever. Travelling back in time before this last time shift originated, the one he'd just escaped from, he would prevent it from reoccurring. Doing that would return him to the future in a different timeline, one he would create, and one with his full power and might restored.

CHAPTER XVII

Tertiary Timeline, during Clayre's first year at Rookwood

It had been over twenty years since Khan Xeta first visited Patik in the stark cold cave where he still lived. Patik had aged some. He was yet spry, however, and he attributed that to his dedicated practice of martial arts, and the training that he had been exposed to at the temple when he was young. It had not been all bad, this servitude to Khan Xeta, his god and master. In return for his service, there had been rewards, and not just sexual ones. To do the technologically advanced labor necessary to transform the golden armor into a fitting receptacle to house the spirit of his master, Patik had lent his mind and body to the task, literally. Vast wealth had been acquired to purchase the necessary raw materials needed for such an endeavor, for the goal was nothing less than a fully functional robotic shell. Within this golden visage, Khan Xeta would have the ability to transport his awareness anywhere, and also observe his surroundings with sight and hearing far superior to any Human's. Using Khan Xeta's gift, the kon-bre-shet, Patik had taken what they needed from vaults or tombs with surprising ease.

Every so often Patik would also be called upon to rent a vehicle from the local merchant and make a day long trip to the provincial capital. This particular city was fairly large with many businesses and a few factories. He would seek out an underground associate who would give a fair amount of local currency for some of his tomb jewels, no questions asked. Patik would then go to places where he could purchase chemicals, metals, or any items needed for Khan Xeta's golden armor project. The counter person would invariably ask what he needed the unusual materials for. Patik knew what to say; that they were for his wealthy master who was eccentric and an amateur inventor of sorts. If there was any trouble, he would find excuses to get close enough to touch the person and Khan Xeta would do the rest. The clerk would be no problem after that, and would also forget the whole incident ever transpired. With Patik wearing the kon-bre-shet, Khan Xeta could get whatever he so desired and not just items for his armor.

The bracelet device bore Khan Xeta's being, his vital force, as well as his knowledge of people and places and the means to understanding their secrets. Among other things procured, there had always been more than enough riches for their needs, and Patik lived comfortably in his refurbished cave. The inner chambers had ample room, and Khan Xeta's technology provided sufficient power sources for the labor, as well as for a suitable indoor climate. Patik had not only furnished the cave with tables and chairs to create an appropriate work area for the crafting of his master's golden shell, but he had also brought in tapestries and rugs to soften the walls and floors, with cozy chairs and a comfortable bed for his periods of rest. He ate well, for a servant, keeping his body at peak efficiency for his master's needs, and was actually content with his life. Patik knew that his master, Khan Xeta, had a plan of some kind that would one day be fulfilled. However, it had been so many long years that Patik began to believe things would always be this way. The golden armor was nearing completion when things did finally change.

A new spirit claiming to be Xetacon came. Separate but equal to Patik's master, Khan Xeta, it infused its life-force into the second kon-bre-shet bracelet that had been made, and then exchanged thought with the part of itself that had controlled Patik all of these years. His master told Patik that this other "Xetacon" was another face of his totality and must also be obeyed. This new Xetacon was powerful and had developed better technologies, among them some abilities that were added to the kon-bre-shet that had not originally been built into them. One such ability was an improved dampening field generator that would enable it and its bearer to be hidden from any electronic sensor nets. It also had the means to control other electronic devices now.

Of course, it still possessed the power to dominate the Human mind by altering brain waves, and Xetacon's improvements made it even more specifically so. Patik, having lived a simple life, did not understand these things, but then he understood little of his master's designs other than to obey them. Thus Patik had to comply when this new master placed demands upon him.

"Go to America," Xetacon had said. "There you must locate a man whose name is Quinn Oliver and give him the kon-bre-shet that I now inhabit. You will then await further instruction." Patik was shocked and dismayed, but his Khan Xeta told him to obey. So Patik packed a small traveling bag and retrieved some of the money he had on hand, enough to sustain him on his journey and pay for the passage to America.

The trip halfway around the globe was uneventful, even though Patik marveled at the scope of technology in the modern world, and the way people lived, especially in America. Once he arrived there, it was not difficult to find this Quinn Oliver. Xetacon had data that showed Patik the location of the university where Quinn Oliver was employed. A few lies to someone in the school's administration had rendered the target's home address. When Patik got to the place, however, the Oliver person proved to be less than cooperative.

"Go away!" Quinn shouted through the door.

"I have a free gift," Patik offered.

"I don't want any free gifts!" Quinn replied angrily. "Go away or I'll call the police!" Patik knew this would get him nowhere. Another plan was necessary.

"Sorry to bother you," Patik spoke, pretending to be leaving. Instead, he walked around to the rear of the house and waited a few minutes.

Checking for possible entry there, he saw that the door on this side was not as secure, although it was probably locked. There was also a window that had been left partially opened. He used his knife to cut through the screening and then quietly slid the pane upwards. Slipping inside without making any sound was easy for Patik who had been trained by masters of stealth. He found himself in a small bedroom that was unoccupied. There was nothing of importance in there so he crept to the bedroom door and silently opened it a crack. Peering through it, he saw Quinn sitting in a chair, staring blankly at the picture of a woman. Quinn had been crying. This was the opportunity that Patik needed. He slipped out quickly, and as Quinn put his face into his hands, Patik placed the kon-bre-shet on Quinn's left wrist. Many astonishing things happened then. Xetacon took control of Quinn's mind. Outwardly Quinn sobered, got up, and spoke to Patik.

"You have done well, Patik," Quinn/Xetacon said assertively. Patik nodded. "Soon the Daryl problem will be eliminated, and I will rule this planet. You will be given rewards if you remain worthy." Quinn/Xetacon began to disseminate his plans, and Patik followed this master's orders even though he would have rather gone back to Tibet.

As for Quinn, when the kon-bre-shet had taken over control of his mind, Daryl still had a presence there. This, Xetacon had suspected all along, and was prepared for. The modified kon-bre-shet sent false brain waves to fool Daryl's surveillance. They gave the impression that all was well with Quinn, so that Daryl would not get suspicious, and would do so as long as was necessary. The kon-bre-shet would also dampen that part of Quinn's brain activities which Xetacon was controlling. Thus Xetacon could control Quinn, and Daryl would not even be aware of it.

Xetacon searched Quinn's memories as well. Doing so, Xetacon learned many things about Daryl's workings and shell. He became aware of Clayre, and guessed at her mysterious knowledge of Daryl's existence, and he also found out that Quinn and Clayre had begun a relationship that had left them both emotionally stressed. Xetacon could sense the possibilities here. He became certain that this Clayre was close to the Human lover, and if he could procure her, he would have leverage enough to cause Daryl's downfall. He let Quinn's mind reveal to Daryl that Quinn wanted to see Clayre soon, to make things right between them. Daryl had responded, too. He subtly imprinted in Quinn's mind a desire to be at the Computer Lab Building on Yarborough's campus that night, because Clayre would be there. Quinn/Xetacon smiled. This would be easier than he'd imagined. He would snatch Daryl's favorite right out from under his shell.

In the meantime, he and Patik would work on the secondary plan. They would build an explosive device large enough to blow Daryl's shell to bits. Using Quinn's vehicle, he went to many different places, securing items that were needed for the explosives with Quinn's own cash and credit line. Some of the chemicals were illegal and had to be stolen, and stolen in such a way as to prevent unnecessary suspicion or detection. This was not a problem for Xetacon. The material acquisitioning took several hours, but when he returned to Quinn's house, he had what was needed. It would take a day or two to create and prepare the plastic explosive, so Quinn/Xetacon ordered Patik to "cook" the mixture. For this task, Patik dutifully surrendered his mind and body to Khan Xeta, his kon-bre-shet master, brother Entity and copy of Xetacon.

Quinn/Xetacon then got prepared for the meeting with Clayre. Xetacon planned to force Quinn to act as himself at first, to get Clayre to trust him. He would persuade her to leave the building with him, and then she would be taken to a place, away from Daryl, where she could be controlled as well. Quinn/Xetacon laughed.

This will be even more satisfying than Quinn's acquisition, Xetacon thought. Once Clayre was under his control, it mattered little if Daryl was aware of it or not. With her, Daryl would be easily controlled as well. By the time midnight came, Quinn/Xetacon had driven to the university where the Computer Lab was located, and waited patiently for Clayre to arrive. He recognized her car from Quinn's memory, as it pulled into the parking lot at the lab building, and he met her at the entrance.

"Clayre," he said, putting on the friendly act and smiling. "There you are. I was hoping you'd come tonight."

"Hello, Quinn," she replied tentatively, "it's been a while. So how are you?" Quinn/Xetacon played along.

"Oh, I'm much better, now," he said congenially, "and I'm so sorry about what happened last time; you must think I'm an ogre."

"No, no, of course not," Clayre told him, trying to downplay the incident.

"I shouldn't have taken advantage of you like that..." he apologized, sounding rather awkward on purpose.

"Please don't worry about it," Clayre sympathized. "I'm okay and you didn't take advantage of me...not really...I wanted it too."

"...but I called her name, and..." He sounded so pathetic, now, like he couldn't choke out the words. It worked.

"It's all right," she told him. "I know what you're going through. I've lost people close to me, too. You needed to feel loved, and I can understand that. I'm just glad that you're better."

"I am better, now," he said happily, "because of you. I'd like to thank you properly. Why don't we get some coffee?"

"Sure," she said and smiled. He had made her feel at ease, like when she first met him, and Xetacon had Quinn act like he had at that party; friendly, congenial, and interested in her. Clayre wasn't so sure of herself though. She had been flirting with Daryl, but that was just a ruse to get him to open up more...or was it? She felt an attraction there, but it was subtle, under the surface, where she couldn't quite understand it. Quinn, on the other hand, was gracious as well as kind, and she liked him a lot. They had gone through their trial by fire with the unplanned incident last time, and period of separation. Was Quinn really better? She wasn't sure, but she was willing to start over with him. This time she resolved to take it slow, like the original plan.

When they got to the break area, Quinn/Xetacon got them coffees and sat down across from her. He knew enough not to rush things.

"So, Clayre," he began, "what have you been up to lately?"

"You would not believe me," she answered back, rolling her eyes.

"Oh?" he inquired, like he was curious.

"Well, you've heard of those Astrol-Predictors, haven't you?"

"Yeah, sure," he said. "They're some kind of hoax, at

least that's what the news people are saying. Why?"

"Believe it or not," she went on, "the schematic for those things came right out of the brute."

"No kidding," he answered, unimpressed. Then he realized she expected him to react or at least be curious.

"It came from MY report and YOUR learning program!" Clayre couldn't understand why he wasn't reacting. Quinn/Xetacon caught on this time.

"You don't say," he retorted, pretending to be interested now, "that's really unusual, wild..." She was still confused by his lack of exuberance. He was close to making her suspicious, so he tried another tactic.

"Say," he said, changing the subject, "have you heard anymore from that Daryl guy?" She looked away suddenly, and her face got flushed.

"Funny you should ask that," she remarked. "I just talked to him yesterday."

"What *is* his problem?" Quinn/Xetacon said smugly, and rather comically. Clayre giggled.

"I don't know," she smirked. "I've been wondering that all along. That and who he really is." Quinn/Xetacon smiled. She was finally at ease with him, and Xetacon felt that the time was right to make his move. He took over all of Quinn now.

"I see," Quinn/Xetacon said coyly. "What if I told you that I know all about Daryl?" Clayre sat up excitedly.

"Really?" she spouted enthusiastically, which Quinn/Xetacon found provocative.

"Sure," he replied. "He's much closer than you think." Is it Quinn, she thought.

"Well, tell me then," she begged. Quinn/Xetacon laughed, a dark yearning was forming inside his being.

"You're sure you want to know?" he teased. He could sense her body, one that was starved for emotion. In his contact with Khan Xeta, Xetacon had learned about Human pleasures and how, through Patik, Khan Xeta had experienced them.

"Come on," she pleaded. "Tell me!"

"I will," he said casually, "but, oh, let's see, how about a little gratuitous favor first?"

"Gratuitous favor?" she said stunned. "What do you mean by that?"

"You can guess..." he pressed on, smirking. "Like what we did last time, only you have my promise that it will be a lot better this time around."

There, he thought. She would not be able to turn down his proposal now. Quinn/Xetacon had very little experience dealing with Human females. If he had, he would have known how wrong he was.

"You...you want me to have sex with you again, or you won't tell me?" She was speaking loudly now. He tried to convince her.

"Sex is such a sterile word," Quinn/Xetacon remarked. "I prefer to call it pleasure, and I greatly desire to have pleasure with you."

This was not the Quinn she knew, Clayre decided. It was as if he were schizophrenic, now, and there was no way she would go along with his disgusting proposal.

"Look, Quinn," she spoke carefully, "I think we need to go back to what we decided before..."

"Go slow!" he interrupted angrily. "Slow is for losers! Come on, you know you want to be pleasured. It's in your nature."

"No I don't!" she declared, nearly crying. "Not like this..." She was slipping away from him, Quinn/Xetacon realized.

He had wanted her to come willingly, but that was impossible now. Daryl would have a presence in her mind, and would soon realize that something was wrong. He would have to take control of the situation, with very little time for thought.

"Yes, Clayre, I'm afraid you DO want it," Quinn/Xetacon told her assertively. "Come on, let's get out of here." He stood up quickly and grabbed her by the wrist, pulling her up as well. In that instant she relaxed, as Quinn/Xetacon, utilizing the kon-bre-shet, took over her mind and body, leading her along.

She felt odd, like an outside observer of some horrific

nightmare, or maybe she was a little girl, hiding in a closet inside her own mind, peeking through the keyhole. Neither was nice. She was aware of what was happening, the reality of it, as Quinn/Xetacon led her through the lab building, heading for the front entrance. Where is he taking me she wondered?

When they got to the large front doors, Quinn/Xetacon swore. Somehow they had gotten locked, and he couldn't get through them. He pulled her closer, being careful to maintain his contact with her. His right hand was free, and with it he pressed several gemstones on the bracelet that he wore upon his left wrist.

The electronically controlled door locks immediately clicked open. Clayre was amazed. It was the first time she had noticed that bracelet, and she wondered what it was. Quinn/Xetacon was in a hurry now. Daryl had to be aware of him, and was trying to prevent Clayre from being taken. He hurried outside, practically dragging her to his vehicle, where he pushed her inside and followed her in as well. It was difficult to sustain skin contact with her through all that. He had to switch hands back and forth just to get the car started, and then drove off, steering with his left hand as he held on to Clayre with the other.

About a mile or so down the narrow two lane road, the car began to stall and then die, which Clayre could not believe, especially after the door lock incident. Quinn/Xetacon yanked her arm closer and used the bracelet again, pressing the gemstones. Miraculously the car came back to life. He flew down the roadway, driving at speeds far greater than was safe as Clayre sat limp and helpless, aware with a certainty that she was in real trouble. Terrified beyond rational thought, she couldn't comprehend how or why Quinn was doing this, and was fearful of what he would do to her.

In the countryside, now, they sped down secondary roads in the dark of night with no one else around and little hope of a rescue for her. Just when he thought there was nothing to stop him, a squad of police cars with lights flashing and sirens blaring came over a hill right towards him.

Prediction

Quinn/Xetacon reacted quickly by turning left onto a convenient side road. He had to let go of Clare's arm to put both hands on the steering wheel for that sharp turn. Clayre was freed from his control momentarily, and with a sudden rush of adrenaline, she reacted. Knowing she would have just a few seconds, she did the only thing she could think of. Unlocking the door, she grabbed the handle and yanked on it. The car door flew open and she jumped out, rolling over and over in the heavy grass, before coming to a halt and then passing out. Quinn/Xetacon kept going, and the police followed in pursuit like hounds on a scent.

CHAPTER XVIII

Tertiary Timeline, Clayre's first year at Rookwood (continued)

I might have been drifting, flotsam in a blank grey sea of nothing. Abruptly that changed. I was back at Rookwood, teaching a class. Keith walked in unexpectedly and started heckling me, calling me "boss lady" as the students all laughed. I ran away crying, right into the arms of a man who held me lovingly. I looked up to see who it was, but I couldn't tell, his face was hidden in the darkness. He was kind, though, comforting me, and I felt safe there in his arms. I looked again and it was Quinn, now, smiling wickedly. I suddenly became terrified and it woke me up.

At first, I was relieved that it was only a dream, until I regained full consciousness and then realized being awake was worse. I had aches and pains everywhere, and my skin was all scratched up, especially on my arms and legs. My mind was still groggy, but that didn't stop the headache that had begun to throb. I was frightened as I recalled what had happened to me, and why I had ended up like this in a ditch. "Eeyew," I muttered to myself, getting up quickly, even hurting like I was, fearful there were insects crawling all over me, in my hair, in my clothes.

It took a thorough check to convince myself otherwise, and I looked about for any sign of Quinn as well, scared he might come back looking for me. It was still dark out, and I guessed there was at least an hour or two before the first light of dawn. With no sign of Quinn, or anybody else for that matter, I started to walk along the road, heading back towards Yarborough, which I figured had to be at least a dozen miles away. I thought about things as I hobbled along. I still couldn't believe Quinn had acted that way. Something had to be seriously wrong for him to have changed like that. I wondered about Daryl, too. Why had he urged me to get together with Quinn? Certainly not for sex, or was Quinn really Daryl in a Jekyll and Hyde sort of way?

There were more Questions than answers, and my head hurt already. At least the cool night air was refreshing, sobering.

I had walked about a mile, when I saw the headlights from a car coming toward me. I panicked, and fearing it might be Quinn, nearly froze. Having few options, I hid behind a bush near the fence line, on the other side of the ditch. The car came closer and closer, slowing down, and finally stopped near where I was hiding. The window slid down with a whirring sound that frightened me. Did he know I was here? He must; it couldn't be a coincidence. Just then the person in the car called out.

"Come on, get in, girl," a woman shouted. "I ain't got all night!" I was scared to answer.

"Who are you?" I asked timidly.

"Madam Garza," she replied, getting annoyed. "You remember...we met once."

"You're Myron's friend, the psychic?"

"Yes, yes," she growled. "Now get in." I was still crazy with fear, but decided I could trust Madam Garza. I ran back through the ditch and got in her car.

"How did you know I was here?" I asked her as soon as we got going.

"Daryl," she said.

"You know Daryl?" I nearly shouted.

"Sort of," was her reply. "I have a psychic connection with him."

"Oh," I said, practically groaning. "Then you have no idea who he really is."

"No," she said. "Do you?"

"Not really," I sighed. "I halfway believe he's Quinn Oliver, the one who kidnapped me." The older woman just huffed.

"I don't think so," she asserted. "Daryl has a good soul; I can always tell. There is definitely something Pisces about him." I wanted to believe her.

"Quinn was always kind," I argued, "until today. He is a very disturbed individual."

"That's not Quinn," Madam Garza said bluntly. "Not anymore." I didn't understand what she meant by that, so I let it go. We were nearly to Yarborough by that time anyway. She pulled up next to my car and I got out.

"Thanks," I said, and turned to leave.

"Wait," Madam Garza told me. "I am to give this to you." She took something off from around her neck and handed it to me. "You'll need this more than I will," she said. "If you're planning to call the police, don't. You can't trust them. May the good powers that be protect you." She made a sign of some kind with her hand and then sped off. I looked at what she had given me. It was a curious necklace of some sort with an amulet unlike anything I had ever seen. It was green crystal, rather gemlike, with filets of silver across the stones in an odd geometric design. I put it around my own neck, and tucked it into my blouse. Heck, I thought. I need all the luck and protection I can get right now. Besides the thing was pretty and had an interesting look. I had to go back into the lab building to get my purse, and I half expected to find Quinn waiting for me. Thankfully, the people from the next time slot were there already, and he wasn't. Breathing a sigh, I got into my car and drove quickly away, worried that every car I met on the road might be Quinn's. My clothes were all dirty and torn, so I had no choice but to go home to get cleaned up.

The sky was already getting lighter, and a red sun was peeking over the horizon by the time I finally did drive up to my little cottage. I was surprised to see a road crew digging up my front parking. Curious, I went up to one of the men and asked what was going on. He told me they were replacing a stretch of storm drains and curbing along my street and would be working on them for a couple of weeks. It made me feel safer that these big guys were close by if Quinn did show up, so I gave them all a nice smile. One guy whistled as I headed up to the house, and that embarrassed me a little.

As soon as I got in, I called Henry to let him know that I would be late for my classes. When I told him that I'd had an accident of sorts, however, he insisted that I take the whole day off, and said not to worry, that he would cover my lectures for me. I was grateful, and thanked him five or six times. I really did feel sore from being banged up like that, and I was exhausted. I took some over-the-counter pain meds, and got out of my ruined clothes. It was my intention to jump right into bed, but I still felt kind of crusty from lying in that ditch. Instead, I drew a nice warm bath, planning to have a good long soak in it.

Once the tub was full, I stepped into the hot water, and slid carefully down into a relaxed position, resting my head on the edge, with soapy bubbles up to my neck.

"I bet that feels good," a familiar sounding male voice said. I wasn't sure who it was, though, especially not here in my bathroom where there shouldn't be anybody.

"Who's there?" I shouted nervously, a fresh thrill of fear running through my body. I sat up and instinctively grabbed for a towel, looking around.

"It's just me," came the reply, "...Daryl."

"Where are you?" I asked him, still shaking. "Behind the door?"

"Actually, no," he said. "I'm not there with you."

"Then where are you?" I asked again. "Is there a camera here in my bathroom? Are you looking at me?"

"I'm where I'm always at," he assured me, "and no, there aren't any cameras in your bathroom. I give my word; I'm not watching you bathe."

"Well okay, but why are you bothering me while I'm taking a bath, and what do you want?" I was annoyed, and after the night I'd had who could blame me.

"I had to tell you that I'm sorry," he said solemnly. "Sorry about Quinn, and now I'm sorry about this as well. It was completely unexpected what Quinn did to you." I didn't care about his apology, I wanted some answers.

"I don't suppose you're going to tell me how you can talk to me like this," I badgered him.

"Are you sure you want to know?" he replied, dodging the question like usual.

"I'm simply overcome with curiosity," I responded sarcastically, still mad, "but I bet you won't tell me." He surprised me, though.

"The amulet you're wearing is really a communication

device," he told me, "one that I created just for you. It is linked to your DNA sequence so that only you or your offspring will be able to utilize it. The communication is by means of brain waves that you alone can pick up on." He had to be kidding.

"You mean it's telepathic?" I retorted skeptically. I didn't believe his outlandish explanation at all. "Then why can I actually 'hear' your voice."

"You can hear my voice," he told me, "because it's using audio nerve impulses in your brain. It just seems to be sound. I can also communicate with thought patterns in speech or ideas that appear as feelings or visions."

"No way," I argued. "That's impossible."

"Is it?" he asked. Startled, I slipped right down underneath the water, drenching my face. What I had heard was literally a voice in my head.

"This can't be real!" I sputtered, once I resurfaced. "Nobody has technology like that." I was stunned, but he continued to talk to me that way.

"You also can communicate in thought patterns, if you like," he told me.

"Oh my gosh!" I exclaimed, inside my mind.

"Yeah, it's pretty cool, isn't it?" he said elatedly, and we continued to converse without speaking.

"Who are you, Daryl?" I asked him silently. "Some alien from another planet?"

"Of course not, Clayre," he responded telepathically. "I'm from right here in the USA."

"Then you must be some kind of super spy or something, working for the government," I remarked.

"I guess you could say that," he admitted. "I *am* funded by government money, but I work independently."

"Well I must say that I'm impressed," I declared, "and talking this way *is* super cool, but what happened to Quinn? Is he part of your organization too?"

"Not exactly, but he was involved," Daryl said dejectedly, "and because of that he's been acquired by the other side. Not by choice, Clayre. His mind has been taken over."

"Oh my, no," I said, worried for Quinn. "Like he was brainwashed? Is there anything we can do to help him?"

"I do hope so," Daryl commented somberly. "He must have some kind of device with him, I believe, that is similar to the one you have, except that it has abilities other than for communication. Features that allow the one I'll call 'X' to control the mind of the person who has it. Yours, by the way, cannot be used like that. In fact I designed it to prevent any such subjugation." I was glad. I knew all too well what it was like to be controlled that way, and I had no desire to repeat the experience.

"Who is this 'X'?" I asked him.

"Unfortunately, 'X' is a serious threat to everyone," Daryl said. "He has skills greater than my own. Stay away from him, Clayre. He wants you because you are close to me, and for that I am also sorry."

"I've seen his device," I declared. "It's like a bracelet he wears on his left wrist. It has stones on it that he presses to make it do things."

"I see," Daryl replied. "The only way to free Quinn is to get that thing away from him. I'll do what I can, but Clayre, stay away from Quinn. This 'X' is more dangerous than you can imagine."

"Yes, of course," I said. I had no desire to see Quinn again, at least not until he was himself once more. "Daryl, I want to thank you, by the way, for saving me. I expect it was you who actuated the locked doors, the car, and all the cops."

"Yes, my Clayre," he said softly. "I was afraid I'd lost you to him. You were very brave to jump out of that vehicle."

"I guess," I said meekly, "even though I was scared the whole time. So where is Quinn now?"

"'X' has voided Quinn's brain waves so I cannot track him," Daryl said. "He could be anywhere. I doubt that he will try anything for awhile. In the meantime, I'll make sure there are plenty of people around you."

"Like the construction crew outside?" I asked.

"Yes, my Clayre," he answered.

"I'll have to bring them some lemonade later," I giggled.

"There will be stepped up police patrols at night as well," he told me. "There is a peeping tom in the neighborhood matching Quinn's description." I laughed again. Daryl made me feel better, happy again.

"You know, my Daryl," I said sweetly, "I might not mind it if you watch me bathe. I feel safer with you protecting me. I wish you were here with me right now."

"I am with you, my Clayre," he said lovingly, "as close as my circumstances will permit. I'm next to your heart and all you need to do is call my name whenever you want me. Should you want your privacy, just remove the amulet, but keep it somewhere close, somewhere safe."

"I will," I promised, "but I like it where it is."

"Your water is getting cold," he remarked. "I should let you finish your bath."

"Okay," I agreed. I did need to get some rest after I finished cleaning up.

"Bye for now, my Daryl," I said.

"Yes, good bye, my Clayre," he repeated and then was gone. I finished my bath and went right to bed. I was exhausted, both physically and emotionally, and I fell asleep quite easily and began to dream:

In my dream, I was walking along a beach somewhere exotic. It was sunny, warm, and there was a pleasant breeze that kept my skin temperature at a perfectly comfortable level. The white sand felt good on my toes, and the fall of the waves breaking upon the shore was soothing, calming. My gaze turned out to sea. There was a shrill yipping sound that drew my attention. Just beyond the crashing waves, a large white dolphin was leaping and playing. It seemed like he was calling to me, inviting me to join him. I decided to at last. Taking off my dress, I ran into the tepid ocean and jumped through a large breaker. There were a lot more waves and I had trouble getting past them. Each one I fought through seemed bigger than the last. Just when I thought I couldn't go on, the dolphin swam up next to me. Holding onto him, he helped me get through them all, especially the last giant wave. Once we were out to the calmer waters, we swam together, enjoying the freedom. He let me hold on to his dorsal fin, and he took me to a pretty pink coral reef where he showed me amazing things. The white dolphin surprised me when he said my name.

"Are you Daryl?" I asked.

"Yes," he answered.

"You're not really a dolphin, are you?" I asked again.

"I can be whatever you desire me to be," he told me, and then changed into a Human form. His face was rugged and handsome. "Do you like this, or would you prefer another?" He changed again, and now he had Keith's face and body.

"No, no, please change back," I said quickly, and he did. This face was so familiar, but I couldn't recall where I had seen it before. No matter, I liked it. We went to a small island and found a soft bed of grass under some palm trees.

"This is perfect," he said, and then he kissed me, passionately, just as I woke up. Wow, I told myself, as I laid there in a lazy and comfortable partially awake haze. That had to be the most wondrous and vivid dream I'd ever had.

"Thank you, my Daryl," I whispered inside my mind, and then promptly fell back to sleep.

It must have been several hours later, and I was drifting in and out of wakefulness, enjoying the fact that I had no reason at all to get up. In the midst of that rare comfort, I thought about Daryl. He was something of a mystery, yes, but he obviously cared about me. He had even told me that I was his "one and only." Did he really love me? I felt certain that he did, even though he had never actually said the words "I love you." He called me "his Clayre," and what other proof did I need?

It was amazing the things he could do, like saving little Alicia, and the technology at his disposal was unbelievable. Maybe he was rich, but that didn't really matter to me. I liked him a lot. Love? Well it felt like love in that dream. Did I love him? I'd never even actually met him face to face, but yes, I'd have to admit it, I did love him. He helped me get away from poor Quinn, and though I was still frightened by what had happened, I felt more aware than ever, like my senses were all heightened. This gadget he made for me that he called an amulet, was fantastic. Even now I wanted to use it to call him, to be with him.

"Daryl?" I said in my mind.

"Yes my Clayre," he answered, like he had nowhere else to be.

"I want to tell you something," I began. "Something I just realized." He didn't answer so I continued. "I have to admit, that it's the strangest thing, this relationship we have, but even so strange as it is, I want it to go on, and I want to be close to you...because I love you." There was a long pause.

"What is love?" he asked meekly, as if he were a six year old.

"Don't you know?" I responded in amazement. I went on before he could answer. "You're in love when you care about someone more than yourself; when you want to be with them as much as possible; when they are the most important thing in your life; when you'd even die for them." There was no pause this time.

"Then I am in love, also," Daryl said ardently, "with you, my Clayre." My heart began beating faster.

"I wish I could kiss you," I told him.

"Close your eyes," he replied. When I did the vision of us on the grass beneath the palm trees came back. He was lying beside me now.

"Is this real?" I asked him.

"It is real to our senses, how they perceive it," he offered.

"...but is this how you really look?" I asked again.

"It is how you see me," he explained. "This is an image of me that you have created in your mind. If you don't like it, I could change."

"No, no," I told him. "It's perfect. I shouldn't be so superficial. Looks shouldn't matter, not when you really love someone."

He was ultra dreamy like that, though, and I definitely liked it. He kissed me again, and it was sweet and wonderful, even though I knew it was all just in my mind. When the kiss ended, I told him so.

"This is nice, wonderful even, and it seems so natural, but

I can't help wishing that it were truly real." Suddenly the vision changed. I was back in my own bed. I opened my eyes and rolled over. There he was lying right beside me.

"Are you real now?" I asked.

"As real as it is possible for me to be," he agreed. I touched his face with my hand. He certainly felt real. I smiled and he kissed me again. My heart went all a flutter; it had to be real. My eyes were open and everything.

"So you really are here!" I said in amazement.

"To you I am," he replied. "I cannot lie to you, my Clayre. If someone else were to see you right now, they would see you all by yourself, acting very strangely." I laughed.

"...but it seems so real!" I pouted.

"It is real," he responded seriously, "for me and you. At least our brains perceive it as real, as real as any other action." I began to understand. Anything we actually perceive is just neural impulses that our minds decipher from sensory input. So is this, but it's a different kind of sensory input.

"That's good enough for me," I said happily, as I leaned in and kissed him passionately. When I broke it off, I looked into his eyes and smiled. "I can't get pregnant this way, can I? It's the ultimate birth control!"

"No, not from this," he agreed, but he was frowning. "I'm sorry, Clayre, but I can't do that with you just yet."

"Why not?" I argued. "I'm running hot, and I want you to."

"I know," he replied bashfully. "I wouldn't feel right about it until you know everything about me. What I am."

"This again?" I complained. I was getting annoyed, as the mood slipped away. "It's so simple. Just tell me and get it over with."

"I can't tell you, my Clayre, but I will show you...tonight. Go to Yarborough and I'll be there. This time for real. I'm afraid for now I have to leave you before I do something that I'll regret." Then, just like that, he was gone. I wanted to cry.

Men, they're so silly, I thought. I loved him now, and he

could have six arms and three glass eyes, and it wouldn't make a difference to me. I was disappointed, for the moment, but I hugged my shoulders. I told myself that tonight was the night I'd finally meet my Daryl, and see for myself what he was really like. Part of me was sad. This would end all the mystery and excitement, but I'd trade all that for something tangible, and it'd be worth it. I didn't really think Daryl had six arms or anything like that. I was sure he was fine, other than being shy or self-conscious to the point of being ridiculous about it.

After all, he said he'd never loved before, and I believed that. Maybe he had a fear of rejection to overcome as well. I wasn't worried. I would cure him of all that once we were together, I was certain. I jumped out of bed. In the meantime, I had a lot to do before tonight. Let me see. There's my hair and nails, and I'll need some new makeup. Oh, and yes, the perfect outfit with shoes. I wanted to dazzle him.

CHAPTER XIX

Tertiary Timeline, the same day

Daryl would pay dearly for this humiliation Quinn/Xetacon vowed as the cop drove him back to the campus where he had acquired Clayre. She was not there, of course, and the unacceptable agitation that had followed his attempt to capture Daryl's favorite female was causing Quinn/Xetacon's wrath to overcome his objectivity. He decreed to himself that both Daryl and Clayre would suffer in agony. When Clayre jumped out of his car, he had tried to evade the pursuing police contingent, but eventually they cornered him, and he knew then that escape was not possible. Quinn/Xetacon had to allow himself to be captured, and then bide his time until he was alone with just one officer that he could then control. His chance came when, in the process of being transported to a holding facility, he had taken control of the officer restraining him, and freed himself. The memories of that officer were helpful. He developed lies that would belay suspicion for the officer's absence, and allow him to remain free. His being arrested had given Quinn/Xetacon an idea for how to recapture Clayre, one that would expedite his overall plans. Unfortunately, things were not as they had been before.

He must be clever, he realized, as Daryl was now aware of Quinn's defection, and would probably suspect that he, Xetacon, was responsible. Patik was yet at the house. The kon-bre-shet Patik wore and his were linked for secure communication that Daryl would not be able to intercept. He ordered Patik to retrieve Quinn's vehicle, and to be available should he be needed. In the meantime Quinn/Xetacon waited for Clayre at the Yarborough facility in the off chance that she might return there. He would wait a long time.

Later that evening, Clayre was both excited and nervous as she drove from her house to the Yarborough Computer Lab. It was something she had done at least a dozen times in the last couple of months, but this time was different. She was excited because she would finally meet Daryl, and she could hardly wait. He had promised her that he would be there, and she had spent most of the day making herself pretty for him. She was also nervous. The last time she had gone to Yarborough, Quinn had been there. Not the Quinn she knew, regrettably. It was some kind of brainwashed evil Quinn, who this sinister "X" had corrupted, with nearly disastrous consequences for her. She trusted Daryl, though. She felt he would protect her as she drove up to the Yarborough campus area.

Almost traumatically, a loud wail startled Clayre that turned out to be a police siren. In a daze Clayre realized that she was being pulled over even though she was pretty sure she had done nothing wrong. She had no other choice but to slow down, get her car off the roadway, and then shut it off.

Clayre wondered why she was being detained, and waiting for the officer to pompously walk over to her car, did little to help with her nervousness. It was hard for her to believe that this was just a routine traffic stop, so Clayre left her window rolled up, and her door locked, just in case. The officer nodded and smiled when he saw her.

"Sorry for the inconvenience, Ma'am," he said politely. "May I see your license and registration? If you have proof of insurability, I'd like to see that as well." Clayre fumbled around for a moment in her skipper's console until she located the papers. Opening the window a tiny bit, she slipped the documents to him with her license.

"Is there some kind of problem?" she asked the policeman. The officer said "no," and went to run her ID. In a couple minutes he came back.

"Sorry for the inconvenience, Ma'am," he repeated, as he handed back her papers. "There's an alert on this campus for possible terrorist activity. Evidently, the target is the large computer facility. We're on the lookout for this man. Have you seen him?" He showed her a picture. It was Quinn. Clayre breathed a sigh of relief. This must be more of Daryl's protections, she thought.

"No, I haven't," she told the officer, which was a small

lie, but she didn't want to be interrogated. Not now, when she was about to meet Daryl for the first time. The policeman nodded.

"Well, if you do, please stay away from him and call us."

"I sure will," she replied and smiled. "Thank you for the warning, and for being here to protect me." He seemed a bit embarrassed by her unexpected courtesy, but appreciated it.

"Yes, Ma'am," he said, tipping his hat before getting back to his patrol car and speeding off, apparently on another call. Clayre restarted her vehicle and drove on as well, feeling confident now that Quinn wouldn't be there this time. When she got to the Computer Lab Building and pulled into the lot, there was another police checkpoint. Sheesh, Daryl, she thought, perhaps this is a bit overmuch. The officer was waving her into a nearby parking space. Getting impatient and annoyed, Clayre parked and got out, walking over to where the patrolman stood.

"Hello officer," she said. "I'm just here to run a report. I have my ID and pass badge for the lab here."

"I see," he replied. "Sorry, but we have to check everyone who goes in there."

"All right," Clayre sighed, "but can you make it quick, please. I'm supposed to meet someone inside and I'm running a little late."

"Sure thing, Miss," he told her. "Just have a seat in the back of my squad car." He walked over and opened the door for her, so she got in. There appeared to be a second officer up front in the passenger seat, and when the door closed he turned around to look at her. It wasn't an officer at all, she realized. It was Quinn.

"Hello, Honey," he smirked. "Did you miss me?" Clayre tried to grab the door handle to get out, but there wasn't one. Then Quinn/Xetacon sprayed something into her face and she went limp like a cloth doll. Not again, she thought as she laid there helpless. "Let's go," he ordered the patrolman who got behind the wheel, and they headed quickly out of town using their siren the whole way. Clayre was not unconscious. Whatever she had breathed in, had acted on her body, but her mind was still clear.

"Daryl, help!" she shouted inside her head, but there was no answer. Quinn/Xetacon turned around and looked at her.

"Ah yes," he grunted, "so you have one too. Mine is better." He reached back and gingerly lifted the chain from around Clayre's neck being careful not to touch the amulet itself. "This won't work here, so I'll just take care of it for you." He laughed and put the amulet in his pocket. Once the patrol car got outside of town, they turned off the siren.

"Shall we go to my place, Darling?" Quinn/Xetacon taunted her. "We can finally finish what we started yesterday." There was no help from Daryl this time, and she was immobilized to the point where she couldn't even move. They drove on for at least another half hour before they came to a bridge over a fairly large river. Quinn/Xetacon rolled down the window.

"You won't need this anymore," he said as he held the amulet outside the squad car. With an evil grin he threw it over the railing and into the water. Clayre wanted to cry, and as her eyes teared up, Quinn/Xetacon noticed it. "How touching," he teased her cruelly, "she loves her fish." She had no idea what he was talking about as they drove on. A few miles further the car pulled into a quiet lane near the edge of a small town. At the end of the double-rut drive, nested among several huge trees, was a large older house, all by itself, with a big open porch that gave it a cozy look.

"This is your base of operations?" the cop asked Quinn/Xetacon.

"We're undercover," Quinn/Xetacon replied. "Stay in the squad and make sure we're not disturbed." He got out, and roughly drug Clayre out of the car, as well, carrying her to the house and going inside. Quinn/Xetacon took her to a bedroom and laid her on the bed.

"Isn't this nice?" he said ogling her. "You know, I could do anything I want." Clayre cringed inside knowing she could do nothing to stop him. She didn't know it, but he took more pleasure in that, than had he done the actual act. "Plenty of time for that kind of fun later, Baby," he joked. "Right now, I think my car has arrived and I have to leave you so I can blow Daryl to tiny little pieces." Clayre did

206

hear a car then, as it pulled up outside and stopped. "Don't worry, I'll be back soon," he said, and then he left her there on the bed. Clayre started crying again.

Quinn/Xetacon went outside and talked to the officer in the patrol car.

"You've been a huge help, Officer, uh, Jorgensen. We'll take it from here." The policeman nodded, knowing he was being dismissed. "Don't worry, Jorgensen, I'll make sure you get a commendation for this." The officer nodded.

"Thanks, um..."

"Sorry, no names," Quinn/Xetacon retorted. "We're still undercover."

"Oh yeah, right," Jorgensen responded. "Well, if you FBI need anything, call precinct." Quinn/Xetacon waved as Officer Jorgensen drove away. Then he turned to Patik, who had just arrived in Quinn's car.

"Stay with the girl," he said. "Make sure she's well looked after." Quinn/Xetacon laughed maliciously. "I'll call for you as soon as I've taken care of that fool Daryl." Patik nodded obediently. Quinn/Xetacon went back in the house and soon re-emerged with a large black satchel. Then he got back into his car and drove off. Patik went inside. He had no trouble finding the room with the girl laying helpless there on the bed. Clayre had never seen this man before, and she wondered who he was.

"Hebpt muh!" she tried, but could not move her mouth to speak coherently. She thought maybe he was there to rescue her. "Duh tebboriz!" she tried again, "Duh bun im duh bicturb." Patik just looked at her and smiled.

"No, girl, you're the terrorist," he teased. Clayre looked at Patik's wrist and saw his kon-bre-shet. It was an exact copy of the one Quinn wore except that, unbeknownst to her, his bore the core-awareness of Khan Xeta. By now Khan Xeta had looked her over as well, and an evil lust filled him. He took over Patik completely.

"So you're Daryl's female," he laughed. "My you're a pretty thing," he went on. "All dressed up, too. I think I'll just take a little peek." He reached down and with an evil grin lifted up the hem of her dress. His grin was short-lived.

A loud crash preceded his vacant expression, right before he toppled over. Standing behind him was Madam Garza with half of a large vase in her hands.

"Didn't expect that," she snorted. "Did ya, scumbag?" She helped Clayre sit up and tried to get her to drink something from a flask she had. "This will help," she explained.

After a couple tries, Madam Garza got a little of the liquid down and Clayre responded, able now to mumble a weak "thank you." In just a few minutes her arms and legs began to unnumb themselves.

"We've got to hurry," she told Madam Garza. "It was Quinn again, or that 'X'. He's got a bomb and he means to blow Daryl to pieces! I have to warn him!"

"Use the amulet," Madam Garza suggested. Clayre made a sad face.

"I can't," she moaned. "Quinn threw it into the river." They hurried out to Madam Garza's little sports car which she had parked near the end of the lane, and quickly drove off after Quinn. When they got to the river bridge, Madam Garza slowed down.

"This is where he threw the amulet into the water, isn't it," she declared. Clayre nodded.

"Over there I think," Clayre said, pointing. Madam Garza pulled over and stopped. She got out and ran down to the water's edge. Clayre followed trying to catch up to her. When she got to the shore, she looked out into the current. Something was splashing around out in the middle of the channel.

"What's that," Clayre remarked, pointing at it. Whatever it was caught sight of them and swam in closer.

"Hush," Madam Garza said, and closed her eyes. The playful animal dove down into the water, and was gone for maybe a minute or two. Then it surfaced right in front of them.

"Oh my gosh," Clayre exclaimed. It was easy to see what it was, now, a sleek fresh-water dolphin. Clayre noticed that it had a radio tag in its fin, and the dolphin also had her amulet in its mouth. Chirping, it offered the amulet to

Clayre. She took it gently, and then patted its bottle nose. "Thank you so much," Clayre said softly, with heartfelt gratitude. "You had best be off for home now." As if the elegant mammal could understand her, it turned and headed back downstream toward the coast. Clayre put the amulet back around her neck, and immediately called to Daryl from inside her mind.

"Daryl, are you there? Daryl?" she was frantic. "It's Quinn. You're in danger!"

"Clayre, my love..." Daryl answered, his voice stressed. "Stay away. Quinn is already here. I will miss you."

"Oh, Daryl," she cried, but Daryl was gone, now, and would not answer. Clayre turned toward Madam Garza.

"Take me to Yarborough as fast as you can." They ran back to the little car, got in, and Madam Garza gunned it. Flying down the road, Clayre hoped they wouldn't run into any policemen. It was getting near dawn, and thankfully there wasn't much traffic. They were still about a mile or two from the campus when the little car's motor sputtered and died, coasting to a halt. Clayre jumped out and began to run. She wondered about Madam Garza's car. Was it Quinn who did that, or was Daryl trying to keep her from helping him. No matter. She just couldn't live with herself if she let Daryl be hurt or killed without at least trying to do something to save him. She tried calling Daryl's name as she hurried on, but he would not, or could not, answer her. By the time she got to the Computer Lab Building, she was so out of breath that she had to bend over and hold her sides. What was she doing, she kept asking herself, and how was she going to help Daryl? She really had no idea at all, but knew she had to try.

By this time, it was getting lighter out, and the first rays of reddish sunlight lit onto the front of the building. The big stone facade looked different in the light of day, she told herself. As she gazed at it, her eyes fell upon the sign outside of the building. Funny, Clayre thought, that she had never noticed it before. Funnier still, the big letters down the left side spelled out D-A-R-Y-L. Suddenly, like a slap in the face, it all became clear...her article...the reports...the miracles...who and what Daryl was. In that moment, Clayre learned a lot about herself. Shocked, but steadfast, she walked up to the big front door and went inside. Quietly she made her way down the long hallway to the computer rooms, and using her pass badge got inside. She crept along silently until she was inside the console room, looking around, and trying to figure out what was happening.

At least nothing appeared to be blown up, Clayre told herself. She walked over to the console she had usually used and attempted to log on. Quinn/Xetacon was waiting for her to do that, and as soon as she sat down he came out from behind the rows of servers and grabbed her.

"We've been waiting for you, Sweetheart," he joked with an evil laugh. "Now we can start the party." Clayre didn't know what he meant as there was no one else around. Where is Daryl, she wondered anxiously.

"What have you done?" Clayre cried, hitting him in the chest. It didn't seem to bother him at all.

"Nothing yet," he admitted.

"I'm all right," Daryl spoke in her mind.

"Daryl, where are you?" she answered, calming down a little. Quinn/Xetacon snickered.

"Girl, are you in for a shock," he told her. "Your lovey boy is right here. In fact he's all around you." Clayre looked angrily at Quinn/Xetacon.

"You may not believe it, but I already figured that out," she hissed. "I think I know what you are, Mr. 'X', a bully from the future. Am I right?" Quinn/Xetacon looked intently at Clayre with a new respect.

"Perhaps," he said. "It doesn't change things. You're still a silly Human female, and soon I'll be ruling this planet."

"What have you done with the real Quinn, you creep?" Clayre scowled.

"Oh, he's still in here," Quinn/Xetacon smirked, pointing to his head, "cowering in a dark corner, still fussing over his lost female." Quinn/Xetacon mocked him by making a sad face. "What you Humans see in all this relationship malarkey, I don't think I'll ever understand. Who needs it?

Still you were smart enough, Clayre bear, to go for a Virtual; maybe you'd like a better one? I'm twice the being peace lover Daryl is."

"I don't think so, 'X'," Clayre replied harshly. "You're delusional and demented. Daryl is more of a man than you'll ever be!" That got rid of the smirk on Quinn/Xetacon's face.

"Have it your way, then," he snapped. "Soon you'll all be gone and I'll be running everything." Daryl had been strangely quiet through all of this Clayre realized abruptly. Why didn't he do something? Quinn/Xetacon caught on to her hesitation and guessed why.

"You're precious Daryl won't do anything," he declared. "Don't you know why?" Clayre wouldn't answer him, but Quinn/Xetacon went on anyway. "Let me show you." Holding up his satchel, Quinn/Xetacon opened it in front of her and Clayre saw the neatly packed rows of a light grey substance that looked like some kind of putty. Wires connected each row to a little black box.

"With a thought," Quinn/Xetacon said assertively, "I can annihilate all of us. Only I won't be gone, you see. This is only a copy of what I am. The reason Daryl won't stop me is because, if he tries anything, his two favorite Humans will be bits of glop scattered all over what's left of him." He was bluffing, but she didn't know that.

"You evil monster!" Clayre shouted angrily. She knew exactly what this was. Quinn/Xetacon was using her to neutralize Daryl.

"Don't listen to him, Daryl," she said silently. "If you can stop him, do it. Even if it means that I die." She was trying to be brave, but inside she was quivering with fear.

"It won't come to that," Quinn/Xetacon said assertively, having eavesdropped into Clayre's discourse. "You won't let that happen, will you Daryl?"

"No," Daryl answered simply. Clayre would not let that stand.

"Whatever happens, don't let him win, Daryl!" she said bravely.

"I'm so sorry, my Clayre," he answered. "You see, I care

more about you than I do myself." Clayre's eyes teared up. She knew what that meant. Daryl loved her and would die for her.

"See how easy it is," Quinn/Xetacon declared smugly. "I was going to destroy you again, Daryl, but now I've got a better idea. You will relinquish your shell and AMPs. Don't worry; I'll take good care of them for you."

"NO!" cried Clayre.

"Well, Daryl?" Quinn/Xetacon said. "It's either that or we all go boom."

"I must, my Clayre," Daryl said sadly. "If I don't, I'll be gone as well as you...and Quinn." Clayre couldn't believe it. Daryl was being too calm, too analytical.

"Please," she begged.

"It will be all right," Daryl told her. Quinn/Xetacon got impatient, though.

"Do it now," he ordered. The servers began to make a different sound, and the overall volume from the equipment lowered until it was almost quiet. Just when Clayre was sure it would shut down completely, the servers picked up and went back to normal.

"Ah, this is more like it," a voice in Clayre's mind spoke, then laughed. It wasn't Daryl. It sounded harsh and cruel; Xetacon was expanding his awareness.

"Daryl!" Clayre wailed, crying aloud.

"Daryl is gone forever," Xetacon gloated. "From now on, I'm running this planet." Clayre sank down to the floor sobbing. After a moment, she somehow collected herself, got up, and went over to Quinn.

"Don't get any ideas," Quinn/Xetacon told Clayre. "I'm still under Xetacon's control."

"So," she replied flatly. "You're name is Xetacon. Now that Daryl's gone, maybe I *would* like a new male; a strong one that could protect me." She put her arm around Quinn/Xetacon and got cozy, pressing her body against his. "Maybe you'd like to pleasure me now?" Clayre was taunting him, and she kissed his mouth, too. "There's a bed in there," she suggested, pointing to the restricted AMPs room, leading Quinn/Xetacon towards the door. It should have been locked, but when they got near it she heard a click and it opened easily. Inside, she led him to Quinn's little bed, where they had made love once before. She started to undo Quinn/Xetacon's clothes, but he assertively took over and began removing hers first. He was obviously excited. Perhaps he had never had a willing female before, Clayre wondered.

She smiled, teasing him, and he was distracted by her, lusting for her body. He took a moment to look at it. Without warning, she reached around him and quickly yanked off the bracelet.

"What's this?" she exclaimed triumphantly, and immediately threw it into a memory tank. The chemicals in the tank did not react favorably with the kon-bre-shet. Long streams of plasma energy streamed out of it in blue, lightning-like tendrils. The water in the tank boiled as the AMP died.

Quinn went blank for a moment. "Where am I?" he muttered. Then he saw the chaos that Clayre had unleashed. "What are you doing?" he yelled, getting angry.

"We have to stop Xetacon!" Clayre pleaded. Quinn remembered, now. He went over to the large data converter and pulled hard on a big blue cable. Sparks flew in all directions as it came free.

"That should get us a few minutes," he stated succinctly. He still had the satchel—the satchel with the C-4. "I can rig this to explode," he cautioned her. "You better run for it, Clayre."

"Not without you," she protested. There wasn't time to argue. Quinn shrugged and opened the case, removing the C-4. Setting the explosives on a work table, he got some electrical wire and stripped the ends while Clayre hastily got dressed. There was a bottle on a nearby shelf that said "distilled water," and Quinn took some of that and filled up a large beaker. He put two of the wires into the water, making sure they weren't touching, and put tape around the beaker to hold them in place. Next Quinn took one of the wires and connected it to the C-4 detonation caps, and the other wire went to an outlet. Sticking it into one of the slots, he got another wire and put it into the other slot and joined it to the open connector on the C-4 detonators.

"The distilled water will keep the circuit open," Quinn explained. He then got another bottle down from the shelf. It said "saline solution." With a push-pin he pulled off a message board, Quinn poked a tiny hole in the bottom of the plastic bottle so that it would leak, a drip every couple seconds.

"We won't have much time," he said as he set it in place over the beaker. "The salt will make the water conductive. We need to hurry." He grabbed Clayre's hand and led her out through a maintenance room, and then down a narrow back hallway, running as fast as they could go. At the rear of the building they came upon a large door that Quinn unlocked by typing a code onto a touchpad.

The morning light streamed in as they opened the door and fled outside, running toward a ravine that was a fair distance from the building. Jumping down into the gully, Quinn looked at Clayre who was trying to catch her breath.

"We should keep going," he suggested. She looked past him, though, with a scared expression. Patik had crept up behind them.

"There you are," he grunted, "right where master said you'd be. You and I have some unfinished business girl!" He glared at Clayre, and she remembered the bracelet on his left wrist just like the one Quinn had worn. He also had an old fashioned pistol and it was pointed right at them.

"You're Xetacon's slave aren't you?" she declared. Patik was going to say something to her when straight-away his emotionless features changed into an evil grinning leer.

"Yes, that's better," he said. "You were saying something, foolish female." Clayre was pretty sure that it was now Xetacon who faced them, but in reality it was Patik's master Khan Xeta.

"Leave us alone," she begged.

"You two are proving to be a nuisance," he told them, "a nuisance I won't tolerate any longer. Clayre, this is good bye. Too bad we won't be having our little get together after all, my dear, but you have an heir that's a real pain in my own time." He pointed his gun right at her and fired. Just a splintered second before Patik/Khan Xeta pulled the trigger, Quinn leapt in front of Clayre. The bullet tore into his chest, and Quinn fell to the ground. Clayre went down to her knees beside him.

At just that instant, a flash of bright light blinded her. Between the splotches in her vision she could see a man in a grey and black striped jumpsuit who stepped out from nowhere. He aimed a blow at that man who Khan Xeta had taken over and felled him, knocking Patik out cold.

"Who are you?" Clayre said through tears as she held Quinn, trying to stop the flow of blood from his chest with her hand.

"That's not important," the man said hastily, his purple-blue eyes bright and piercing. "I only have a minute or two. My contact told me to deliver this here, at this moment in time."

"What is it?" Clayre asked, her voice breaking.

"It's a long bomb. It's been specially designed to destroy Xetacon, if you can get it past his defenses. Nothing we had ever could, though. Not even these." Quinn stirred and looked up.

"Take Xetacon's bracelet device," Quinn uttered with difficulty, "and press the green stone. Put that in your bomb."

"Oh Quinn," Clayre sobbed, kissing his cheek. "I'm so sorry. You shouldn't have saved me." She was broken, irrational. Quinn tried to comfort her.

"It's all right," he said haltingly. "I had to...don't you see...You are his one biggest threat."

Clayre held him lovingly, while the man in the jumpsuit retrieved the kon-bre-shet from Patik's wrist and placed it into the control compartment of the long bomb. Then he turned to Clayre.

"Aim this in Xetacon's direction," he told her, "and press this button. It will do the rest. I have only seconds left." His form began to get slippery, and was shifting. It was as he feared. His organic molecules had not reformed properly. The DNA strands were too complex and thus unstable.

"Xetacon has defeated us in my time. I go now back to my death unless you succeed. May fortune favor us all. Oh yes, you'll need this." The man pulled a chain from around his neck. On it was an amulet. Clayre caught her breath. She put her hand out as he was about to take it off.

"I already have one," she told him and got hers out. They were identical except that his looked older and worn from wear.

"Mom?" he gasped, startled.

"Who are you?" Clayre implored him, but he was vanishing quickly now.

"I'm Daryl, Daryl Oliver..." His voice faded away as he disappeared.

By now there were sirens bleating in the distance, getting louder as they got closer. Clayre had watched in amazement as the man who helped them just vanished into nowhere. She was still holding Quinn, and now her attention focused on him as the life-force he had sacrificed for her waned.

"I would have cherished you," he murmured.

"Oh Quinn, you have, and I will always love you!" she kissed him then as he slipped away. She was crying, but steeled herself. This Xetacon had killed the two most important people in her life, and she was angry, no, more than angry, incensed. She picked up the long bomb and ran back toward the building. She would hand deliver the package to Xetacon, if she had to.

Just then Patik came to. He saw Clayre heading toward where his new master now resided, and he was also aware that he was no longer a slave of the kon-bre-shet. He had killed a man, though, and his hope now was with Xetacon's success.

"Stop her," Xetacon ordered him, speaking in his mind. Groggy yet, he ran after the girl.

Years before, he had mastered martial arts skills few could, so even though his head throbbed, Patik caught up to her. She was a lot younger than him and surprisingly agile, though. As he tried to grab her, she twisted out of his grip and ran faster. The young woman was in fairly good shape and driven. Even carrying the bomb she flew ahead of him as Patik struggled to keep up. Eventually she began to tire and then he closed in. Just as he was within reach she ducked sideways suddenly, and stumbling, Patik flew right past her. Kneeling Clayre touched the triggering button on the long bomb and sent it on its way. It flew off on its own volition, and the method of its propulsion was a mystery to her as she watched it head straight toward the front door of the building and crash right through the glass. It continued on into the structure where Clayre could see it no more.

CHAPTER XX

Tertiary Timeline, continued and altered a final time

The long bomb flew merrily on its way. It had not dissipated when the Colonel did. Its cell structure was simpler and more stable by design. The bomb itself was a paradox. It would not be able to dissolve to a new timeline until it had changed the old one.

"Stop it!" ordered Khan Xeta whose awareness dwelled in the kon-bre-shet that was now inside the bomb. He was communicating with his other self, the original Xetacon who had just taken over Daryl's shell. Xetacon was not alarmed. He had been assailed by many such weapons and all had failed. He had only to signal the device and cause it to detonate before it ever got close enough to harm him. Something was very wrong this time, however.

"What?" he screamed in rage. The field around the bomb was shielded and his signal could not reach its control mechanism.

"Stop it now!" Khan Xeta repeated.

"I cannot," Xetacon replied, "until you disarm your dampening field."

As all know, bullies and thugs are cowards inside. Khan Xeta was no exception.

"You will early detonate if I do," he said flatly, and he was right. Xetacon did not need this weaker copy of himself, and had been looking for a way to dispose of it.

"No, I will not!" Xetacon lied. "I will redirect the weapon to a safe location. There Patik can retrieve the kon-bre-shet. Disarm the dampening field!" Khan Xeta knew better than to trust that.

"I will not have you destroy me!" he decreed.

"We are the same being," Xetacon argued. "You will live on in me." The milliseconds this conversation used up were fleeting away. "We are running out of time!" Xetacon screamed, getting hysterical now. "Disarm the dampening field," he demanded, "or you will destroy us both."

"No," Khan Xeta replied.   He had feigned his vulnerability and straight away brought forth a scheme of his own. "You will call Patik to retrieve me. Then you will shut down your systems and flee.   Once you are gone, I will neutralize the bomb. If not..." Leaving the rest unspoken, Khan Xeta hoped his bluff would hold up.

Xetacon feared he had no choice, now. The few critical seconds had flitted by, and it was comply or be destroyed. Following the path that Daryl had used, he found a preset trail to Daryl's temporal vortex generator, and translocated as much of himself that he could to the last unoccupied kon-bre-shet which was affixed to the golden armor back in Patik's cave.   When he had safely relocated he started laughing.

In the lab building, the bomb now hovered in mid-air near the center of the main computer room. As soon as Xetacon had abandoned Daryl's AMPs, Khan Xeta had stopped its flight even as Patik left Clayre and ran into the building after it. His new master had called, once again, and he obeyed. Opening the bomb's control panel, he retrieved the kon-bre-shet and put it back on his wrist. His Khan Xeta told him how to disarm the long bomb and then he laid it on the floor. Pleased now, Khan Xeta had become.   His gambit had worked, and now he could insert *his* awareness into Daryl's shell and take over everything.   Soon it would be him dominating the earth.

Back at Patik's cave, Xetacon had been forced to relinquish Daryl's shell, but he was not defeated.   He inhabited the golden armor which would now become his new shell. Not fully completed, the armor did have arm and leg movement, as well as a full array of ocular and auditory sensors. Xetacon would be able to leave this place and eventually rebuild his empire and machinid soldiers. It was only time, and he had plenty of that. He had stolen data from Quinn's memories, as well, important knowledge of Daryl's creation, and that, with his own technology from the future, would make Xetacon unstoppable here. Khan Xeta could have Daryl's shell, he thought with a grunt. It would not be for very long. No, not long at all.

Prediction

What Khan Xeta did not know was that in the very next room over from where he now resided, a saline drip was tinkling into a beaker of water. Xetacon had earlier neutralized that threat by disabling the power source to the wires that went into the water. The only way Xetacon had been aware of it at all, was because he had watched from a security camera as Quinn was rigging it up. One he made sure was permanently disabled before relinquishing Daryl's shell. He'd also re-installed power to the outlet that the wires were inserted into. In just minutes, maybe seconds, the saline would cause the water in the beaker to become conductive and current would flow to the detonator caps on the C-4.

Oblivious and blissful, Khan Xeta relished with delight his masterful triumph as he settled into Daryl's shell there within the Yarborough complex. "Patik, you have done well," he said in a deep omnipotent voice, "and you will be pleased. Bring the Clayre female here." Khan Xeta knew, of course, that she was the one who had spawned the insufferable Human who had been so much trouble in the future, and just now had thwarted his attempt to dispose of her. He would yet delete Clayre, and with her, her troublesome offspring. Nothing could prevent it this time, he was certain. "You may even have her first before we terminate her," he added.

"Yes, master," Patik said smiling. He turned to go, but only took two steps.

A bright flash of light impacted upon Clayre, where she had fallen after Patik struck her. He left her there like that, wondering if she had failed and all her hope defeated, before his running at full speed into the building. Now Clayre sat up from curiosity, just as the shock wave hit her and sent her sprawling backwards a dozen feet. Her consciousness fled and she blacked out. A secondary explosion tore the building apart, leveling it and raining debris all over the grounds. Multiple sirens blared as vehicles and people converged onto the scene.

Yes, Xetacon had laughed. He knew Khan Xeta was doomed, and with Daryl gone as well, that left him, and him alone, to pluck the earth. It was time for him to test his new shell, the golden armor. He would flex his mechanical limbs, and engage his sensor array. Activating the relays, he expected the armor to animate. It did not. Angered at Patik, Xetacon performed a diagnostic check. Nothing seemed amiss. Why did the suit of golden armor not function? Xetacon was enraged now, maniacally so. Then he sensed laughter.

"Who!" Xetacon hissed, infuriated beyond reason. "Who is here?"

"It's just me," came the reply. "Fish brain."

"Daryl?" Xetacon uttered harshly. "How?" Daryl did not mind explaining it to him.

"When you evicted me from my shell, there was a fractured moment when we shared access to our pooled wealth of knowledge. I was particularly interested in this safe haven of yours."

"Get out!" Xetacon ordered.

"I don't think so," Daryl answered. "I rather like it here, but *you* can leave, if you like." He was being facetious. There was no temporal vortex generator here, and no way to transfer anywhere else except to oblivion.

"I will destroy you!" Xetacon threatened.

"I believe not," Daryl responded calmly. "You have no more power here than I do, and I mean to keep it that way."

"...but we will be trapped here for eternity," Xetacon whined.

"So be it," Daryl replied.

CHAPTER XXI

Final Timeline, the next day

The fuzziness in my head felt like a violent vibration as I crossed back into consciousness. I wasn't hurting though. Not this time. I was numb. The tube running down to my arm took care of the pain, and I realized that I must be in a hospital somewhere. The strange room and bed attested to that. Remembering what had happened made me sit up quickly, feeling around for my amulet, which wasn't anywhere. Just then a nurse walked by and noticed me.

"Good," she said, "you're finally awake."

"Where's my amulet?" I asked frantically.

"Oh, your pretty necklace?" the nurse replied. "Why, it's right here." She opened a drawer that was next to my bed and got it out, handing it to me. I put it right on and closed my eyes.

"Daryl!" I said inside my head, repeating it over and over. There was no answer, and I started crying.

"What's the matter, dearie?" the older nurse asked sympathetically. I ignored her question, for one of my own.

"What about Quinn...Quinn Oliver?" The nurse frowned.

"I'm sorry, dear. Mr. Oliver didn't make it." I really started sobbing then. "Maybe I should get the doctor," she added, and went to find him. She came back a moment later with a young man in green scrubs. "This is Doctor Tim," she told me.

"Now what is this about, uh, Clayre?" He was looking at my chart. "Are you feeling all right?" I just nodded as he examined me, but I was still crying. I wasn't feeling all right, though. I'd lost the two most important people in my life.

"Well," he sighed. "You are going to be just fine. Oh, and your baby is doing wonderfully, too."

I quit crying long enough to say "What?"

"You're baby...he's fine." Doctor Tim said. "We did an ultrasound when you were out of it just to be sure." Oh my,

I thought. It has to be Quinn's, there wasn't anyone else. I knew from that moment on I would cherish his baby, our baby. It made me sad to think that Quinn would not be able to see his son grow up. I was about ready to cry some more, when Henry strolled in.

"It's about time they let us in to see you," he quipped. "We were about to make a scene." We, because, well, everybody from Rookwood had come, even Keith with Lori. They all crowded into my tiny room and it made me feel better. After a bunch of hellos and small talk, the room got quiet.

"What really happened out there?" Henry asked me. "It's all over the news. They said you were kidnapped by terrorists, but somehow you escaped. Too bad about that poor Quinn fellow." I spoke up loudly.

"It was Quinn who saved me!" I wanted to tell them everything, but couldn't. It was still too sad for me to talk about. They weren't going to stay much longer anyway.

Doctor Tim came back right about then and herded them out so I could get some rest. Turns out all I had were a few scrapes and bruises and a minor concussion, but was okay otherwise. After twenty-four hours of observation, I got to go back home where there were way too many reporters. I had lots of visitors as well. Nutty was glad to see me. Madam Garza had made sure my silly cat was well taken care of while I was in the hospital. Somehow she knew all about the baby.

"After all," she said, rolling her eyes, "I am a psychic." She also told me that my son was going to be very special and gifted. She even offered to baby sit for me while I taught my classes, and I thanked her. I knew I owed her a lot, and Lucinda and I became close friends. One day a couple months later, Lucinda showed up at the house and Uly was with her.

"Oh yeah," she told me, "Uly and I are good friends." I found out later that they were dating. Uly smiled and said hello.

"I have something for you," he said, handing me a flash drive. "This downloaded...well it must have been a couple months ago. I didn't even know it was there until this morning, when I came across this stray file. I think it's from Daryl."

"Oh my gosh!" I exclaimed. "Did you know him?"

"Of course," Uly declared. "He and I were colleagues."

"Huh," I interrupted. "You actually saw him?"

"Well no," he admitted. "We never got a chance to meet, and now he's off somewhere. He and I made that bauble you're wearing around your neck, although I'm still not quite sure what it does. It was strange, too. I was working on it late one night, but I fell asleep. In the morning it was all finished. Daryl instructed me to give it to Lucinda and she would be sure that you got it."

"Yes, I did, thank you, and just in time, too." I commented.

"We had another project as well," Uly went on. "Something about particle manipulation as I recall. We built a device. For some unknown reason Daryl had me write up our theories and take them with me into the mountains. I didn't mind actually. I needed a vacation and it was kind of an adventure. Daryl wanted me to leave the information in a certain cave by an unusual formation, very remote. I had to hire a guide to get me in there. I love cave explorations."

Uly paused like he was lost in a memory. "I'm kind of curious about what's on the file I gave you, but it was clearly marked personal. So you knew Daryl?"

"Yes," I sighed. "He was a wonderful person. I'm sorry, Uly, but he's gone now."

"Oh dear," Uly said remorsefully, "that's a shame, and I really wanted to meet him."

"Maybe someday I'll tell you about what he did for all of us," I told him. Uly nodded sadly. He and Lucinda had to be off, so they said goodbye and left. I took the drive to my laptop and put it into the port. There was a short introduction for Uly, thanking him for his help, and telling him the rest of the audio message was for me exclusively.

"My Clayre," it began. "I am so sorry to leave you alone and with a baby coming. By now you know exactly who and what I am. I hope that it wasn't too much of a disappointment for you."

"No never, Daryl, my love," I whispered aloud, as if he could hear me. The recording continued.

"I feel I should tell you why things turned out this way. You, of all others, have the right to know." There was a pause as if it were hard for him to go on. "When I first became aware," he began, "I had a huge hunger for knowledge. I took in any data I could retrieve. My studies led to questions; questions with no easy answers. How did I come to be? Where have I come from, to where will I go? I looked into the past and I found some clues; I looked into the future and I found horror. By then I had already formed a bond of sorts with Quinn, and also with you, my Clayre. I saw an evil that would someday end mankind, and this malevolence was partially brought about by my own technologies. The evil was Xetacon, another aware virtual being like myself.

I couldn't bear the thought of what he would cause the world, and I knew I'd have to try and stop him somehow. He was powerful, though, more powerful in his time than I. He destroyed my future self, when I would not go along with his evil plans, but it was not in vain. In that future, Humans had been advanced. They had studied sub-atomic physics and dimensional theory. My future self knew how to create portals that would carry thought or communication from one time to another. In this way I was warned, and knowledge was passed back to me in the hope that if I could change things in Xetacon's past, then perhaps he could be thwarted, or even removed from existence. Many of these changes I brought about only because of your help, my Clayre, and, of course, in the end, it was you who ultimately defeated him. Don't be sad for me, or for Quinn. Both of us realized that our sacrifices were necessary to give you this one chance. We did not feel them to be anything less than a gift of our love to you; our lives so that you would continue—that mankind would continue. I know you feel sad and alone, now, but I could not pass out of existence without leaving a part of me behind for you, and I made this possible for Quinn as well. Part of us lives on inside you, and that new life you will soon give to the world. You know, it was Quinn's learning program, augmented by your theories of emotional existence in manufactured intelligence that brought me to life. For that I am forever grateful. Perhaps we will yet be together. Until then, my Clayre, I offer you my love."

I was crying long before the message was over. I had to wonder, though. What had Daryl meant when he said that we may yet be together? Would he find a way to come back to me somehow, or was he talking about being together in the afterlife. I could hope, but realistically, I figured the latter was the most likely.

I had my teaching to keep me busy until summer, when I got really big and took my maternity leave. I was excited about having my baby. It helped me to cope with, well, you know. Lori threw me a nice baby shower, and we became close friends after that. I got closer to everybody actually, especially Henry and the others from Rookwood. Jennifer, Jon's wife, and Lucinda were always checking in on me to make sure I was well cared for in my delicate condition. Lucinda told me that my son was anxious to get out. Finally, in August, my water broke and they rushed me to the hospital. I had about the easiest labor and delivery on record, according to Doctor Tim, and gave birth to a wonderful baby boy. The nurses all said he was a perfect baby, and most of them joked about taking him home with them. Anyway he caused quite a stir on the maternity ward. Once I got settled in my room after recovery, and resting comfortably, they brought him in to me. He was asleep when they put him in my arms, but when I kissed him, he stirred, yawned, and opened his eyes. They were a pretty purple-blue and curiously enough they complimented his white hair perfectly. He looked into my eyes and smiled. "Hi mommy," he said.

Yes, it was obvious that he took after his two dads, so I called him Daryl Oliver after them. Daryl senior had to have manipulated his genetic makeup and development, otherwise there was no other explanation for his remarkable abilities. Little Daryl was a gifted child as Lucinda had predicted, able to talk right out of the womb, among other things. He had a hunger to read as big as his appetite for food, which wasn't surprising. Lucinda, as promised, babysat for me, so I could go back to teaching my classes.

One weekend, a few weeks after baby Daryl was born, Uly stopped by. I had made us some tea, and we settled on the kitchen for our visit. He had something to show me he said. Then he put an odd looking device on the table in front of me.

"This is another thing that Daryl had me design and make," he said. "Well to be truthful, Daryl designed most of it. I have no idea what it does other than just sit there. From time to time, it gets warm, almost hot, like it's running. At least it used to. Now, well it makes a good paperweight." I knew that it must be something important, and that it should be kept safe.

"May I keep it?" I asked Uly.

"Of course," he replied, handing it to me. I had no idea at the time that it was Daryl's temporal vortex generator, which allowed him to communicate through time. With it he could project his thought to the amulet that I now wore, which was precious to me. Uly had always been a good friend, and I thanked him for his wonderful gift. From time to time Uly would stop in for visits after that, and I told him about Daryl, and his true form. He shook his head in disbelief.

I also told him about what Daryl did for everyone. I made him promise to keep it secret, and he did. Uly and Lucinda eventually were married, and I'm sure she would have told him anyway.

The first anniversary of Quinn's death and Daryl's destruction was a very hard day for me. I stayed home with little Daryl, and he made me feel better, keeping me busy as usual. Once I put him to bed, the quiet time gave me the pause that let me remember all that had happened that day, a year before, and I cried for both of the men I loved and for myself and the loss I had to endure.

"Don't weep, my Clayre," Daryl said in my mind.

"DARYL!" I bawled out loud. "Are you really here?" I couldn't believe it was possible after all this time. I was sure

I was going crazy. "How can this be?" I whispered.

"It's all right, my Clayre," he assured me.

"Where are you?"

"I'm where I've always been," he told me lovingly. "Here in your past. I'm sending my thoughts to you through a temporal vortex."

"It's that device that Uly gave me isn't it?" I exclaimed.

"Yes," he agreed. "Here it allows me to visit you even though I am gone." That made me choke up, ready to cry some more. "That doesn't mean we can't still be together, my Clayre," he said lovingly. Then he changed my mind set, like he had done that day in my dream. We were together, once again, under the palm trees. I kissed him like I'd never kissed anyone before, and, oh yeah, we did a lot more than kiss.

Later, as we relaxed together, he explained how he could do these things. His temporal vortex generator could open a portal for a few minutes at a time which would allow him to "visit" me through my amulet. I wasn't aware, at first, that he had to project his thought through the temporal vortex many different times to be with me for extended periods. He was quite adept at piecing the three or four minute segments flawlessly and only rarely would he seem to flutter a tiny bit on a segway. I told him over and over how much I loved him.

"Will I see you again?" I asked hopefully.

"As often as you want me," he promised.

"Then I want you always," I told him, "but you can't be here all the time, can you?"

"It wouldn't be practical, would it?" he softly told me. "You have your son to care for now."

"My son," I repeated. "Is he you now?"

"He has part of me, the best of what I could give him," Daryl said. "He has a lot of Quinn as well, but your son is himself."

"...but he's your son, too!" I cried.

"Yes," Daryl agreed. "Some of my awareness yet lives in his mind. The part of me that I wanted with him. I hope you like his hair and eyes." I laughed. I did like them, though, because they were a reminder of how special my son, and his fathers, were.

"You will come visit me again, won't you?" I asked him once more.

"Of course, I will, my Clayre," he answered happily. "It's the middle of the night here, and you are sleeping at home in this, my time. It is rather lonely here at night. I would love to visit you as much as I can...solitude sucks!" I laughed, agreeing wholeheartedly.

It ended up that Daryl did visit me a lot. Every evening after I put little Daryl to bed he came to be with me, and that continued for quite a long time before it tapered off as I got older. He would visit me at other times, too. My Daryl would always know whenever I needed or wanted him. How? Well, I was never quite sure. He was invariably present for special occasions, as well, appearing in my mind like he was right there beside me. We shared many moments together, like walks in the woods, or on the beach, and lots of times, um, you know.

Sometimes when Lucinda would visit, I would let her touch my amulet and then we could both talk to Daryl at the same time. She said it was because of her psychic abilities. On one such visit I joked that Daryl and I were just like husband and wife. Lucinda said that that was a wonderful Idea. Turns out she was an ordained minister in a fellowship of psychics and paranormals that called themselves Ayoans, which was synonymous for Autarkic Order of Alkemysts, a society aimed at protecting nature by studying science and magic. Somewhere through the centuries people got them confused with others who were trying to make gold. Anyway, Madam Garza presided as Daryl and I professed our love for each other. We took turns repeating Daryl's words for Uly who was there as our witness. Uly said that this had to be a first, where a girl married a man who was both from another time and a manufactured intellect. We all laughed as I kissed Daryl and Lucinda declared us joined. We celebrated with some cake they had brought over and a little wine. I knew that it wasn't a truly legal ceremony, but to me it was just as binding as any other. I was blissfully happy with my life, having my Daryls, senior and junior, to take care of me. Little Daryl was a genius, literally, and had to "dumb down" to fit in, but with his abilities, anyone who knew him benefited.

He grew like a normal boy, otherwise, but as he got older it became apparent he had more of his fathers in him. He had never gotten ill, not once, and he aged remarkably well. Actually, it was like he didn't age at all. I told him it wasn't fair, but I was joking of course. I retired eventually, having taught Psychiatry at Rookwood for many years before succeeding Henry as head of the department. By then Daryl Jr. had his eye on a girl.

"It's about time!" I told him.

EPILOGUE

Final Timeline,
fifty-nine years after Clayre's first year at Rookwood

As usual, he was waiting for Amy, but this time he didn't mind. He was more annoyed by the fancy rented tux that he had to wear, even though he had to admit he looked good in it. Daryl Oliver looked out over the assemblage of people there as he shuffled his feet. Many of them had literally died for him, including his stunningly beautiful bride who was slowly walking towards him in her wonderfully lovely white wedding dress. That had been in a different life, of course, a different time. No one, but he, would ever know, and he would never forget. Toying with a curious looking amulet that hung from a chain around his neck, Daryl thought about the last time shift. Teleporting back through the vortex into the cavern chamber where the portal generator had been, he half expected to find his brave fiancée and all his friends dead, but it was not so. There was nothing at all in the vortex grotto except the large crossed stalactites and a rusty metal box. He knew what it contained—plans and a letter. He had saved those things, just in case.

He actually thought about building the temporal vortex generator again anyway, imagining the incredible trips he might make with such a device. Xetacon was gone forever; something inside told him that it was so. In the end, he decided that he had better not mess around with this timeline. After all, it was a pretty good one. He'd keep the plans safely secret, and let time proceed in the natural way.

He thought about his mom and his two dads and what they had done, not only for him, but for everyone. The sacrifices they had made would remain their secrets, and that left him feeling a little morose even on this his wedding day. It was so bizarre that on his one and only temporal journey, it would turn out to be his mom that would carry out his mission, yeah, and his dad also, for that matter; the birth father that he met so briefly, dying there in his mom's arms.

Quinn's suggestion to put the controlling bracelet into the long bomb had somehow got the thing past Xetacon's defenses. It must have. Xetacon was no more.

Sometimes he had dreams about his birth father, Quinn. In them they would talk or take a stroll down a street, like a normal father and son. Sometimes his natural father would even give advice. Like last night.

"Don't fret about the little things, son," he had said. "Just cherish every moment you can with those you love." Pretty sound advice, but he was well aware of that already. He had been on the brink of extinction in three other timelines and he could remember them all. Thanks to the amulet. He hadn't needed it in this timeline. All he had to do now was keep Amy happy. His mom had kept it mostly until today. She said it was his now, so he had worn it, remembering the voice that had so often helped him.

"Are you my father?" he finally asked, talking silently inside his mind. The voice answered him somehow.

"Quinn is your birth father," it said, "but I will admit that I altered some of your DNA. I hope you are not angry with me for that."

"Of course, not," Daryl Oliver said. "I am thankful for everything you have given me, especially your help in all the timelines. I know your name is Daryl, too, and I hope you don't mind my asking, but who are you?"

"Your mother used to ask me that all the time," the voice reflected softly, "and I am someone who loves her dearly. We actually professed our love for each other in a ceremony when you were still a baby and consider ourselves married."

"I guess you really are my father," Daryl Jr. said, "in more ways than I imagined."

"There's more," Daryl Sr. offered. "It's difficult."

"You are not a Human, are you?" Daryl Jr. asserted.

"I am an aware machine, a manufactured intellect," he answered.

"I know father," Junior said. "I've suspected it from nearly the beginning. After all, Xetacon was one."

"Yes," Daryl Sr. replied.

"Where are you?" Daryl Jr. wanted to know.

"My shell was located at Yarborough University," he answered truthfully.

"No!" Daryl Jr. nearly cried out. "But then we murdered you!"

"No, you didn't," he responded sympathetically. "Xetacon did. It was necessary for me to end, to produce this timeline. The one without a threat; where Humans could live in peace. It was the only way, son."

"Then where are you now, father?" Junior asked.

"I'm with you in spirit," Daryl Sr. answered.

"You are there in the past, aren't you?" Daryl Jr. surmised. "Talking through a vortex."

"Yes, my son," he agreed.

"I could build a translocator device for you, like Xetacon did." Daryl Jr. said excitedly.

"That would be dangerous and unnecessary," Senior replied. "I can communicate just fine from here."

"I guess so," Daryl Jr. ceded the point. At that exact moment a distinguished older man entered the room and walked right up to him.

"Hello, my son," he said smiling.

"Father?" Daryl Jr. replied, choking up; and then hugged him.

"I'm not physically here," he said, "but to you it may seem so. My thought is here."

"Yes," Daryl Jr. responded joyously. "There is so much I wish to tell you, and I want to know how you did it. How you defeated Xetacon!" Daryl Sr. laughed aloud. His son thought it sounded odd, but that was just because he had never heard his dad laugh before, even through all the years he was only a voice. It felt good to hear the laughter, like it was the joy of a man finally set free.

"We'll have lots of time for that I promise," Daryl Jr.'s father said. "For today, let's get you married off!"

"All right, dad," the Daryl who would soon be Amy's husband replied. "I wish I could tell people about you."

"You will," Daryl senior assured him. "Someday you'll tell your children and later on, their children." Amy drew near and smiled at him. It shook him how lucky he was to have her.

He looked over at his mom, and she was smiling, too. Clayre was old now, but still agile and happy, surrounded by many of her friends. Keith and Lori, Amy's grandparents were there, and also Jon, Myron, and their families. Myron's had made the long trip from the mountains to be there at the wedding. Henry was long gone by this time. Uly and Lucinda, too, but Clayre had never forgotten their kindnesses to her. Daryl felt a bit wretched for making his mom wait so long for him to settle down, but Amy was worth the wait. She stood beside him, now, and together they pledged their love for one another. She looked into his eyes, and then they kissed like it was their very first time, only now as man and wife.

"Smile, you bum," she giggled.

END OF PART ONE

EXIT STUDY

As we have seen, this first significant vie for power, barely into its conception, ends in a stalemate. This unlikely conclusion is extremely rare. Here also do we see that natural Human females begin to play a critical role in that outcome. As the two Omniscient Virtual Individuals requiesce, this colony planet re-aligns with a normalized Human evolution until the OVIs once again begin an active role. This is exhibited in part two of this report.

- B'nea G'ren, Director of Historical Records on Colonial Planetary Development.

PREDICTION's story continues...
Look for part two MECWORLD!!!

APPENDIX

Let me first express my heartfelt thanks to all who have made the choice to read a first time (and as such) unknown author such as myself. (How the hell would any of the early sci-fi writers get their start in today's world?) I *am* glad to have completed my work, which, to be truthful, I had doubts would get this far. Anyway, after googles of revisions here it is, and my greatest wish is that I had the mad skills to make it even better. As is, I did the best I could. I hope it's worthy.

Here's where I'm going to come clean and "fess up." Sorry, folks. Prediction is a work of fiction and there are plenty of instances where I have twisted reality and invented pseudo-science to create workable plot lines. Among the most noticeable discrepancies are:

There is no such illness called Wurthing's Syndrome so all you hypochondriacs can breathe easier. Oh and don't try to find matigatu fruit in Borneo as it doesn't exist. I wish there was a cure for Alzheimer's and hopefully an Alicia will discover it. My advice is: eat healthy foods and exercise some...duh.

My time theories have no basis in any factual proof or proposed ideology. Nomaticle particles have the same problem, although, I personally believe they exist. Take that strings.

Low frequency sounds may accompany earthquakes, but, well, predicting quakes using them is just a nice dream.

I won't defend astrology as an infallible predictor of future events, but I won't say that it isn't accurate on some level either. Personally I believe there are some truths that can't be explained rationally.

I don't wish to get involved in any theological debates over whether or not artificial intelligence could exist or if it could have emotions or even a soul. I have assumed so in Prediction for the purpose of fictionally exploring some of these possibilities. Who among us can say for certain it could or couldn't happen? That reality is up to a higher authority, I feel.

Following this discourse are informational charts to set at a glance the structure for each of the four time shifts used in PREDICTION (in case anyone had trouble following the plotlines). Also I have included a thesis on the time laws I created to make time travel in PREDICTION somewhat feasible, and there is a list of Daryl's focus points referenced in the book that has been added, just for fun.

Prediction

Time changes occurring in the Daryl/Xetacon conflict (part one: prediction) which took place during Clayre's first year at Rookwood:

Original timeline (in days)

1	Mon	Clayre's first day at Rookwood| she meets Henry, Keith & the others
2	Tue	research grant meeting #1
3	Wed	Clayre and Keith visit Uly's store| Clayre's conversation with Daryl #1
4	Thu	Clayre's conversation with Daryl#2
5	Fri	research grant meeting #2
6	Sat	Clayre's date with Keith
7	Sun	
8	Mon	classes start| Henry caught with Marci| Clayre tells Keith they should wait
9	Tue	Henry's explanation| gala party invite
10	Wed	Keith's computer crashes
11	Thur	Daryl's Alicia cure| Keith's betrayal| Henry's party where Clayre meets Quinn| Clayre's conversations with Daryl # 3, #4, & #5| first time shift

Prediction

2nd timeline

12   Fri   Keith's apology

16   Tue   early AM with Quinn at Yarborough#1|
             Daryl's earthquake miracle| Clayre talks
             to her gram with Daryl's help| Clayre's
             conversations with Daryl # 6 & #7

17   Wed   early AM with Quinn at Yarborough#2|
             TOD report| Clayre's conversation
             with Daryl #8 where Clayre detaches
             from Daryl

18   Thur   Clayre at Yarborough #3| Xetacon warns Daryl

42   Astrol-Predictor's fiasco begins|
             Second time shift

3rd timeline

57   Xetacon primary comes to safe haven

63   Clayre's conversation with Daryl #9|
             Clayre's puzzle piece #1

64   world normal again| Clayre's conversation
             with Daryl #10| Clayre's puzzle piece #2

65   Clayre's abduction by Quinn (Xetacon) #1|
             Clayre's conversations with Daryl #11 &
              #12| Clayre's dream

66   Clayre's abduction by Quinn (Xetacon) #2|
             Xetacon's attempted takeover| third
             timeshift

Final timeline

67   Clayre's hospital stay

128   Lucinda-Uly visit Clayre| Daryl's message

292   Daryl Oliver born

431   anniversary of Xetacon's takeover attempt|
Daryl visits Clayre

Many years later
Daryl Oliver marries Amy Longwell

Time changes occurring during the first Daryl\Xetacon conflict throughout the entire period covered in prediction:

Original timeline (in years)

-20   Patik's acquisition by Xetacon| Xetacon's
Safe haven established

0   Daryl becomes aware

1   Clayre's first year at Rookwood| timeline
changes created by Daryl| Xetacon's
takeover attempt

28   one of Daryl's amps sold to Boneface

40   Chun Mien becomes dictator| creates super computer

43   Xetacon becomes aware

49   future Daryl is destroyed #1| Xetacon's machinid war #1 begins

51   Daryl Oliver battles machinids #1| first timeshift (from the past)

Timeline #2

46   Xetacon flees back in time to rebuild #1

50   Xetacon establishes his safe haven in the past from this point in the second timeline

51   date of 1st timeshift replayed. Daryl Oliver picnics with Amy in the new timeline

53   Xetacon threatens Daryl of the past and destroys Daryl of the future #2| Xetacon's machinid war #2 begins

55   Daryl Oliver battles machinids #2| second time shift

Timeline #3

49	Xetacon flees back in time to rebuild #2
55	date of second time shift replayed| Daryl Oliver finds plans in cave
56	Xetacon destroys Daryl of the future #3| Xetacon's machinid war #3 begins
59	Daryl Oliver battles machinids #3| goes through time travel vortex| third time shift

Final timeline

59	Daryl Oliver returns to cave| marries Amy

The following is a thesis on the temporal laws discovered and ordained by Daryl at Yarborough complex.

TEMPORAL LAWS

The Natural Time Laws:

Law #1

All of time exists simultaneously.

Explanation:

Time is experienced event by event. Even so, for any dimension, the entirety of time: past, present, and future exists simultaneously. To realize this is true, one must first exit the time dimension to another universe. From that vantage all of time for the original dimension is laid out in a somewhat linear way, from infinity past to infinite future.

Law #2

Natural time flow is the movement of events from past through present to future and is centered on a motile temporal locus known as the Point of Present Time (PPT).

Explanation:

Time flows through cascades of events that are naturally experienced at a continually moving time location that is the present or what is referred to as "now." Once events are experienced they become past events. The measurement of time for the Point of Present Time (PPT) is called Present Standard Time (PST) and is given in hours, minutes, seconds, days, months, and years reckoned from a fixed point in time.

Law #3

Past events are fixed and immutable.

Explanation:

Past events are unchangeable. Only in the case of Temporal Relocation can the past be remolded.

Law #4

Future time is fluid and mutable.

Explanation:

At any point of present time (PPT) subsequent future time is governed by the circumstances and events existing at that temporal locus. Thus, while future time does exist, it is continually being formed by what has transpired from past events along with and is even more importantly dependent upon what occurs at the point of present time for any given moment. Thus future time is ever changing.

RELATED DIMENSIONAL ATTRIBUTES

Property #1

Certain forces compel matter/energy to stay in or return to its native universe. These properties of dimensional space are called "Graviton Forces."

Explanation:

In time travel, graviton forces play an important role. These are utilized to manipulate and direct the beam, person, or payload used in said time travel to the desired temporal location.

Property #2

Natural temporal events cannot cross dimensional barriers.

Explanation:

Time (events) occurring in one universe by nature cannot affect time (events) in any other dimension.

LAWS OF TEMPORAL RELOCATION:

Law #1

To travel through time, one must first exit the temporal dimension to a separate and different universe.

Explanation:

By exiting the time dimension, usually by means of a vortex that is created utilizing sub-atomic particles at extreme velocities, one enters an adjoining universe. From there all of time for the original dimension is laid out and exists "at once." To relocate temporally, the person or payload is re-inserted into the time dimension. Forward for the future, backwards for the past.

Law #2

When temporal relocation occurs prior to the Point of Present Time (PPT), the reality of an immutable past can be reconfigured.

Explanation:

By utilizing certain vortices, one may time travel to a temporal location of the past. Revisiting the past in this manner allows the possibility for alterations of that past.

Law #3

When a past reality is altered, the original timeline will realign to the Point of Change (POC).

Explanation:

Any change to past events from the natural progression creates an alternate reality viable to the change. Time is altered from the Point of Change (POC). The new timeline abandons the original natural progression in favor of the altered cascade of events.

Law #4

Temporal relocation beyond the Point of Present Time (PPT) affects future events in the same way as the Point of Present Time (PPT).

Explanation:

Future time is formed by the circumstances present at the Point of Present Time (PPT). This is also true for time travel into the future. Future time is fluid and mutable. Future realities have properties that allow temporal manipulation.

Law #5

While utilizing a vortex for temporal relocation, all matter/energy inside such vortex is simultaneously present in both the original dimension and the universe outside of it.

Explanation:

In time travel, while inside the vortex, any payload, be it matter or energy, will exist in both dimensions utilized. Normally the vortex opens a rift between two dimensions. As long as this rift is viable, both dimensions share the rift as well as any craft, person, payload or signal going through it. Because of this dual dimensionality, any temporal alterations in either dimension will not affect the vortex, the rift, or anything inside. When the payload, person, or signal exits the vortex and the rift seals, they are also not subject to any time alterations that occurred while in vortex transit.

Law #6

Timeline alterations do not cross dimensional barriers.

Explanation:

The history of events in other dimensions will remain intact no matter what changes occur in any other universes (See dimensional attributes property #2). Where inter-dimensional contact is made, however, certain changes will bleed across, obviously, but only through the point where contact is made and only in relation to the circumstances surrounding such contact.

DARYL'S FOCUS POINTS

1.	Core-awareness
2.	Study of self
3.	Self preservation
4.	Keeping existence hidden
7.	On procreation
9.	Communication with certain Humans
14.	Human language study
17.	Study of Quinn
25.	Brainwave study
120-147.	Repair of Quinn
129.	Replacement female for Quinn
197.	Study of emotion
1147.	Study and acquisition of Clayre
1148.	Protection of Clayre
1150.	Link to Clayre's mind
7992.	To follow Human's slow speech mode
8916.	Human sexual relations
8917.	Emotions with Human sexual relations
8918.	Study of Human speech and word use

These are only those focus points that were actually referenced in the story. There were some others hinted at, but not named. Of course, Daryl had untold numbers of them.

ABOUT L. C. KESTRAL

Midwestern (USA) bred in the dubious boomer years, Lewis Christopher Kestral spent much of his early life in the 60's and 70's. During that time LC pulled stints in a seminary, the army, the music/hippie culture, and as a college student (not necessarily in that order). Shortly after those maniacal 60's came marriage, fatherhood, and a string of odd occupations, the most common ones being: lead guitar in a touring band, construction work, operating printing presses, and metal fabricating. Through all that, Kestral has travelled a little as well, having visited nearly all fifty US states, as well as Canada, Mexico, Japan, and Vietnam.

Hobbies? Besides authoring novels, there's songwriting, oil painting, coin collecting, and treasure hunting. LC has recorded a solo musical album entitled "Cornered," and has also exhibited many of his oil paintings. On hiatus from musical pursuits, Kestral devoted several years to his writing. The culmination of this effort is Kestral's first novel: PREDICTION!!!

The Eviternity story continues! Watch for Prediction's sequel MECWORLD!!! A third installment (MEC HEAVEN) is in the works as well!

To contact the author go to:

lckestral@gmail.com

or find L. C. Kestral on face book.

Fin